DEATH
AMONG THE
DIAMONDS

BOOKS BY FLISS CHESTER

DEATH
AMONG THE
DIAMONDS

FLISS CHESTER

bookouture

Published by Bookouture in 2022

An imprint of Storyfire Ltd.
Carmelite House
50 Victoria Embankment
London EC4Y 0DZ

www.bookouture.com

ISBN: 978-1-80314-645-4
eBook ISBN: 978-1-80314-644-7

For my dad, who loved crime fiction too
Malcolm Chester 1949–2021

PROLOGUE

The grey, creeping light of the early dawn danced around the edges of the grand hall of Chatterton Court. It slipped down the wide stone staircase that wrapped its way around the circular space, emphasising the shadows in the niches behind the stone busts of Chatterton ancestors.

Whatever lay up those stairs was no business of his, however. Those ladies sleeping soundly and those gentleman snoring in their comfortable, warm beds. No, his mission was to climb that scaffolding as quickly and quietly as possible. He eyed it up; the hollow steel pipes and rough wooden boards had held his weight before. He ran his sleeve over his slightly runny nose then started his climb with the agility of a steeplejack, reaching and pulling and shifting his weight from foot to foot.

He'd built this scaffold tower, this starkly utilitarian edifice, in the middle of the elegant grand hall. Built it with his own hands, his workmate and he keeping their effing and blinding to a hushed hiss whenever a bolt snagged at their overalls or a finger got caught between a heavy board and an unforgiving pole. He hadn't wanted to offend the ladies with any cussing. He'd needed this job. But then his partner had gone and gotten himself the 'flu. Just what they'd needed... but, for the best, perhaps, that no one else, not even his friend, had been around to spy what he had. All that pain, all that hard work would be worth it if his inkling was correct. He knew what he'd seen.

The sparkle of the chandelier, each glass bauble glinting in the first rays of the spring sunshine, caught his eye. He'd polished hundreds of those blooming things these last few days, each one making his shoulders ache as he'd reached up from the top platform to get his soft cloth around their facets and edges. It wasn't that he didn't like his work; life could be worse. But if he was right... after tonight, he might be able to jack this job in, move to London and buy a car! Get a nice girl and treat her right, like the lords and ladies in their beds just along the wide landing that he was now level with.

He knew better than to look down. No point scaring yourself with the distance between you and those hard, marble tiles below. He shook his head and made his final pull to the top platform. The light was brightening by the minute and he knew the housemaids would be up and about soon. If they asked what he was doing here so early, he didn't have an excuse planned, save that Her Ladyship had asked so nicely for the cleaning to be done before the weekend. But on his own he'd had no chance to finish up, even though he'd been here till late last night.

A wobble. *Steady now son*, he told himself. No point killing yourself when the prize is within your grasp. He righted himself and planted his feet squarely on the boards. A shudder again. He looked around, but the burgeoning dawn that lit the hall created spots of light and deep shadows that were strangely disorientating. He blinked and held out a hand to grip the grand light fixture above. He kept his other arm behind him, a counterbalance. But he couldn't quite reach. He nudged his feet further towards the edge of the platform, the toes of his work boots precariously peeping over the edge of the boards.

He felt unbalanced, another tremor rumbling beneath him,

but all of his concentration was on the task at hand. His balancing arm came forward and he leaned, dangerously, teeteringly, as far over the edge of the platform as he could.

He mumbled a curse as he pulled himself back. Why hadn't he brought a hook or some sort of stick? And that shudder again. This scaffold had been up too long; it was weakening. They must have missed a bolt here or there. He had no choice, he had to climb down and sneak into the kitchen, find a wooden spoon or a crowbar from the coal hole. He turned around, annoyed at himself for not thinking it through.

Then he froze.

Was that a figure, shrouded in shadow? Who was this up here with him, up his scaffold? His mouth formed the question, but before he could disturb the silence of the hall, he was struck with a thought.

Those tremors and shudders... the scaffold wasn't weakening under his weight; someone else had been climbing the tower. Before he could react, two strong hands came towards him, a square push to the chest that sent him completely off balance. His arms wheeled, trying to get some purchase on the air, his fingertips brushing the very furthest edge of his salvation as his body plummeted from the tower, falling, falling... no sound came from him, the air sucked out of his chest as he fell like the dead weight he was. The figure looked down from the very top of the tower in time to hear the crunch of bones breaking on the marble tiles below. Then all was silent again. The grand hall was quiet as a tomb.

1

If anyone knew how important sunlight was, it was the Hon. Cressida Fawcett, who at this very moment was admiring how it dappled across the ceiling of her bedroom. She understood light. Not the science behind it exactly, though her friend Peter 'Boffy' Boffington had lectured her at length about waves and refractions during a soiree at the Royal Society once. No, she understood how it worked in a more *practical* sense. How it changed the colour of a painted surface, reflected off a silk brocade, or how it could even be manipulated through mirrors or windows to quite change the feel of a room. Light had an effect on people's moods too. Flickering, golden candlelight could make otherwise sensible people rashly propose marriage, while cold, bleak, grey light could put the jolliest person into a terrible fug for days. This morning, however, the sunlight was playing mischievously across the coving and it made an already simply perfect morning even better.

Cressida watched as the dappling faded away. A cloud must have just breezed over the sun, stopping it from bouncing its rays off the gently churning Thames, London's great river that meandered through from west to east and, most importantly for

Cressida, only a few yards away from her delightful little pied-à-terre in Chelsea. This small flat by the river was her home from home, a London bolthole for when she wasn't with her parents in the grand surroundings of Mydenhyrst Place, their sprawling estate full of heirlooms, servants and dark, Tudor panelling.

A wet nose and a grunting snuffle disrupted her musings and Cressida absent-mindedly reached out and patted Ruby, her pug, on the head. Ruby had been a gift from Lord Canterbury, along with a proposal of marriage almost a year ago, in the June of 1924. Cressida had accepted the one without the other, being as indisposed to marriage as a silk footstool was to a muddy shoe. Ruby, unlike a potential husband, had never questioned her love of a good party, or where she spent her considerable allowance, why she'd decided against keeping a lady's maid or how fast she drove her rather snazzy little motor car. A pug, Cressida had thought whimsically, was in fact a much better match for her than a man and so Ruby had stayed and Lord Canterbury, as far she knew, was off digging up artefacts just outside Cairo – a place that would no doubt have played havoc with Cressida's shingled bob, not to mention her social life.

With the ceiling no longer a focus for her attention, returned to the plain off-white it was painted, she flicked through the large broadsheet newspaper she had been reading before she became distracted and reached out for her cup of specially blended Indian tea. Ruby snuffled into the crook of her arm and the bells of Chelsea Old Church struck the hour as Cressida read about various goings-on in parliament before switching her gaze to the more jovial columns that mentioned friends and acquaintances of hers in often quite scandalous ways.

'Henry Molyneux, you old rogue...' Cressida muttered, putting aside the paper and setting her teacup down before stretching her arms up above her head with an exaggerated yawn. Ruby snorted her disgust at being ousted from her cosy nook... and Cressida snorted back at her.

It was ten o'clock in the morning and she really should consider getting dressed... yet last night had been rather a late one and sitting here with her pup, her tea and still in her silk pyjamas with pillows propping her up and nothing to do except read the paper, well, it was louche and lazy and idle and indolent and... utterly, utterly wonderful.

Cressida reached over for her tea again and sipped from the delicate china cup. With her other hand, she flicked up the corner of the newspaper and continued reading the society columns. The dreaminess of her morning was brought up short, however, and her elegant teacup sent clattering back to its saucer on the nightstand, when she noticed one particular headline.

DIAMOND HEIST AT CHATTERTON COURT – POLICE NONE THE WISER

Jewellery worth in excess of £2,000 has been stolen from the stately home of Lord and Lady Chatterton, near Newbury, Berkshire. Police attended the burglary at Chatterton Court when the alarm was raised by Lady Honoria Chatterton. Her heirloom diamonds – a necklace, earrings and bracelet – were taken in a heist-like manoeuvre late the night before when the power to the house was cut. Police have alerted the ports, but no sign of the intruder has been found...

'Gosh!' Cressida exclaimed, and then jumped as the loud bell of the telephone receiver started ringing next to her. Having it installed at all in her flat had been quite a luxury, but having it wired into her *bedroom* had caused the chap from the London Exchange to blush like a freshly boiled beetroot and she'd had to insist that she wanted it there, rather than in the hallway like most folk. Now, having it so alarmingly (and deafeningly) close made her doubt her choice, especially with Ruby's added yaps and yelps, but she did at least appreciate not having to leave the comfort of her bed to answer it.

'Chelsea 221,' she greeted the caller while raising a finger to her lips to try to shush Ruby, and then... 'Ah! Dotty! I was just reading about you.'

Lady Dorothy Chatterton had been Cressida's dearest friend since they'd both charged around the hockey pitches at one of southern England's premier academies for young ladies in their formative years. Other sensible, and generally educational, things they'd been taught included how to alight from a train carriage with poise and élan (pause, raise your chin as if alerted to a piquant aroma, glance each way along the platform, dismount with calm purpose); how to walk with the collected works of all Brontë sisters atop your head (the literal and literary weight was quite something); and, of course, how to balance the other sort of books, the financial ones, which had come in very useful last night, as a matter of fact, when the bill for all those cocktails had landed in Cressida's lap. This rather sensible and grounding education must have had a jolly good effect on Dotty, as she remained remarkably calm on the other end of the telephone line as she told Cressida about the theft of her mother's diamonds only two nights before.

'Mama is desperately upset, of course, and the police haven't a clue who it could be. Oh, and the house is in chaos as the annual mop-and-bucket brigade are still in residence and they really should have blown through the spring cleaning by now. And we have everyone coming down tonight for the weekend, too!'

'*Who* has your mother got in, Dotty? A mop squad?'

'Oh, you know what Mama's like. The annual dust and bother. It's the chandelier that's taking one of the chaps the most amount of time, you know the biggie in the great hall that dangles down from the cupola?'

'My word, do you get that cleaned every year?' Cressida was impressed.

'Oh yes. To the day practically. Mama is most adamant about that. I must say, though, the young cleaner chap is doing a spiffing job. It takes a scaffolding tower to get up high enough for the poor blighter to scramble up it and spit and polish each and every crystal. Honestly, Cressy, he's as able as a mountain goat, clinging onto those poles. None of the household staff will dare go that high, and I don't blame them. Still, he's taken his time, so that dratted edifice is still in the hallway causing Mama the heebie-jeebies every time she sees it, knowing full well that by Martini o'clock she'll have a house party on her hands. What's worse, she went and ordered some new curtains for the ballroom and the scaffold is needed in there, too, to hang them and, Cressy dear, they are *ghastly*.'

'Oh dear, Dotty, they must be really quite objectionable if you're finding them more offensive than a burglary. But your poor Mama... are you sure she wants all us bright young things descending on you this weekend? Sounds a frightful mess down there with you. And truth be told, I'm not sure my constitution is strong enough after last night to come face to face with any hideous curtains.'

'Nonsense. Dinner tonight at eight as planned, cocktails before. I'm simply dying to see you and I *am* upset about the horrid break-in too... it's made everything feel so rummy and we're all terribly out of sorts.' There was a pause. 'And you must get to know Basil a little better before we're married. He's found a bathroom on the second floor with an excellent view of the arboretum and is taking potshots at squirrels with the four-ten.' Dotty paused again and Cressida caught herself raising her eyebrows to an inquisitive-looking Ruby. Luckily, Dotty's voice soon carried on at the other end of the line. '... But I'm happy that he's happy. That's what relationships are all about, isn't it?'

'Don't ask me, chum, I'm more than happy with Ruby and my little motor car. Speaking of which, you're in luck and it's all fuelled up and ready to go. I need to do a few chores, then I'll motor down this afternoon.'

'Oh super, yes.' There was a noise that Cressida assumed was Dotty blowing kisses into the receiver and it made her laugh.

'I'll brace myself for the brocade and see you later, dear.'

Cressida heard more lip-smacking come down the line and she hung up the candlestick-style receiver still laughing. *Darling Dotty...* She didn't know of anyone so pure of heart or good of nature. Why she'd fallen head over heels for the shotgun-wielding Basil Bartleby and agreed to marry him was a mystery to Cressida, but she would support her friend no matter what, even if she couldn't get excited about this whole marriage business. It baffled her how anyone could let a man ruin what was a perfectly wonderful solo existence, but she had to admit that romantic notions were a failing of her sex and even perfectly sensible women like Dotty had to succumb to them once in a while.

Thoughts of Dotty and Basil were put to one side, though, as Cressida slipped out from under the eiderdown and picked up her teacup again. She walked over to the large sash window that looked over the tops of the trees and across to the river. There was something much more exciting than suitors who shot squirrels out of second-floor windows to think about. There had been a theft at Chatterton Court and the felon was on the run. According to the newspaper and Dotty herself, the local police had no inkling of the lowlife who had done it, but Cressida, despite being a lady of the most elevated order, thought she might just know a man who would.

2

Cressida was known among her friends and acquaintances as having a rather good eye for interior decoration. Chums of hers from her schooldays, and indeed their mothers, often invited Cressida to stay at their homes for weekend parties and, while there, pressed her for her thoughts on what sort of fabric might be best for reupholstering the chaise longues; whether the colour above the dado rail really should have been such a bright shade of yellow; or, her personal favourite in the case of Mrs Appleton-Smythe of Lower Weston, Dorset, whether it was frightfully infra dig to tone her drawing room to her favourite shade of hyacinth. And fill it with hyacinths. Cressida's answer to these three specific problems had been 'anything tough enough to withstand your cat's claws', 'no' and 'thankfully yes and yes', in that order. And they had all been much debated and chortled over with her friend Mr Maurice Sauvage, who she was now visiting in the fabric cutting room at Liberty of London.

Liberty was one of those department stores that could never fail to delight. Its mock-Tudor prettiness dominated the corner of Great Marlborough Street, just off Regent's Street in

London's West End, and the reclaimed black and white timbers reminded Cressida of the genuinely Tudor ones at Mydenhyrst Place. Apparently, Liberty's ones had been foraged from long-destroyed warships and she hoped their salty past had done more to rid them of the dreaded deathwatch beetles that haunted the dry old beams at her parents' house. Still, she liked to touch them and feel the smoothness of the centuries-old wood under her fingertips as she climbed the great staircase between the floors. Silk scarves, porcelain dinner services, sandalwood soaps, Charles Rennie Mackintosh furniture, boxes of the most tempting Turkish delight... all this could be found in the hallowed halls of Liberty and Cressida found herself drawn to the shop time and again for life's little essentials. And every time she came, she made sure to pop up to the third floor to see Maurice.

Maurice was of French Huguenot descent and was proud of his heritage, which spun back to the original silk weavers of Spitalfields in the seventeenth century. He, like his forebears, lived and breathed fabrics, and although he found himself on the retail side of things here at London's smartest department store, Cressida had realised over the years that he had his well-manicured fingers on the pulse of all the other branches of the rag trade, from the dockside warehouses where silks came fresh from the Far East and India, to the East End dye houses where the women chattered over the vats of coloured, bubbling liquid as their arms turned the same indigo as the cloth in their hands. He told her how he listened to the talk of the duchesses in Mayfair drawing rooms as he measured up for their new drapes, and gossiped with the porters at Euston station after a day of loading bails of raw cotton onto carriages bound for Manchester. Maurice Sauvage was a man in the know and, luckily for her, Cressida was one of his favourite clients.

'Mr Savidge!' The shop girl's voice rang out over the wide cutting table. Cressida had announced herself at the entrance to the department and now smiled to herself as the young apprentice butchered her friend's French surname.

'Sauvage, dear girl, *sew-varge*... Oh I don't know why I bother.' He greeted Cressida and took her hand in his, gently raising it to his lips but barely letting it touch. He was a short man with dark brown hair that was lacquered tight to his scalp with the barest hint of a wave curving around his forehead. His moustache was just as well tamed, its tips raised upwards and often twiddled with whenever Maurice paused for thought. He wore a simple white apron over black pinstripe trousers and a similarly sombre waistcoat – sombre from the front at least. Today, like most days, the silk back of his vest was a vibrant clash of colours and patterns, a hint to his certain style of flamboyance. 'How can I help you today, Miss Fawcett? Another commission from a friend?' Maurice was well used to Cressida bringing her ideas to him, when she had been tasked with finding the perfect fabric in the most fitting shade as a favour for someone or other.

'Not yet, dear Mr Sauvage,' she pronounced his name perfectly and he gave her a brief nod in recognition of the fact, a definite twinkle of amusement in his eyes. 'But I have a feeling I may be burdened with the chore of helping to choose some new curtains for the mother of a dear friend quite soon. By all accounts, Lady Chatterton has gone rogue and chosen something frightful that might haunt the ballroom of Chatterton Court for years to come unless I can persuade her otherwise this weekend.'

'Chatterton Court?' Maurice queried, and Cressida saw his eyes glance across to where today's newspaper lay open on the cutting table.

'Yes... *that* Chatterton Court,' Cressida confirmed. 'Heard anything?'

'Not a *sausage*.' He pronounced it to rhyme with his own name and Cressida laughed at him. He smiled at her, but then twiddled one of the fine points of his moustache as he carried on. 'In all seriousness, though, when something like that happens you usually get some chatter, if you'll forgive the pun, somewhere along the line. Diamonds of that value missing for two days now and no word of it on the grapevine? It's very strange.'

'Hmm. Very strange indeed. Lady Dorothy Chatterton is a dear friend of mine and due to be married. I've no doubt those diamonds would be forming a large part of her trousseau.' She glanced down at the glaring headline on the newspaper's front page again, taking a moment to admire how calm Dotty had been in recounting their loss to her earlier that day. 'Poor Dotty. I'm going there tonight, a whole bunch of us are in fact. And I wonder...'

'Miss Fawcett.' Maurice picked the newspaper up from the cutting table and folded it over, hiding the front page and its salacious headline from view. 'I've had the honour of knowing you for a few years now...'

'Yes, since you helped me convince Mrs Wicker-Flyte not to go full orange silk in her spare bedroom. That sage green we found was much more sensible.'

'Indeed, Miss Fawcett, but don't you remember the trouble you got into when you started delving into the reason for the redecoration? I believe it's no longer a *spare* bedroom, but now that of Mr Wicker-Flyte himself.'

'Well, the silly man shouldn't have left his collar studs in the maid's bedroom then, should he?' Cressida crossed her arms in indignation. She'd merely been trying to fathom the situation when Mrs Wicker-Flyte had demanded to know what she'd found.

'And perhaps you, dear Miss Fawcett, shouldn't have been nosing around in the servants' quarters?' Maurice, if he'd been taller than Cressida, would at this moment have been peering down his nose at her. Instead, he cocked his head slightly to one side and Cressida shrugged an acceptance. Maurice continued with his warning. 'The theft of two thousand pounds' worth of diamonds is a somewhat more serious matter, Miss Fawcett, and if you poke your nose, as elegantly aristocratic as it is, into the whys and wherefores of their disappearance, I fear you might be placing yourself in more danger than merely being struck off the Wicker-Flytes' Christmas card list.'

'Their cards were very dull anyway,' mumbled Cressida, her arms still crossed in front of her.

'Miss Fawcett,' Maurice stepped towards her, his tone avuncular, 'burglaries can be a nasty business and perhaps, just perhaps, the reason I've heard nothing about the fencing of those diamonds yet here in London is because the truth of it all lies closer to home.'

'Maurice!' Cressida raised her hand to her mouth in shock. 'But none of the Chattertons would ever... I mean... no, quite out of the question!'

'Miss Fawcett, in my humble, but long experience, *nothing* is ever out of the question when a sum of two thousand pounds is involved.' Maurice stepped back and placed the newspaper in a wastepaper basket under the counter. 'Please, do be careful.'

Cressida nodded, his words chilling and thrilling her in equal measure. The problem was she couldn't help it if she was naturally inquisitive, even when it might be dangerous...

3

With Maurice's warning still ringing in her ears, Cressida found some suitable stockings in the Ladies' Wear department (who knew that riding on the running board of a Rolls-Royce last night would have been so torturous for one's rayon?), along with a snazzy new hat with a fancy feather sticking out of it. The shopping made her rather hungry, so she took a late luncheon at The Ritz. Finally, refreshed and refuelled, Cressida made her way back to Chelsea, congratulating herself on only diverting three times into friendly-looking boutiques in order to catch up on the latest spring fashions. It was in the last of these, when a superbly jazzy pair of polka-dot, wide-leg trousers had tempted her, that she'd remembered her friend and gasped audibly, 'Oh heck! Dotty!' and dashed out of the boutique and headed back to her flat.

She packed her weekend case in a hurry, helped along by Ruby, who sat on top of it so that she could do the clasps up, and doubted momentarily her decision to not keep a lady's maid in town, who could have done all of this for her while she'd been shopping. Once valise, hat boxes, several pairs of shoes and Ruby had been heaved downstairs and loaded into Cressida's motor car, and the busy streets of west London navigated (not helped by Ruby taking a liking to a cat they passed along the Cromwell Road and almost jumping out of the car in her excitement), the drive across country to Newbury went relatively smoothly.

Cressida loved her little motor – a Bugatti Type 30 in a glorious nail-polish red – and forgave Ruby most indiscretions in the passenger seat for never once during the meeting with the salesman raising her little wrinkled brow in consternation at the price. As far as Cressida was concerned, it was worth every penny, especially as it took the corner into the driveway of Chatterton Court with barely a gear change – though Cressida did think she may have to apologise to Lady Chatterton later for the slight damage to the lodge house's gate, what with the spray of stones kicked up from the rear wheels after what could be described as one of her more 'sporting' turns.

'Here we are, Rubes, Chatterton Court – the scene of the crime.' Cressida kept a tight grip on the steering wheel as she avoided the potholes illuminated in her headlights on the long driveway – having a spare wheel affixed to the side of the car and knowing how to change one were two completely different matters and she didn't intend to find out how to do the latter at this very moment. 'And look, there's Dotty come to say hello to us. Halloo!' Cressida waved a gloved hand through the open window at her friend, who was waving vigorously back as she stood on the steps of the great house that was Chatterton Court, framed in light by the open door behind her.

Dotty looked positively puny in comparison to the stately marble caryatids that were doing a splendid job of holding up the portico above them and her. She was rather short, though, maybe in truth, anyone would have been dwarfed by those great marble goddesses. The rest of the house, though grand, was a little less fancy, being made of red brick and constructed in the classic William and Mary style – vast sash windows facing out for three storeys, with another layer of mansard ones in the tiled roof.

Cressida pulled to a stop at the bottom of the stone steps and gracefully slipped out of her car, Ruby not so elegantly descending behind her with a plop onto the gravel, and greeted her old friend.

'Oh Cressy, there you are! We were all so worried about you. Oh, hello Ruby.' Dotty bent down and rubbed the small dog's head as she snuffled and licked her hand. 'Just the two of you?'

'Yes, Mama says I really should bring Agnes with me when I come to these shindigs, but you know how I can't stand being fussed over. Still, I have to admit to wishing I had a maid to pack for me. Am I terribly late?'

'Yes, terribly.' Dotty pointed emphatically to her wrist.

'Oh dear. Sorry, Dot. Time got away with me. I fear I've missed cocktails, yes?' Cressida started to rightfully feel quite ashamed of her lousy timekeeping when Dotty burst out laughing.

'Cocktails, dinner, port... but don't worry, Cressy, Papa opened a rather good bottle of whisky and the boys are all ensconced in the billiard room with it. Mama's still up and she'd love to see you before bed. Speaking of beds, you'll be more than comfortable in the Blue Room, I hope? I asked Mildred to put an extra cushion or two on the bed for Ruby, and I know you like that room.'

'Picked the patterns myself, chum,' Cressida noted, pulling off her leather driving gloves finger by finger as the two of them walked up the steps to the open front door of the house.

'And jolly nice they are too,' Dotty agreed. 'I really am almost too embarrassed to show you Mother's new curtains...'

'All in good time, Dot. And speaking of time, I am sorry about being so horribly late. You can blame London, where things don't get going until Big Ben has at least struck ten.'

'I forgive you, Cressy, and your fashionable timekeeping.' Dotty slipped her arm inside her friend's, shaking her head affectionately. 'It's only just gone nine. Climpton can send some cold cuts in if you like?' Dotty offered and Cressida smiled at her friend, who always took such care of those around her.

'No, don't bother poor Climpton. I had rather a splendid late lunch at The Ritz. A nightcap wouldn't go amiss though if you're pouring?' Cressida raised an eyebrow and Dotty laughed.

'You're as bad as Basil.' Dotty shook her head and, with that, the friends – one tall and willowy, her blonde shingled hair peeking out from under her cloche hat, the other shorter and stouter, her smooth brunette bob bouncing as she walked – entered the great house that was Chatterton Court.

'So, this is the cause of your mother's heebie-jeebies then, is it?' asked Cressida, eyeing up the huge scaffolding tower that stood plumb in the middle of the marble-tiled hallway. A hallway that in daytime was flooded with light from the great glass cupola at its height, yet tonight was simmering in the flickering golden glow of dozens of candles. They were placed in the niches next to the alabaster busts of Chatterton ancestors, along sideboards and most effectively up the balustrade of the great stone staircase, which curved its way around the edge of the hall, climbing to the first-floor galleried landing, which, too, had candles shimmering along its length. It was hard to imagine such a hallway, in such a house, had been the scene of a dastardly crime only a couple of days previously.

'Yes, and sorry about the candles. We do have electricity most of the time, but, well, as you can see...' Dotty gestured up to the rough tower of planks and poles, where one of Lady Chatterton's 'mop-and-bucket brigade' was still hard at it cleaning the crystals of the chandelier, even at this late hour.

'I must say, Dotty, it's a rather romantic look.' Cressida took in all the glimmering candle flames around her, casting her eye up the staircase, its solid stone softened by the gentle light, before following Dotty's indication up to the young man in a blue boiler suit lying on his back on the very top of the tower, a polishing cloth in his hand. 'Gosh though, he must be finding it hard to see what's what?'

'Yes, and bless him, he's insisting on working late in order to get it done tonight so the scaffold can be moved.'

As she spoke, the scaffold wobbled slightly and Cressida and Dotty instinctively moved closer to each other. They both released a breath at the same time when they realised it was only the cleaner adjusting his position. He gave a friendly wave down to them and they waved back. He seemed pleased with this and Cressida heard a jaunty tune being whistled from the heights of the tower.

'So there you have it, Cressy.' Dotty rolled her eyes and all but laughed. 'Chatterton Court in chaos as usual. Oh, Jacob, would you see to Miss Fawcett's car and luggage?'

A footman had appeared, handsomely dressed in the Chatterton livery of a light gold waistcoat and dark blue morning coat. He nodded to Dotty and Cressida threw her keys at him.

'Ignition switch should still be warm and I haven't locked the doors. Thank you, Jacob,' Cressida said and then winced as the poor footman mistakenly thought Ruby was to be taken below stairs too and suffered a few nips around the ankles in what was Ruby's own special way of protesting.

'Come on, Cressy.' Dotty led the way once car and pup were sorted out. 'Mama is around somewhere, but once you have nightcap firmly in hand, you *have* to see these ghastly curtains...'

4

'I think Mama is regretting her colour choice now.' Dotty frowned, looking at the gaudy purple-and-gold-striped curtains that were carefully laid out on trestle tables in the ballroom to stop them from creasing. 'She says she can't find anything to match them, for the upholstery and such.'

Cressida took a sip of her whisky before answering. 'I'm not surprised, Dotty. I don't think anything's been designed since Emperor Nero ruled Ancient Rome that could match those.'

'They are a bit Imperial, aren't they?' Dotty agreed. 'I think Mama was trying to channel neoclassical, but got something a bit more circus tent instead. Cost an arm and a leg though. She'll be frightfully cross if they have to go.'

'And it's a shame in a way, as they're beautifully made.' Cressida ran one hand across some of the interlined backing fabric down to the expertly stitched hemline. 'I only wish your cleaner chap had turned the electrics off in here too; I think I could just about stand them in candlelight.'

'Maybe the village fete committee would like them for the tea tent?' Dotty mused. 'Though they might put everyone off their scones and jam.'

'I did warn Maurice at Liberty to be on standby,' Cressida replied to her friend. 'He could send samples and—'

'Cressida dear,' Lady Honoria Chatterton, wife of Lord Francis, Earl of Chatterton, entered the room and walked towards her daughter's best friend with open arms. 'We're so terribly pleased to see you. We thought something tragic might have happened to you on the road. Was it a miserable journey?' Lady Chatterton looked like an older, slightly plumper, version of Dotty. Her silky chestnut hair was greying at the temples, and while Dotty's was cut into a fashionable bob, hers was tied back in a stylish chignon that complemented her evening wear. She was looking elegant in a black and silver crêpe de Chine dress with a long string of pearls, but she was clearly tired, and not just from an evening of entertaining. Dotty may have been doing a sterling job of 'business as usual' having not even mentioned the diamond robbery, but Cressida wondered if Lady Chatterton was more affected by it than her daughter. She decided now might not be the time to delve more deeply into the story.

'Utterly terrible journey, yes,' Cressida winced as she lied, then couldn't help but rectify it. 'I got slightly waylaid in some boutiques, too...' Noticing the look of disappointment on Lady Chatterton's face, she took a quick sip from her crystal glass tumbler to stop herself from talking and digging herself into any deeper holes.

'Well, we're glad you're here now.' Lady Chatterton was gracious enough to ignore Cressida's excuses. 'And with Ruby too, how delightful. And look,' Lady Chatterton forced a smile and spoke more brightly, 'what do you think of my new curtains? Frightfully avant-garde, aren't they?'

'They're frightfully... something,' Cressida agreed, her need to give her opinion over the horrendous things straining against her good breeding and excellent manners. 'They are very well made,' she decided on, hoping to leave it at that.

Lady Chatterton, however, gave a long and cheerless sigh.

'Mama?' Dotty asked, moving to her side and placing a supportive hand at her elbow.

'Oh, I'm quite all right, Dorothy dear, just a little exhausted from all the goings-on. That wretched scaffolding tower is still looking like some sort of revolutionary barricade in the hall and this ballroom looks like a fabric trade fair...' She waved a hand over the curtains. 'And those... oh, who am I kidding. They're foul, aren't they?'

Cressida caught Dotty's eye, and although neither of them would have admitted to starting it, a snort became a snigger, which became a chortle and then a giggle and in no time at all the three of them were hooting with laughter over the whole silly mess.

'Oh, it does me good to laugh. Thank you, girls. And I suppose there'll be nothing else for it,' Lady Chatterton said, running a hand along the weighted hem. 'I shall have to see if I can sell them and start all over again. Cressida, dear, you will help me this time, won't you?'

'Of course, Lady Chatterton. It would be my pleasure.' Cressida looked at Dotty, who rolled her eyes.

'I'm afraid these will have to go up pro-tem,' Lady Chatterton admitted. 'What with the scaffold being in situ and all that. Curtains like these take such an age to order and make, I simply can't have the windows bare for all that time.'

'Fear not, Lady Chatterton.' Cressida reassured her. 'I'm sure we can have new curtains chosen, designed, stitched and sewn by midsummer at the latest. And scaffold or not, we'll get them up!'

As the three ladies came to a natural break in their conversation about fabrics and finishes, Cressida thought it the time, finally, to ask Lady Chatterton about her diamonds. Leaving the striped monstrosities on their trestles, they moved over towards the large fireplace that dominated one of the longer walls in the room and sat in front of it on a pretty little suite of gold-rimmed chairs, each one upholstered in a dark red velvet.

'I'm so sorry about the burglary,' Cressida said. 'It all sounded so dramatic in the press: broken windows and midnight flits by the thief and not a trace of his whereabouts and all that. Was that how it all really happened?'

'Yes, well they do like to exaggerate a bit, don't they, these so-called "gentlemen of the press". But on the whole the reports were accurate enough.' Lady Chatterton sighed and glanced at the ormolu clock on the mantelpiece. 'Oh dear, is that the time? I really should head up to bed.'

'Mama, stay a little and tell Cressy all about it.'

'Very well,' Lady Chatterton played with her long string of pearls as she spoke. 'Cressida dear, you have a sharp and bright mind, you tell me what you think after you've heard it all.'

'Oh, I shall. Do go on.'

'It was Wednesday night, wasn't it, Mama?' Dotty started the story for her beleaguered mother. 'We were dining, weren't we, just you, me, Papa and John...'

'Yes, Alfred was in London,' Lady Chatterton agreed, and Cressida nodded. She'd seen him at The Savoy on Wednesday night, though only briefly. 'We dined and then did the usual evening things. John was planning his trip to Europe, and I think you and I were about to go and do a stock check of the cheese in the pantry, weren't we, Dotty, when the lights all suddenly went out.'

'Gosh. The press did mention that the power was cut.' Cressida tucked one leg under the other and pulled Ruby up to her chest for a cuddle. The small dog gave a little snort in excitement. 'Best you continue, Lady Chatterton, before Ruby decides to add more to the conversation.'

'That's quite all right, Cressida dear, I've had similar conversations with Francis. Anyway, that's one of those little exaggerations of the press. You see the power wasn't *cut* so much as *turned off*. At first, we thought it was only a blip. The poor cleaners, who are taking *so* much longer than I hoped, have been fiddling with the power on and off and on and off as they clean the lights...'

'Hence the candles out there now,' Dotty said to Cressida, then turned back to her mother. 'You can't really blame them, Mama, it is a frightful job cleaning that chandelier. Or electrolier, as I think it's correctly called these days. And, Cressy, you have to understand, we have power cuts here all... the... time.' Dotty's voice echoed the ennui the family obviously felt about Chatterton Court's precarious relationship with its wiring. 'We're not so close to that lovely new power station over the river from you at Battersea, Cressy. We're a little more tin can and wire from the coal hole here in Berkshire, you know.'

'Believe me, I understand,' Cressida nodded. 'Ma and Pa are always blaming their power outages on the Kaiser, even though the Germans never got anywhere near West Sussex. Anyway, do carry on, Lady Chatterton.'

'Thank you, dear. Well, you see the power outage was a trifling nuisance really, since we had the fire burning. We stayed put and chatted amongst ourselves for a while until it really became intolerable and I sent John off to find Cardew.'

'The butler,' Dotty added for clarity. It was a name Cressida was unfamiliar with and she cocked her head on one side.

'I thought you had old Greystoke? Or am I behind the times?' Cressida asked.

'Mr Greystoke shuffled off this mortal coil this winter just gone. Working til the last, though we tried to pension him off years ago. Bless him,' Dotty answered.

'Oh poor Greystoke, such a loyal man. But we have Cardew now and he's terribly efficient,' Lady Chatterton continued. 'He's been with us a few months or so and is a godsend. I hadn't realised how slow Greystoke had got until Cardew came and did all the same tasks in a fraction of the time. Anyway, John went and found him and, of course, all of a sudden, there were the lights all back on again. I still can't get used to this electricity. When I was a girl, you knew where you stood with an oil lamp and a nice candelabra.'

'Usually sweating like one of our racehorses, Mama, with all those naked flames around.' Dotty stifled a giggle.

Lady Chatterton sighed and shook her head. 'Honestly, dear, I sometimes wonder whether that terribly expensive school did anything for you at all...' The words were said with warmth and kindness and were met with an indulgent grin from Dotty.

'So the lights came back on?' Cressida pressed.

'Yes, and with them John, who came back with the oddest piece of news, which was that the main switch had been *thrown*. It's down in the kitchen corridors somewhere, one of the old pantries was turned into a sort of switchboard cupboard, I think. Anyway, turns out Cardew was down there about to flick it back up when John found him.' She paused. 'Cressida dear, you might think this a little odd, but I'll tell you what I told the local police, and that was that at the time we really didn't think anything of it. Some of the servants are new and still getting used to the wiring. Of course, looking back, it's all bit strange, but there seemed no harm done and we continued the evening. It was only when I retired to bed that I...' Lady Chatterton paused and Dotty leaned over and placed a hand on her arm.

'Go on, Mama, it's good to talk about it, I think.'

Lady Chatterton nodded. 'You see, as soon as I walked into my bedroom, I could tell something was horribly wrong. The wardrobe doors were open and my clothes flung all over the room, the ottoman at the end of the bed was upended, its stuffing pulled out, the rug flipped over like one of those French pancakes and the drawers of the tallboy and my dressing table were pulled out and tossed around, their contents everywhere. And, of course, I knew what had happened when I saw the black velvet box that my diamonds came in lying open on the floor – empty.' Lady Chatterton wrapped her arms around her and shuddered. 'So they're gone. Quite gone.'

'Lady Chatterton, I'm so sorry.' Cressida could see how affected the older woman was by the theft.

'It's the violation, you see. Someone, in cover of darkness, rifled through my personal belongings. Not that there's a salacious thing to be found, my dance cards are spotless, as it were, but it's all rather tawdry, isn't it? Having a stranger in one's inner sanctum.' Lady Chatterton pulled at her pearls again, so obviously in distress over the whole thing.

'Horrible, yes,' Cressida agreed.

'It's the wondering what might have happened had one of us disturbed him.' Dotty's shoulders shuddered at the thought and Lady Chatterton blanched at the mention of it.

'Dorothy...' She closed her eyes, drawing on some inner strength. 'Perish the thought, darling. Though it's the fact that none of us were harmed which is keeping me from mourning the loss of the diamonds so much, special to me as they were.'

'The value of things can't always be measured in pounds, despite what the newspaper headlines want to say,' murmured Dotty.

'Were they of huge sentimental value too then?' asked Cressida, looking at Dotty and then her mother for the answer.

'Yes, dear,' Lady Chatterton answered. 'Given to me by my own mother before she died. Irreplaceable – in my heart at least.' Her Ladyship pulled a handkerchief from her sleeve and dabbed her eyes.

'I'm so sorry.' Cressida hated seeing dear Lady Chatterton so upset. 'How do you think he got in?'

'Via the kitchens, we suppose, which weren't locked for the night at that point. Then past the electric switch, of course, up the stairs, to my suite of rooms, and out the window, which he left open, not broken, as the press delighted in saying. There's a rather sturdy drainpipe to the right of the window and it seemed he used it to shimmy down, leaving two boot prints in the soft ground below, before dashing off across the lawns in the direction of the icehouse, I suppose, and then the back lane to the village and station.' She shrugged resignedly. 'He might as well be in Peru by now.'

'Nothing at all picked up by the local police?' Cressida asked.

'Nothing.' Dotty intervened. 'Those prints were apparently those of a standard Army-issue boot, which could be worn by almost any man in the country, what with so many of them having recently served.'

Despite hopefully living up to the expectation of being both sharp and bright-minded, Cressida was stumped. She had, however, all weekend at Chatterton Court and she was sure her keen eye for details would help turn something up. She said as much to Lady Chatterton, who thanked her with a squeeze to the shoulder as she got up.

'This whole affair has been so wretched. I shan't sleep a wink tonight, I'm sure.'

'Let me come up with you, Mama.' Dotty went to her mother's side. 'One of the maids can have some hot milk sent up. Cressy, you'll be all right finding your room, won't you? Name's on the door.'

'Of course. Goodnight, both, and do sleep well, Lady Chatterton.' Cressida raised her glass to them, while still holding onto Ruby on her lap. 'If there's a clue, we'll find it, Rubes,' she whispered to her pug once they were out of earshot, then drained the last drop from her glass and placed it on one of the side tables. 'But first it's time for bed, and who knows what tomorrow will bring?'

5

Tomorrow brought with it a scream so loud that it penetrated the walls and doors, carpets and curtains even, of Chatterton Court. A scream that awoke the still slumbering Cressida, who was further being roused by the efforts of an overexcited pug.

'Calm down, Rubes, what's happening?' Cressida pulled her velvet eye mask up and blinked into the morning. She pulled Ruby away from licking her face, telling the young pup that she was now 'more than awake, thank you very much', flipped the bedclothes off her and padded to the door in her silk pyjamas, her eye mask now acting as a headband keeping her tousled hair off her face. Beyond, out on the landing, she could hear sobbing and shouting; not at all the usual morning routine in an English country house where the servants were prized for their softness of tread and hushed voices.

She pulled the door open and peeked out, noticing that several of the other bedroom doors were currently being used to shield the pyjamaed bodies of her fellow guests, their faces, some familiar and others not, as perplexed as hers. With a nod to Dotty, who had just appeared bleary-eyed from her own bedroom, Cressida tiptoed out into the corridor and met her friend, taking her hand by instinct as they walked along the carpeted landing towards the top of the large staircase and the stone balustrade that edged the balconied landing.

Light was streaming in through the glass cupola above the hallway, glinting off the sparkling crystals of the chandelier. Guttered candles from last night's overtime peppered the pale grey stone, while the scaffolding tower still dominated the grand space of the hall. Sobbing and shushing were coming from below and Cressida recognised a couple of the voices. There was Mrs Climpton, the Chatterton's cook, along with Dotty's father Lord Chatterton, and someone she assumed was Cardew, the new butler, and several hysterical housemaids.

'What on earth...?' Cressida and Dotty reached the top of the stairs and peered over the reassuringly solid balustrade, recoiling almost immediately as they witnessed the scene below.

'Dear Lord!' Dotty pressed her hands against her face, covering her eyes, but Cressida knew nothing could erase the memory of what they'd seen. She peered over again, bracing herself this time for the grisly spectacle below her. There was a body, crumpled on the marble floor, one leg bent at a wholly unnatural angle, while the head and arms were haloed by a dark red pool of blood.

'Dotty...' Cressida recognised the blue boiler suit but had to ask, 'is that... the cleaner?'

'Yes, it's H-H-Harry. Harry Smith.' Dotty was shaking and she looked distinctly green around the gills. Cressida knew the best thing for her friend would be to get back into bed and drink some warm sweet tea, but, to her surprise, Dotty dropped her hands from her face and moved closer to the balustrade. 'He seemed so jolly last night.' Dotty trembled.

Cressida nodded silently, remembering the cheerful whistle as he'd polished the crystals. But there would be no more whistling now. He was dead, that was for sure, and judging by those injuries, he'd fallen from the very top of the scaffold, plummeting to his certain death on the cold, hard tiles below.

Dotty pulled back from the scene and Cressida wrapped her arms around her friend in a hug.

'I'm so sorry, Dotty.' Cressida couldn't think of much else to say but peered back over the balustrade one last time. The scene was quite sickening and even Lord Chatterton was now standing back and mopping his brow with a handkerchief, while Cardew and several footmen tried to calm the housemaids, one of whom had no doubt been responsible for the scream that had awoken the household.

'He seemed such a nice young man,' Dotty mumbled into Cressida's shoulder. 'One of those cheeky chappies with a "how's you?" in the morning.' Dotty sniffed and then pulled away from Cressida and wiped her nose with her pyjama sleeve. 'Made me laugh, you know the sort.' She started crying again, so Cressida, who was starting to shake a little herself with the shock of it all, slipped her arm around her and guided her back to her bedroom. Ruby, who had snuck out of Cressida's bedroom and was panting expectantly in the corridor between the two doors, obediently trotted in behind them as they entered Dotty's room.

Once a really rather pale Dotty was tucked into bed, Cressida rang the bell for her maid, hoping that she would be able to respond and wasn't too caught up in the tragedy below. Before long, they were both settled, Ruby snuggled up between them, pillows propping themselves up and steaming cups of English Breakfast tea and buttered and jam-covered fingers of toast reviving them from their shock.

'That poor young man,' Dotty said before she took another sip of tea. 'To fall from such a height.' She shuddered.

'It doesn't bear thinking about, does it,' agreed Cressida, pulling Ruby up to her chest and resting her chin on the pup's thick rolls of fur.

'I'm sorry this isn't the sophisticated weekend you hoped for, Cressy.' Dotty looked at her, her chestnut eyes brimming with tears behind her round glasses.

'Oh Dot, please don't spare a thought for that. I'm simply glad I'm here for you. This would be ghastly faced alone.'

'I'm glad you're here too, Cressy.' There was a snuffle from near Cressida's chest. 'And you too, Ruby, of course,' Dotty added. 'So very glad.'

Once the tea and toast had done their restorative work, Cressida left Dotty to wash and dress and headed back across the landing, Ruby in tow, to the Blue Room. She'd known her way to it last night well, not only because she was a frequent visitor to Chatterton Court and had stayed in that room before, but because she'd helped Lady Chatterton design it when Her Ladyship had first embarked on her grand plan of redecorating the house 'for the modern age'. Cressida didn't mind being asked to help, in fact she adored designing room schemes, plus she sometimes found the endless leisure time of the upper classes infuriatingly boring and she did like to be *doing something*. Helping her hostesses with their interiors was to her a far better way to spend a morning than dawdling around playing cribbage or shooting things out of second-floor windows.

Or watching footmen cover a dead body with a sheet…

Why she'd let herself glance down once again into the atrium as she'd left Dotty's room, she didn't know, as the addition of the sheet had done nothing to wipe the gruesome image of the broken body from her mind.

Cressida could at least take some comfort from the elegant decor in her bedroom and as she turned the large brass knob of the antique wood-panelled door, she felt a sense of much-needed calm wash over her. She had arrived in darkness the night before, and it was natural light that so brought this room alive. Named the Blue Room in the eighteenth century when the house was built, it was a large west-facing room with two sash windows overlooking the lawns. It had always been blue – a colour too cold for east- and north-facing rooms, but bright and fresh for those blessed with the warmer light of the western-setting sun. She had noticed this when it had come to refreshing the space and had acknowledged that, nine times out of ten, those that had come before had got it right. In the afternoon, when the orange-tinged sunlight would hit the pale blue of the walls, they'd take on a greenish hue, with hints of the pink of the setting sun reflecting off the bevelled edges of the looking glass in the wardrobe and mirror on the dressing table. Come sunset, the colours would give the effect of being inside one massive opal, with aqua, turquoise and rose accents delicately complementing each other all around her.

Cressida thought about this as Ruby scuttled off to wherever little dogs like to scuttle off to. It was a much nicer place to let one's mind linger than on the hellish scene in the hallway below.

'Downstairs shall have to be faced at some point though, Rubes,' Cressida muttered to her pup, who had found a sunbeam and was already lightly snoring. 'All right for some.' Cressida went over and stroked the wrinkles between the snoozing dog's eyes, letting the sensation of it help soothe her after this morning's horrors. 'I don't think you've ever seen a dead body either have you, Rubes? But now I have, and a gruesome sight it was too.' Cressida sighed with a slow shake of her head. 'I'm glad you've been spared it, precious pooch. And,' she gave Ruby one final stroke, 'you lucky thing, you're also spared the chore of having to get dressed.'

A few minutes and one or two tricky button loops in awkward places later saw Cressida wondering once again if perhaps a lady's maid might not be such a bad thing after all. However, with buttons accomplished, Cressida dismissed the idea and turned to face herself in the mirror. A smart tweed skirt, silk blouse and cashmere shawl held in place by a beautiful pearl brooch and she was fit and proper to go forth and meet the other guests at Chatterton Court, and put names to those shocked and sleepy faces she'd seen first thing this morning.

She shuddered. As social as she was and as confident as she normally felt in company, she had to admit that leaving the sanctum and safety of the Blue Room now was easier said than done. Cressida took one or two deeper breaths than usual as she opened the door and faced going back onto the landing, before descending the wide stone staircase to the great hall, where, only until very, very recently, there had lain a dead man in a pool of his own blood.

6

Soulful yet beautiful piano music guided Cressida down the staircase and helped distract her from the maids who were scrubbing hard at the bloodstained marble floor. Ruby, proving that in no way could she have been descended from feral wolves, paid no attention to the blood on the floor and trotted off in the direction of the kitchens, where, in fairness to the young pup, there emanated a tempting smell of grilling bacon and hot sausages.

'Go and find Climpton, Rubes. At least one of us should have the stomach for a cooked breakfast and I'm afraid to say it isn't me this morning.'

Ruby snorted a sort of agreement and Cressida thanked one of the maids who held open the green baize door that separated the main house from the kitchens for the imperious small dog.

The piano music still played and Cressida followed the sound into the drawing room, where she recognised a few fellow guests from Chatterton parties of old, but found it was Dotty who was the musician. A spaniel, Rollo, had his muzzle resting on Dotty's lap as she played and Cressida was pleased that Dotty had him to comfort her. Where Dotty's fiancé Basil

Bartleby was, Cressida had no idea, but the thought crossed her mind that, after the trauma of this morning, the least he could do was be by his betrothed's side. *Still*, thought Cressida, *dogs are usually better than men. Perhaps it's for the best.*

'Cressy!' The music stopped and Cressida waved at Dotty, who was now beckoning her over. 'Off you go, Rollo, find Ruby.'

'She's off pestering Climpton for a sausage or two,' Cressida said, leaning against the grand piano. 'So lovely to hear you play again, Dot. Your tinkling was quite the only thing that gave me the strength to make it downstairs.'

'Ghastly isn't it.' Dotty shivered. 'But, Cressy, I'm forgetting my manners. You remember my brothers, don't you?' Dotty pointed over towards two young men, smartly dressed in country three-piece tweed suits, who were earnestly talking about something, one of them using a pipe to gesticulate his point, while the other stood with his arms crossed, leaning up against the fireplace.

'Yes, of course.' Cressida looked over to where they were standing. She knew Dotty's brothers well. Alfred, the older of the two, was very much in her 'set'. As the eldest son of Lord Chatterton, who was an earl, he was a viscount, and confusingly titled Lord Delafield, that being a subsidiary title of his father's. He preferred plain Alfred though. He was the one waving his pipe at his brother, sucking on it occasionally with intent while he listened to what John had to say. The Hon. John was the youngest of the Chattertons and undoubtedly the most academic of his siblings, if not blessed with their common sense. They were both handsome men and, in fact, Cressida had deflected many a well-meaning suggestion from her mother, and many of her mother's friends, on the subject of Alfred's eligibility.

A third man was sitting on one of the chintz sofas, reading the paper, and though Cressida recognised him, she didn't know him terribly well.

'That's Edmund Priestley.' Dotty filled in Cressida's thoughts. 'He's in that silly dining club they're all members of. The Mutton Pie Club, or whatever it's called.' Dotty carefully closed the fallboard over the ivory piano keys before getting up from the stool and walking with Cressida over to where the young men were congregated.

'Ah, what ho, Cressida,' Alfred greeted her, giving her a kiss on the cheek, which to Cressida's horror made her blush. 'We missed you last night. Decided to forego us and party til—'

'Alfred...'

'What is it?' Dotty quizzed them. 'What have I missed?'

The corners of Alfred's mouth twitched in amusement. 'Nothing, dear sis, just your pal Cressida here entertaining us royally a few nights ago at The Savoy with her rendition of—'

'Yes, yes, Alfred,' Cressida did her best to shush him.

'Did I miss a frightfully fun night?' Dotty asked, wringing her hands. 'Only Basil said it wasn't proper for me to be out dancing every night now we're engaged.'

Cressida frowned, but thought better of voicing her thoughts on that for now. 'No, Dotty, nothing salacious, just one too many Gin Rickeys for me—'

'And the small matter of that bowl of trifle that fell off your head while you Charlestoned on the bar.' Alfred chuckled to himself as Dotty formed a wide 'O' with her mouth.

'Anyway, Alfred.' Cressida crossed her arms and looked at him. Unlike his mother and sister, his chestnut hair had a wave to it and Cressida had to admit to herself that he was looking very handsome in his tweed suit, his pipe now stuck at a rakish angle from the corner of his mouth. 'I'm sorry for the recent run of events here at Chatterton Court.'

'You know it's statistically disproved that bad things happen in threes,' John answered before his brother could remove his pipe from his mouth. He carried on: 'People always say bad

things happen in threes, but it's never been proven. It's merely
the human condition to observe pattern.'

'I think what John is implying is that we all very much hope
that the tragic death of that young cleaner chap, following on so
soon after Mother's diamonds were filched, is the end of our run
of bad luck,' Alfred said and then sucked on his pipe while John
nodded enthusiastically.

'Or so we hope.' The third man, Edmund Priestley, folded
the newspaper he'd been reading and looked up at Cressida
from the sofa. It was hard to gauge his height, sitting down as he
was, but Cressida reckoned him to be a sporting sort of chap.
He was handsome too, and Cressida recognised him now from
various race meets at Newbury and Sandown. He looked
tanned, as if he'd been enjoying the spring weather, and it
suited his dark brown hair and equally dark brown eyes.
'Edmund Priestley.' He finally stood and stretched a hand out to
Cressida. 'Sandhurst with John back in 1920. You must be the
Honourable Miss Fawcett, I presume.'

Cressida shook his hand and nodded. 'That's me. Very good
to meet you properly, Edmund, and not on the other side of the
paddock at the racecourse.' She looked at them all. 'And again,
apologies to you all for my appalling timekeeping last night. I
would like to say that I hit a pothole and blew a tyre, but in fact
I was just waylaid in London and didn't leave in time.'

'You're statistically unlikely to hit a pothole on the Great
West Road, being that it's dual lane for most of the way,' John
piped up and Cressida remembered that Dotty had been
relieved when her sweet-natured, but rather numerically
obsessed brother had been granted a place at Cambridge to read
mathematics after his spell at the military academy at Sandhurst. 'In fact, with a tyre width of approximately six inches and
a circumference of—'

'John, that's enough dear,' Dotty shushed him. 'I don't think

Cressy really needs to know about how likely she is to run into any potholes between here and London.'

'Pretty bloody likely, the state of some of those roads,' Edmund chipped in.

'Oh yes, you've been driving around a bit recently haven't you, Edmund?' Dotty, who had by now slipped her arm into that of her younger brother, who still seemed to be calculating statistics in his head judging by the silent movement of his lips and the narrowing of one eye as he concentrated, turned to Edmund. 'I was busy ringing around all our guests yesterday to reassure them that the party would still go ahead despite the theft and the cleaners still being here.' Dotty paused, her face suddenly falling as her own words reminded her of the morning's tragedy. She collected herself before adding in more of a whisper, 'I couldn't get hold of you, Edmund, but it was jolly lovely that you turned up anyway.'

'Three thousand and forty-nine to one.' John's more forthright voice brought them all back to the room. 'And you needn't have tried telephoning Edmund, I'd told you on Monday afternoon, Dotty, that I'd already spoken to him.'

Dotty squeezed her brother's arm. 'Quite right, John, you did.'

Everyone fell silent again and Cressida wondered if each of them in their own way was struggling to come to terms with the fatal accident this morning. Despite not knowing the man personally, a death had occurred in the house and it had been, at the very least, an extremely unsettling thing to wake up to.

Cressida, who hadn't been at Chatterton Court for more than about twelve hours, couldn't help but think there was something very bizarre about the whole thing. Something she couldn't put her finger on, that wasn't making sense. But before she could mention this to Dotty, or the young men, they were joined by two more members of the house party.

'Petronella, William,' Dotty ushered the two new guests in.

'Cressida darling, I don't think you've met the Harper-Ashes? Brother and sister, not missus and mister though.' Dotty gave a nervous laugh, but Cressida was relieved that she was at least attempting humour again after this morning's grisly discovery.

'Hallo both.' Cressida stuck her hand out.

Petronella took it first and gave it a firm shake. She was one of those tall, outdoorsy types and although her hair was unfashionably long, it was tinged with golden highlights and she looked incredibly healthy and tanned. Cressida, flexing her fingers after such an assertive greeting, wondered if there were perhaps some rather strong muscles under the soft silk of Petronella's tea dress.

Her brother, his hair sandy and touched with golden highlights too, pressed both his hands around Cressida's now wearied one. He, too, was of that outdoorsy sort of build, but thicker set than his sister, taller of course, and more overtly muscular – his tweed sports jacket, though well tailored, sat taut across his biceps.

'We've heard so much about you.' William let her hand go and Cressida thought about cradling it in the crook of her elbow for a little while to allow it to recover. The Harper-Ashes, if strong, were at least friendly, while their accents betrayed them as not being local.

'William and Petronella are from South Africa, Cressy.' Dotty once again seemed to know exactly what Cressida was thinking.

'Oh, how marvellous,' Cressida replied and now could see why they both looked so tanned and outdoorsy.

'We're half-English though,' said Petronella, 'despite what we sound like.' She laughed and Cressida noted to herself how often it was the women in society who dropped a self-deprecating remark in order to lighten the mood and carry the conversation. She decided that this sacrifice shouldn't go unrewarded.

'Well, I think you both look splendidly healthy from all

those days in the veld sunshine. I am green with envy.' Cressida smiled at Petronella, who grinned back at her. To Cressida's shame, she briefly and subconsciously compared Petronella's splendidly white and mouth-filling teeth to that of a horse, but she blinked the idea away.

Luckily, Petronella wasn't as good at reading Cressida's mind as Dotty seemed to be, and she kept smiling at Cressida as she carried on explaining their heritage. 'You're right, we're Veldlanders. Well, Mother is and Father found his way out there in order to manage the family mines. He always says that, despite finding as many gems as he could ever want under the ground, his most precious one was Mother.'

'That is utterly the sweetest thing I've ever heard.' Cressida, who wasn't impressed by romantic nonsense, knew that as a young woman in society, this was the sort of reply that was expected of her.

'Isn't it,' Dotty agreed, and Cressida looked at her, surprised by the lack of enthusiasm in her voice. Dotty was usually the first to fall doe-eyed at romance and yet she seemed distracted and pulled away from her brother's arm as she squeezed past Cressida and the Harper-Ashes. 'I'd better go and find Basil. He did say he'd be down to greet you, Cressy. And I think that's a whiff of cordite I can smell coming from upstairs. At this rate, there'll be no fauna left in the arboretum at all come Sunday night. Will you excuse me?'

'Of course, dear. I'm dying to see Basil again,' Cressida lied, distinctly remembering Basil Bartleby to be an oafish sort of brute. With the horrors that had been going on recently, though, at Chatterton Court, she had convinced herself to try to see the best in him, for Dotty's sake at least. The last thing poor Dot needed was a doubting Thomasina at her side all weekend.

'Oh dear, was it something I said?' Petronella whispered to Cressida, a volume of speaking that was hardly necessary now that all the young men in the room were talking raucously about some card game they'd all played at their club the other night.

'I don't think so, Petronella. Dotty's had a shock. And I don't think Basil's the hopeless romantic she's after in her life. I rather thought he might be comforting her, but...' Cressida tailed off. She thought perhaps it wasn't right to gossip.

Petronella frowned. 'Basil's not...' She paused and shook her head. 'Well, I hope it wasn't mention of Father's mines, what with the family's diamonds being such a sore subject?'

Cressida had almost forgotten about the missing diamonds, what with the ghastliness of the morning's discovery of poor, dead Harry Smith. She let Petronella talk to her about the beauties of the African plains and she nodded along with her recounting of how lovely the supper the night before had been despite Lady Chatterton's recent loss. She'd been delighted to be able to wear her new silk dress, even if her brother had compared it, colour wise, to a silverskin cocktail onion. Basil, according to her, was a super raconteur, while Alfred was simply charm itself. Cressida *oohed* and *aahed* in the right places, but the death and the diamonds were occupying her thoughts. There was nothing to suggest they were linked, but was John really right in saying that events were merely coincidences? Cressida couldn't help but think that they weren't and hoped that John was correct in his analysis that bad things really didn't happen in threes.

7

Cressida's reverie was interrupted by the arrival of Dotty and, in her tow, her fiancé Basil. Where Dotty was short of stature, yet as elegantly dressed as her class and status afforded her, he was tall and lanky with an air of louche entitlement to him. He was, admittedly, exceedingly handsome, if one liked the rugged sort of look. His hair was sandy in colour and not the type to kowtow to a hairbrush and he more often than not had a hand running through it. His clothes were smart, yet worn with a sort of insouciance, and he had obviously neglected to shave this morning... well, perhaps Cressida was reading into it all a little too much, but like a badly done piece of upholstery, there was something not quite right about him. *For someone who spends so long in the bathroom, his lack of grooming is simply unforgivable*, Cressida thought to herself. *It's a shame he hides away up there with a shotgun, not a razor blade.*

Cressida shook the thoughts out of her head and reminded herself that, for Dotty's sake, she was determined to like him.

'Basil, hello.' Cressida stuck out her hand and greeted him.

'Ah, Fawcett. Pleasure to meet you. How do you do?' He shook Cressida's hand and she wanted very much to remind him that they *had* actually met before, but didn't want to embarrass him in front of Dotty. Or, indeed, herself, as she seemed to remember that the last time she and Basil had been in company, she'd ended up placing far too large a bet on the King's horse at Epsom and not come off terribly well from it.

'How many squirrels have you bagged this morning?' Petronella asked Basil, and Cressida thought it awfully sporting of her to try to make conversation with him.

The topic was obviously a hit with him and his face became animated, his pale blue eyes shining, as he talked Petronella through each and every near miss. Cressida couldn't help but be on the side of the squirrels and was pleasantly surprised at how many were apparently still living to eat another nut, or at least be there to amuse Ruby on one of their walks.

Thinking of walks, however, reminded her of what Lady Chatterton had said last night about the footprints in the soft soil of the herbaceous border. She looked down at her insubstantial but elegant enough pumps and frowned. Stouter shoes would be needed, Cressida decided, if she were to retrace the steps of the local village constables and see if maybe, just maybe, they might have missed something. *Something from the robbery, something that might connect it to the death of that poor cleaner fellow*, she thought to herself. Hanging around drawing rooms partaking of idle chat might be what was expected of her, *but*, Cressida thought, *it's not going to get us anywhere.*

'Dotty, do you mind if I get some fresh air? Better go and check Ruby hasn't snaffled all the cold meats too.'

Cressida excused herself from the party and headed back out towards the great hall. As pointless as the drawing-room chatter had been, it had at least been a welcome, comforting normality compared to the gruesome scene she'd witnessed in the hall. She braced herself to see the aftermath of the cleaner's fall, but as she was wincing at the thought of either seeing the claret-red of the blood on the ground or the hunched backs of industriously scrubbing housemaids, she heard the familiar snorting of her own dear pup.

'Oh, Rubes, you are heaven-sent.' She scooped up the small dog and detected the unmistakable whiff of sausage on her breath. 'Good breakfast?'

Ruby snuffled in what Cressida took to be the affirmative.

With her pup nestled into her arms, Cressida felt a darn sight braver crossing the marbled hallway, and keeping the scaffolding tower, and the floor beneath it, as much out of her sight as was possible, she ascended the wide stone staircase and headed back to her room.

Stouter shoes on, and Ruby tucked under her arm, Cressida felt more prepared to start retracing the steps of the local village constables. Quite what she had been expecting to see in the soft mud of the herbaceous border under Lady Chatterton's bedroom window, she couldn't now tell you. However, it was obvious that whatever boot prints might have indicated a single thief shimmying down the drainpipe had been superseded by umpteen clodhopping coppers who had trampled all over the scene and damaged some of the lower branches of the hydrangea too. She only hoped that photographs had been taken, and developed, before the evidence was buried under multiple other prints.

It reminded Cressida of a visit she'd paid to Lady Fishbourne a year or so ago, who was determined to find the original colour of her hallway paint, but it had been painted over so many times, they had ended up chipping away at the wall and analysing the flakes. It would have been a whole lot easier if Lady F hadn't, in the first flush of her tidying and renovations, accidentally thrown out the eighteenth-century work logs that would have just *told* them which colour had been used. It had turned out to be something approaching the colour of an under-

DEATH AMONG THE DIAMONDS   45

cooked crumpet and they had decided to go for cream anyway, but it had been a right palaver.

She sighed at the memory and glanced up at the window and saw what Lady Chatterton had meant about the sturdy drainpipe. She didn't fancy sliding down it herself during a dark night's escapade; green algae like that would be hell to get out of one's evening wear for a start, though she didn't doubt that the thief would have been wearing something more suitable for jumping out of windows than her favourite tasselled silk and satin.

A boiler suit perhaps, like that of the poor cleaner...

She huffed out a breath, turned away from the house and started walking across the terrace towards the lawn, Ruby waddling along beside her. It was a bright morning and Cressida took a few deep breaths, inhaling the gloriously fresh country air. London was devilishly fun and exciting to live in, but the constant burning of coke and coal by her and everyone around her had lent a certain tang to the air and it was only in the very centre of one of the city's parks that one could draw a breath of air anywhere near as clean as this. And it was quiet here too. Unlike London, where omnibuses and cabs roared down the Embankment at almost all hours of the day and night, the voices of revellers often drifted up to her open windows on a summer's evening and street vendors, scrap collectors and traders all joined in the throng come the morning... Well, here there was only the noise of birdsong and the gentle coo of a dove... And some sort of clanking sound.

'Interesting,' Cressida said to herself, following the sound across the lawn and towards the wood as it continued.

Clink, clink, clink...

Cressida pulled her shawl tighter around her and held Ruby close as she entered the shade of the wood and cocked her head to one side to try to ascertain where the noise was coming from.

Clink, clink, clink...

She stepped further into the woods, with the noise guiding her towards what looked like a small brick-built dome rising out of the dead leaves and undergrowth of the woodland floor. She'd seen one like it before; in fact, domes like this were a common enough occurrence in the grounds of large country estates. It was the icehouse, and Cressida soon realised that the clinking sound was one of the staff removing a suitable-sized block from the recent delivery to take back to the kitchens. She recognised him as the same lad who'd parked her car for her last night.

'Hallo there, Jacob, isn't it?' Cressida said as she approached, not wanting to surprise the man with the small pickaxe and cause an injury.

'Hello, miss,' he replied, looking up and giving a little nod of his head. 'That's right. Can I help you, miss?' He was good enough not to mention Ruby's indiscretion from the night before and she appreciated it.

'No, not at all. Sorry to disturb. I was just...' Cressida suddenly felt a bit silly playing the part of the amateur detective and realised her reason for being out here in the woods sounded a little preposterous. She could hardly say that she was hot on the heels of the thief and triumphing where the local bobbies had failed. And especially not start espousing theories on how the theft and the death of the young cleaner were perhaps linked. Still, this young man might know a little of what had gone on, from the staff's point of view, and so she carried on: '... Wondering where the thief who stole Lady Chatterton's diamonds ran off to after he descended the drainpipe.'

As she suspected, Jacob had an opinion on the case.

'Could as easily 'ave been anywhere, miss. There's a lane out yonder, through the woods. I wouldn't like to say for sure, but it's been an awful time it has.' The young lad wiped his brow with his sleeve and sniffed a couple of times.

'Oh, I'm sure. How are you all bearing up below stairs after this morning?'

'Well, it's kind of you to ask, miss.' Jacob nodded in thanks to her. 'It's been a shock, that's for sure. Especially as that lad had such a bright future.'

'The cleaner? What was his name again? Harry...'

'Harry Smith, miss. Yes, that's him. Clever lad, it seemed. And industrious too. It weren't his fault the cleaning was taking so long, as he'd been left all on his own to do it after the other chap went off with the 'flu. It's a technical job, see, unhooking all those crystals. Us lot couldn't help him and it took some doing to even climb that bloomin' thing in the hallway to get at them.'

Cressida thought about it. She had tried her best to avoid looking at the scaffolding tower this morning but had seen it last night, illuminated by candle and moonlight, and had been impressed then at how confident Harry Smith had been up there, whistling away to himself.

'You said he had a bright future? What do you mean? Did he own the cleaning business?'

'No, miss. He took his tea most days with us in the kitchen and hadn't had much to say except cheeky "how dos" to the maids and the odd joke. Then yesterday he said he was about to come into some money and how should he spend it and whatnot. Got some of the maids quite excited with his flirtin', he did, and he was adamant he weren't going to be a cleaner no more.'

'And he didn't say where this money was coming from? Or why he'd suddenly started talking about it?'

'I supposed he was getting to know us before starting to show off, like. And no, he just said he was coming into some money. Or wealth, I think he said. I thought that was a bit odd. "I'm going to be wealthy, you see" is what he said. He even started asking the gents about it.'

This really piqued Cressida's interest. 'The gents? Lord Chatterton, you mean?'

Jacob laughed at this suggestion. 'No, not His Lordship. The younger men. And not Lord Delafield or the Honourable John either. That one with the shotgun in the bathroom and the other one.'

'Basil...' Cressida bit her lip as she thought about it. Harry the cleaner had been blessed with some sort of inheritance, told Basil about it and was dead the next day... She shook her head. Basil didn't need money, she was almost sure of it. *And this didn't have anything to do with the diamonds... unless...* 'Jacob, Harry was cleaning here when the diamonds were stolen, wasn't he?'

Jacob hesitated. 'Y-yes, miss.' He looked uneasy. 'But he wouldn't have taken them, miss.'

'I don't like to cast aspersions either, Jacob, but how can you be so sure?'

'It doesn't make sense, does it?' Jacob looked at her and Cressida cocked an eyebrow at him. There was a small part of her that thought it might make perfect sense for a cleaner to steal the diamonds, far more than any of the trusted household servants or some random thief. The fact that whoever had taken the diamonds knew roughly where they were kept, but not exactly, occurred to her and she made a mental note to hold onto that thought as Jacob continued. 'The diamonds disappeared on Wednesday night, you see, and yet Harry was back in on Thursday, worked his shift among all the police and whatnot interviewing us all, searching the house and all that, then it was only yesterday, miss, a full day after the theft, that he mentioned the inheritance or whatever and looked best pleased with himself. If he'd been the one to steal the diamonds, he'd have been off and out of the country as soon as you could say "first-class ticket to Timbuctoo please, boatman".'

'Leaving the country isn't as easy as all that. He might have a wife and children to think of.'

'Judging by the blushes he caused in some of the maids, I don't think he had a wife, miss.' Jacob himself coloured at his own suggestion.

'I see.' Cressida took Jacob's point. 'And the police didn't suspect him?'

'Not really, miss. They were more concerned that it was one of us, despite Her Ladyship standing up for us and insistin' it wouldn't be, which was decent of her. Then they got all highfalutin about the doors being unlocked and how foolish that was with any Tom, Dick or Harry able to walk in. Asking why we didn't notice anyone come in and all that.'

'Lady Chatterton told me last night that the kitchen door wouldn't have been locked by that point,' Cressida reassured him.

'None of them were, miss. Fine spring weather like this, the doors had all been open during the day, the fancy French ones in the library and all that, as well as our kitchen door. It leads out to a small courtyard by the stables where there's heaps of coal and the like. It's in use until all the hot water is done for the day. It was shut by the time the lights came back on though.'

'And you didn't notice anyone, anyone at all, come in the back passage?' Cressida pulled her shawl tighter around her. The glade of trees that surrounded the icehouse completely blocked out the sun and there was a chill coming off the ice blocks, too.

'No, miss. Though there's whispers that someone heard something from the great hall. That scaffolding tower was shaking when we got the lights back on.'

'Someone knocked into it in the dark maybe?' Cressida ventured.

'Maybe, miss, but who? And another odd thing happened too.'

'Oh yes?' Cressida was intrigued.

'Mildred, she's the one who found the body this morning... she's been given an easy morning of it and holding court down in the kitchen, everyone taking turns to cheer her up with some news or gossip or whatever. Well, one of the upstairs maids said something and Mildred's been telling us all ever since, though we've been scratching our heads about it.'

'What?' Cressida wondered if Jacob was perhaps intended for a life on the stage, his dramatic timing was so *en pointe*.

'Well, it's just that apparently last night, from Lady Chatterton's dressing room, the empty box was taken.'

'The velvet case for the diamonds? How odd.'

'I know, miss. Who'd want an empty box?' Jacob shrugged and turned back to his ice block.

Who indeed? Cressida thought to herself, and hoped that her friend Maurice wasn't about to be proved right about the answer to the theft of the Chatterton diamonds, and perhaps even the death of the hapless cleaner, lying very much closer to home...

8

The sun was now high in the sky and away from the cool of the icehouse its rays were warm on her back as Cressida walked back to the house, Ruby trotting along next to her. She checked her watch to see what time it was, but before she could register what the elegant blue hands against the Roman numerals were telling her, she felt her stomach rumble and she realised that, despite not fancying anything to eat this morning, she was quite ravenous now.

Still, she thought about what Jacob had said. She might not have made much more progress than the local coppers, but she had definitely gained some information about the household, and more especially the late Harry Smith. Jacob had made a point about Harry not really fitting the bill as a thief; he hadn't made a dash for the borders and instead had calmly turned up to work for two days after the burglary. Not the behaviour of an opportunistic thief or a guilty conscience. And the thought that had occurred to her as they'd chatted too was interesting. The thief must have known roughly where Lady Chatterton kept her diamonds, and that there were diamonds of a certain value in the house at all.

'So the thief can't have been that close to the family, else he'd have known exactly which drawer to head to,' Cressida whispered to Ruby, pleased that she'd discounted the Chattertons and their staff.

Ruby snorted and blinked at Cressida and she paused.

'Darn it, you're right of course, Rubes. Someone could have easily faked that rummaging to disguise the fact they knew where the diamonds were. Back to square one, sadly.'

Cressida, a frown on her face, entered the house and headed up to her bedroom to remove her stout shoes and make sure she was decent enough for lunch.

'I think you've had enough excitement for this morning too, eh Ruby?' she said, entering the Blue Room and letting Ruby jump down from her arms in order to scamper across the room and find a sunbeam for a snooze.

Cressida quickly changed and, leaving Ruby to dream of squirrels or sausages, or both, made her way downstairs. The sight of the scaffolding tower in the great hall, skeletal in its make-up, made her shiver with the thought of the accident that had befallen the young man who had worked so hard cleaning and polishing all the crystals that hung from the mighty chandelier.

Accident... there was still something that nudged at the side of her brain that made her doubt, just a touch, that it *had* been an accident. And as she walked down the wide stone stairs, this time really looking at the poles and planks that made up the tower, something caught her eye.

'Hmm.' She leaned over the balustrade that edged the stairs to get a better look, but the scaffold was too central in the great hall and she couldn't see it well enough at all.

Cressida descended the rest of the stairs and once down in the hall, careful not to stand where the body had lain this morning, looked up at the scaffolding and then glanced around her. There was no one around and, despite her own stomach's grumbling, it seemed nobody was milling around waiting for lunch to be served.

With a final check to ensure she was alone, Cressida decided to take the plunge – or rather, the climb. Despite now wearing her soft leather pumps and her tweed skirt, and a cashmere cardigan rather than her shawl (a rough-and-ready boiler suit this was not), she started to put one hand and then another on the metal poles and heave herself up so that her feet could find purchase on a plank below.

The whole tower shook as she climbed and more than once she wondered to herself if this was a good idea, but she kept her eye on the something she was aiming for... As why would there be, snagged on to one of the connections between the poles, a small piece of fabric?

Cressida climbed upwards, muttering to herself about fools running in where angels, or at least sensible people, feared to tread, until she was almost within reach of the scrap. She could at least see it more clearly now, and despite her hands suddenly getting incredibly sweaty, due to her nerves at being almost at the very top of the tower, she knew she only had to reach out an inch or two more... Her fingers stretched and...

'Oh darn.' Cressida reached again, aware that her stretches were causing the tower to shudder rather violently. In fact, the rocking was getting worse, and all Cressida could think of was *how* poor Harry Smith had even climbed it, let alone got high enough to... 'Don't think of it, don't think of it,' Cressida said to herself through clenched teeth.

One last stretch, though, and she snagged the scrap of fabric between the tips of her fingers just as the juddering got considerably worse. Clinging onto the poles, she focused her eyes on those of one of the Chatterton ancestors whose portraits lined the staircase, hoping that finding a steady viewpoint would help balance her and hence reduce the shaking she was obviously causing. It was only as she stared into the dark brown eyes of Sir

Radleigh Chatterton – a Tudor ancestor, she assumed, due to his fantastic ruff and pointed beard – that she realised that the tower was shaking a lot more than it really should be.

'Oh cripes...' Cressida clung onto the pole for dear life. It felt like an earthquake had suddenly and very acutely struck and she was finding it harder and harder to stay attached. She couldn't look down, not just for fear of vertigo, but because all of her strength was going into holding onto the pole and keeping her feet, in these far from sensible pumps, as clamped onto a bar as possible. If only she'd stayed in her stout walking shoes, or if only... Cressida stopped thinking about her wardrobe choices and instead wondered if perhaps her nosiness really had gone too far?

This is far worse than being struck off the Wicker-Flytes' Christmas card list... she thought. Her heart was beating a roar in her ears that was matched only by the scraping and clanging of the metal poles and wooden planks being pushed and pulled all around her. Another thought occurred to her, one much more pressing than seasonal greetings cards...this scaffold wasn't merely shaking, *it was being shaken.* She felt her fingertips slipping from their grip and just as she believed her time had come and she was really done for, she let out a scream. In that very moment, as she felt her fingers loosen and heard her own voice cry out, the tower stopped shaking.

Cressida barely dared to breathe, acclimatising herself to the now still and stable tower she was clinging to, her grip strengthened, though not trusting the whole thing not to shake like fury again at any moment. She clung to it for a second or two longer. Then, just as she was about to release her grip by a fraction in order to start climbing down, the clashing sound of the lunch gong resonated beneath her.

This was enough to elicit another squeal from her and she wrapped both arms tightly around the nearest pole again.

'Oh, miss, my apologies!' Cardew called up from below.

Cressida took a deep breath and steadied herself. His timing couldn't have been worse, almost shocking her from the tower to her own grisly end below. But she breathed in and out a few times and, in what she hoped was her most normal and nonchalant voice, she called down, 'Cardew, would you mind steadying the tower? Yes, that's right, thank you...'

She felt no need to prolong her stay up the tower for a moment more than necessary, so accepted Cardew's help as he handed her down the last few rungs, hoping that she hadn't inadvertently flashed him her undercarriage as she did so. Once down, she stood there, wobbly from the exertion and shock, and wiped her now quite disgusting hands down the front of her skirt.

She could feel Cardew's eyes boring into her with no doubt a hundred questions as to why she had decided to climb the tower, especially now, especially after what had happened, and even more especially right before lunch. But in her best possible stiff-upper-lipped way she merely smiled and said, 'Was that the lunch gong? Wonderful, do lead on.'

And tucking the small piece of fabric she'd found into the sleeve of her cardigan, she let the bemused butler show her into the dining room, where the other guests were now starting to congregate. Embarrassment vied with fear as her primary emotion, and Cressida hoped that no one in the dining room had heard her scream, and that no one would notice the distinct tremble in her hands or the quaver in her voice. But the trembling and quavering could be forgiven, she thought to herself, as she was sure – as sure as she could be – that someone only moments before, someone in this very house, had tried to kill her.

9

Luncheon was being served buffet style, and Cressida was very glad of the bolstering portion of pork pie on her plate. Something about almost falling to one's death from a high scaffolding tower had got her appetite up and she filled her plate before joining Dotty at the table.

Lord and Lady Chatterton were already seated and speaking to each other in hushed tones. Sitting next to Lady Chatterton was a guest Cressida hadn't met properly yet, though his face was familiar. She hazarded that this was the family friend of the Chattertons who used to be quite the schoolgirl crush of Dotty: Major Spike Elliot. The major was older than Cressida and Dotty, though a few years younger than Lord and Lady Chatterton. His moustache was luxurious and of impressive bearing, and Cressida suspected that perhaps a small amount of artificial intervention might have occurred to keep it so glossy and black, especially as the hair at his temples was a shade or two greyer, the rest of it though fulsome, was salt-and-pepper flecked. He was caught up in Lord and Lady Chatterton's conversation, and before Cressida could properly introduce herself to him, Dotty leaned over to her.

'Was that you screaming from the scaffold 58 asked, a worried look on her face. John w: counting the potatoes onto his plate, as Edm and nabbed one from under his nose, popping mouth.

'Yes, sorry. Not my usual pre-luncheon modus operandi.' Cressida flushed, the memory of being so scared hadn't yet left her, but the thought of her behaviour embarrassed her too. What would the Chattertons think of her?

'I thought it was you. Are you all right? I came straight to the door to see what it was all about, but I saw Cardew helping you down and you seemed in one piece, so I assumed you'd tell me all about it,' Dotty said, then forked a piece of pork pie into her mouth.

'And I will, chum. You see—'

'John, come and sit here, for heaven's sake, man.' Edmund, who had helped himself to pie and potatoes and sat himself down, patted the seat between him and Cressida, interrupting her and Dotty's conversation.

John looked up at him and shook his head, while counting the number of chairs round the dining table before finding the one he wanted to sit at.

Edmund sighed but made no more of it and turned to talk to Petronella Harper-Ashe on his other side. She, however, was doing a marvellous job of looking interested in what Basil was saying, and Cressida could hear him showing off about his latest hunting trophies. Dotty, between mouthfuls, was still looking downcast, no doubt worrying over recent events and Cressida was about to say something to cheer her up when Major Elliot leaned over and spoke to her.

'Afraid we didn't meet last night, what?' he said.

'Appalling timekeeping on my part, Major,' Cressida admitted. 'Unforgivable to a military man, I'm sure.' The major graciously shook his head and she carried on. 'And I was sorry to

.ss you all. It's not quite the same making your acquaintance after what happened.'

'Rum affair. Isn't that right, Francis?' The major tried to bring Lord Chatterton into the conversation, but as his mouth was full of pork pie, he merely nodded and then, as if noticing Cressida for the first time, gave her a wave. 'How's that husband of yours?' The major started a new conversation and Cressida looked over her shoulder to check he was talking to her.

'Me? Oh, Major Elliot, you must have me confused with someone else. I'm not married.' Cressida was grateful her mother wasn't here, as this sort of conversation usually sparked off some enthusiastic and encouraging nodding, especially when it was asked by a moderately handsome, and no doubt eligible, gentleman.

'Not married, eh? How have you managed that?' The major turned his gaze on her as if appraising a mare in a field. 'In my day, you'd have been whisked off your feet, fine lady like you. What's wrong with these young men?'

'Miss Fawcett is too keen on her motor car and her dancing,' Alfred interjected, smiling at Cressida. 'You should have seen her at The Savoy last—'

'Yes, thank you Alfred.' Cressida glared at him, annoyed at the blush she could feel rising in her cheeks. 'You see, Major, I choose to stay single. I have my dog, Ruby, my motor car, my apartment in Chelsea and some wonderful friends.'

'And a substantial independent income.' Alfred raised an eyebrow but was silenced by a look from the major.

'It never pays to out a young lady's means, Delafield,' he said kindly, but Cressida could see that even the confident Alfred paid heed to what the major had said and bowed his head in an apology. He turned back to Cressida. 'Well, good luck to you, Miss Fawcett. A woman of her own means and, by the looks of it, her own mind... well, capital, capital. Oh, darn it...' The major looked down to where he had spilled something down his front. 'That's the second waistcoat I've ruined.'

'I know a marvellous man in Notting Hill who helped me get the best part of a bottle of claret out of my... Well, he's a very good cleaner,' Cressida volunteered.

'Afraid last night it was jam from the sponge pudding that went right down my Mutton Pie Club waistcoat, those little raspberry pips just seemed to get deeper into the frills and seams the more I dabbed.'

'Frills?' Cressida had never heard of a waistcoat having frills before.

'New idea of the club. Issued them only recently. Frills down the buttonhole edge to look like the top of a pie. You see William over there got about half a pint of gravy down his the other night. Adds to the authenticity, I suppose.' He chuckled. 'Anyway, it was a damn fine sponge pudding. Must compliment Climpton on it. I'll look up that man of yours though, dear girl. Not fair on the Chatterton maids having me around!' He piled some more piccalilli on a large piece of pork pie and *almost* managed to get it into his mouth before a blob of the bright yellow chutney splattered onto his tie. 'Oh, darn it.'

'I'll send you his card, Major,' Cressida assured him. 'He does an excellent multi-garment discount...'

Eventually, the clattering of cutlery on crockery, or in this case, silver knives and forks on fine bone china, faded away and was replaced by the murmuring conversation of the house guests.

Lord Chatterton was about to say something when John started talking statistics again and, in the end, Lord Chatterton resigned himself to listening to his son's theory of coincidental patterns and their effect on the human brain. Dotty, Cressida noticed, was looking adoringly at Basil, who in turn was telling Alfred how the moles on the lawn outside should be dealt with, namely with a shotgun, which seemed to be his answer for everything. William and Petronella were telling Lady Chatterton about the veld and all its beauties. Talk, however, naturally returned, time and again, to the death of the chandelier cleaner.

'Poor chap,' Major Elliot sighed. 'Not a way to go, not a way to go.'

'Is there a way to go?' Petronella asked, running her turquoise beads through her fingers, her question almost rhetorical.

Edmund shrugged. 'Maybe better that than a lungful of gas in a muddy trench, with—'

'That's quite enough I think, Edmund dear,' Lady Chatterton interrupted him. She in turn was then interrupted by one of the housemaids whispering in her ear. Cressida watched as Lady Chatterton nodded and gently dismissed the maid before turning to the assembled guests. With a brave face, she announced, 'Well, it seems the police are here. Scotland Yard that is. Finally.'

A murmur of excitement rippled through the guests. Hands were clasped to pearls and eyebrows were raised as they all awaited the entrance of the Scotland Yard detective.

'Scotland Yard?' Edmund queried. 'London bobbies out in this neck of the woods?'

'Standard stuff, young man,' Major Elliot beat Lord Chatterton to the explanation. 'A robbery is one thing, not that that wasn't a dastardly affair in its own right, but something as serious as a death, especially in a house of this importance, well, the local force would be superseded by the Flying Squad.' He dabbed at the corners of his mouth with his napkin after he'd spoken.

'But why police at all, it was an accident, surely? The body's gone off to the mortuary in Newbury, I assume?' Alfred asked and received some nods in agreement from those around him.

'I made the telephone call this morning, Alfred, dear,' Lady

Chatterton replied to her son. 'After the young man had been... removed.'

'You said "finally", Lady Chatterton,' Cressida stated. 'Why was that, if you don't mind me asking?'

'I telephoned Scotland Yard when the diamonds were stolen, but they dismissed it as a job for the locals. Evidently a death, although it was most probably accidental of course, is enough to get their attention. They've promised me a full search of the house again, which I'm afraid will mean bedroom rummages.' She looked awkwardly down at her clasped hands and Cressida was pleased to notice Lord Chatterton place one of his own over hers to ease her anxiety at this breach of social etiquette. She hoped Lady Chatterton wouldn't worry herself unnecessarily; for surely there could be no complaints from the guests in the circumstances.

An 'ahem' at the door announced the arrival of a man in his mid-forties, with a military sort of bearing, tall and straight-backed. He was neatly dressed in a brownish tweed suit, a watch chain hanging from his waistcoat pocket, and his shoes, Cressida noticed, shined to a brilliant polish. His neatly trimmed beard framed his face, which, despite its seriousness, was pleasant enough to look at. A far younger and fresh-faced uniformed sergeant entered the room behind him and stood to attention, his hands behind his back, his chin raised to keep his helmet strap from garrotting him.

'My lords, ladies.' The policeman nodded a formal greeting to them. 'My name is Detective Chief Inspector Andrews from Scotland Yard. This is Sergeant Kirby.' He paused. No one responded, so he continued, 'I know our presence here is a stark reminder of the tragedy that occurred this morning, but Sergeant Kirby and I will try to keep our intrusion into your weekend to a minimum while also doing our duty by the victim.'

'Victim?' Petronella sounded rather strangled, and indeed

she was pulling quite hard at her turquoise beads now. Perhaps sitting next to Basil for the whole of lunch, despite how brave and happy a face she'd put on it, had taken its inevitable toll.

Basil, who had seemed exceedingly pleased with himself to have someone so willing to hear about his triumphs over the squirrels with his four-ten, entered the conversation, his voice booming and arrogant. 'Victim, man? By Jove, it was an accident, eh what? Plain as day.' He ran his hand through his wayward hair as several of the others nodded their agreement with this assessment, but they all turned to look at the policeman as he calmly pulled his notebook out from his pocket and flicked through it. When he spoke again, they all listened.

'As far as we know, Harry Smith, the young lad who died, was found at 6.34 a.m. this morning by Mildred Spiceall, one of the maids. Now, although there is nothing out of the ordinary about a housemaid starting her rounds at that time in the morning, it is highly irregular for a contracted cleaner to be in the house before his shift should start at' – he licked a finger and checked back a page – '8 a.m. In fact, time of death is estimated to be even earlier this morning.'

There was silence in the dining room. It was broken a moment later, a moment that had seemed like an eternity to all gathered, by Alfred, who had stood up from his seat and moved over to place a comforting hand on his mother's shoulder.

'Am I right, Detective Andrews, that you believe this Smith man might have been murdered?' he asked, as Lady Chatterton brought her own hand up to rest on his.

DCI Andrews answered in his clipped, militaristic tone. 'That, Lord Delafield, is what I'm here to find out.'

10

'Well, that was quite the entrance,' Cressida said to Dotty as they walked across the terrace, taking the air after the commotion that had broken out due to DCI Andrews' proclamation. Lunch had very quickly broken up after his arrival and Cressida, having popped upstairs to see if Ruby fancied a walk, decided it was very much time to go outside and clear their heads in the spring sunshine while the policemen set up in the library.

'A murder at Chatterton Court... Cressy, this is terrible.' Dotty shook her head and Cressida passed Ruby to her so she could cuddle the pup as they walked. Dotty thanked her and carried on. 'Murder... it's such an ugly word, isn't it? And such a horrible thing to think about. I know Mama's been wanting Scotland Yard here since her diamonds were stolen, but... but I can't see how anyone could have had anything to do with that poor boy's death. And yet that detective chap seems convinced it's murder, Cressy! I simply can't imagine it, I really can't.'

Cressida nodded but was inclined to agree with the policeman. The idea that it hadn't been an accident had been brewing in her mind too, and it was only when DCI Andrews had so clearly spelt out the oddities of the timing of the fall that she realised *that* was what had been bugging her. Harry Smith had been working late last night to finish the cleaning, so why come into work before six this morning? She voiced this concern to Dotty. 'What was Mr Smith doing up that scaffolding so early?'

'Maybe he felt like he should impress Mama, this being his first job here, and decided to come in early to see the chandelier once more in daylight before the scaffolding was moved? Or maybe he hadn't finished by last night and didn't want to keep Mama waiting any longer than necessary. We used to use a different company, I think, a local firm, but the old man retired and his son was injured at the Somme. Luckily, Edmund's parents, the Priestleys, live just the other side of Newbury, so they recommended this new company. But Harry was let down by the other fellow who was here with him, 'flu apparently.'

'So Mr Smith had never worked at Chatterton Court before?' Cressida asked.

'No, but I don't see what that's got to do with it?' Dotty looked confused.

'Well, only that I was thinking about your Mama's room and how it was ransacked. Someone who knew there might be something valuable, but not exactly where or what they were looking for...' She let her train of thought sink in with Dotty.

'Would he really come back to work in a house if he'd recently made off with the goods?'

'That's what young Jacob the footman said too, and it's a good point. But Mr Smith was certainly agile enough to get down that drainpipe if his gadding about up that scaffolding tower was anything to go by. And apparently he'd been bragging to the servants about suddenly coming into a large amount of money. No, not money... wealth. That's what Jacob said. He even went as far as asking your Basil and Edmund or William, one of them in any case, how to spend it.'

'Gosh. That does put a spin on it,' Dotty said. 'I still don't think he was that type though.'

'Dotty darling, you see the best in everyone. Even "Six Sugars Sheila" at school and her filching of the teacher's sweet treats.' Cressida smiled at her friend.

'Sheila couldn't help it if she had a condition,' Dotty, kind as ever, defended her.

'Her only "condition", chum, was a sweet tooth!' Cressida laughed and even Dotty begrudgingly nodded in agreement. 'Forgetting Sheila for a moment, did you know that the empty box that belonged to the diamonds has gone missing?' Cressida asked.

'Missing? No. Who said that?'

'Jacob. He said Mildred had been holding court and had heard from another of the maids that all of a sudden your mother's black velvet case, the one that had been emptied by the thief on the night of the crime, was gone.'

'How bizarre. And poor Mama hasn't mentioned it. But who would steal an empty case?'

'It certainly baffles the brain cells,' Cressida agreed. 'But there must be some meaning to it. Boxes don't simply disappear, like rabbits out of hats or magicians' handkerchiefs. Oh Dotty, that reminds me!' Cressida blurted out and rummaged up her sleeve for the small piece of torn fabric she'd found on the scaffold. 'Look at this. Not a handkerchief, that's for sure, but I had to hide it somewhere. I had no time to tell you at lunch, and quite frankly I didn't want anyone else to see, but I found this up the scaffolding tower.'

'Oh yes, we got a bit interrupted earlier, didn't we.' Dotty's round-framed glasses slipped down her nose and manoeuvring Ruby around in her arms, she freed up a hand to slowly push them back up. 'What on earth were you doing up the scaffolding?'

'I know it seems macabre, but, you see, I'd spotted this fluttering up near the top, so, hothead that I am, I simply had to find out what it was.'

'So, what is it?' Dotty and Ruby peered at the small piece of fabric in Cressida's hands. 'It looks like something from a quilt perhaps, or a piece of clothing.'

'I'm not sure. But it's certainly not blue boiler suit material, so couldn't have come from our dead body, on the way up or the way down the tower.'

Dotty blanched. 'Oh Cressy, that is a horrible thought. On the way down...' She buried her face in Ruby's rolls of fur, then looked back up at Cressida, her eyes wide as if suddenly remembering something. 'You screamed too... why? What happened?'

'It was horrible, Dot. As I was reaching out for it, the most almighty shaking started to happen on the tower. Now, I know I'm no acrobat, or indeed a seasoned climber of scaffolding—'

'Though didn't you once climb a fire escape at the back of the Garrick in order to—'

'Yes, yes... no need to get into that now though,' Cressida blushed. 'As I was saying, I'm no seasoned scaffold climber, and I was getting a tad nervous at the height so may have been shaking a little, but not enough to cause the whole structure to sway like that.'

'Are you saying someone shook you?' Dotty looked aghast.

'Yes. No... well, I couldn't bear to look down to see. But I think someone must have done. And jolly violently too.' Cressida paused as the realisation set in again. 'Perhaps to kill me...'

'Oh Cressy!' Dotty grabbed her friend's arm. 'Kill you?'

'Or more likely scare me.' Cressida placed a hand over her friend's to reassure her she was very much still alive.

'Not just high jinks?' Dotty asked, her voice full of hope.

Cressida softened, realising how horrible it was for Dotty to think that one of the Chatterton Court guests could be responsible for such a heinous crime. Despite not agreeing with her friend for one second, she smiled and nodded. 'Yes, perhaps it could have been high jinks.' She folded the piece of silk up and slid it back up her sleeve for safekeeping.

High jinks, my... If that was a joke, she thought to herself, remembering the sheer terror she'd felt as she'd almost lost her grip so perilously high up that tower, *it wasn't a terribly funny one.*

The two women walked on in contemplative silence for a while. Chatterton Court was a large house, but still, it wasn't too long before they found themselves back on the terrace, onto which the doors to the drawing room opened and where they had begun their walk. The terrace was long enough that it also bordered the library and ballroom, and Cressida could see through the windows the trestle tables with the ghastly new curtains lying on them. Voices could be heard drifting across from the library and Cressida and Dotty instinctively walked over to see if they could hear what was being said.

'Good a place as... desk and paper... one at a time...' the voice of the Scotland Yard detective was recognisable, being more gruff and not so refined as that of the guests or senior male staff of the house.

Dotty was about to say something, but Cressida put a finger to her lips and then led Dotty back to the other end of the terrace.

'Sorry old thing, but I didn't want us to be rumbled.' Cressida took a squirming Ruby from Dotty's arms and set her down on the terrace, where the small dog instantly sat herself down and gave one ear a good scratch with a back leg.

'Flea in her ear?' Dotty asked, looking at Ruby.

'Maybe... and now that really has given me an idea. I say, Dotty, how interesting do you think it would be to be able to listen in later, on what everyone has to say to Inspector Andrews?'

'Cressy! That's... well, that's so sneaky.' Dotty looked visibly shocked by her friend's suggestion.

'How else will we get an idea of what on earth's been going on, though? If we can hear what everyone's telling that detective, we can start to work it out on our own.' Cressida was getting carried away with her idea and failed to notice that Dotty was looking downcast.

'You really think one of *us* had something to do with it?'

Cressida was halted in her tracks and suddenly felt terrible at how crestfallen Dotty seemed. She reached out a hand to touch her friend's elbow. 'Not necessarily. But something's going on, Dot, and let's not forget there was a robbery too. Perhaps with the real detective asking some pertinent questions, it might trigger a memory or something that might help with the missing diamonds, as well.'

'Poor Mama is still so terribly upset about her diamonds being stolen. But, Cressy, don't you think we've all already wracked our brains and tried to work out what might have happened that night? And what happened this morning is simply too horrible to contemplate at the moment. And... are you sure listening in on private interviews with policemen is legal?'

Before Cressida could answer, Lady Chatterton came upon them and asked Dotty for her help with the seating plan for dinner that evening, leaving Cressida, perhaps unwisely, to her own devices.

11

Dotty had a point, there was a moral ambiguity in Cressida's suggestion to listen in on the interviews. However, the Fawcett family motto ran along the same lines as the famous idiom 'fortune favours the brave' (but with a few more digs towards the French scattered into the Latin phrasing), and she couldn't help but begin to formulate a plan. It was this doggedness of thought – and doggedness of dog who decided she mustn't be separated from her mistress at this critical point – that meant a few minutes later Cressida and Ruby were sitting on a small upholstered stool behind a wooden three-panel folding screen in the corner of the library. She'd snuck in when Sergeant Kirby had gone off in search of Alfred to interview and while the inspector was called away to talk to Lord Chatterton.

'We must stay silent as the grave,' Cressida whispered to her pup, who suddenly waggled her tail and panted hard in anticipation of something. 'Grave, Rubes, not gravy.' Cressida wagged a finger at the disappointed dog, who luckily settled quickly and quietly onto her lap with barely a snore coming from her.

Moments later, Cressida heard the wide panelled door of the library open and the assured footsteps of DCI Andrews enter the room, followed by what she took to be Sergeant Kirby, or perhaps Alfred. She mentally counted three of them through the door and the sound of two men sitting down. She assumed the sergeant would stay standing, perhaps to take any notes.

Oh, notes... darn it... Cressida chastised herself, realising that with Ruby on her lap and no paper or pen to hand she was going to have to rely on remembering everything she heard. *Focus then, Fawcett*, she scolded herself. *Focus...*

An hour and a half later and Cressida was so famished that even the unmistakable whiff of a fish paste sandwich – obviously some sustenance brought in for DCI Andrews, poor man – was tempting. Ruby had been asleep on her lap, quiet as anything, but Cressida was sure that at any moment either her tummy rumbles or the soft, almost imperceptible snore of the pug would alert the policemen to her presence. She had, however, heard some interesting things; and some exceedingly boring things.

Alfred had been the first one to recount his side of the story from the night before, and, as expected, he'd told the chief inspector that he'd retired to bed at around ten o'clock, due in some part to overdoing it with his father's Scotch and coming off the back of a few late nights out in London. He'd rather touchingly mentioned that the house party had been worried about her, Cressida's, whereabouts, but had then gone on to list several times when she'd been late to various balls and dinners. Cressida thought this was rather unchivalrous of him.

It's not like Gwendoline Moorhead's parties ever start on time anyway, she'd harrumphed to herself.

Alfred had also mentioned seeing the cleaner up the scaffold when he went up to bed and had had a cheery word with him. In a similar way, he had said his goodbyes to the policemen and finished his interview.

Next in was Lord Chatterton, but before he could say anything Cardew had beckoned him out as there was a problem with one of the horses in the stable, so he'd been replaced soon after by his wife, Lady Chatterton. She had confirmed that the cleaners came from a new firm she'd employed for the first time this year and were from Newbury, which was over ten miles away, hence not usually starting before eight o'clock in the morning, but that, yes, they did have knowledge of where the main electricity switch was located. She had also mentioned the bizarre nature of her jewellery case going missing last night too and all but pleaded with the chief inspector to perhaps look into the disappearance of her jewels. Cressida had welled up with tears as Lady Chatterton had described how her mother had handed them over on her deathbed and how she had assumed she'd do the same for her own daughter.

After her, Major Elliot was brought in. He had claimed to have been sozzled by ten, and said he had taken a nightcap to bed at around half past the hour.

And now John was in the hot seat while Cressida wondered if in fact the fish paste sandwiches were a ploy by DCI Andrews to put people off guard, the smell of them hastening confessions in order to be out of scent, if not sight, of the hateful things.

'I've got a good memory for numbers, Chief Inspector,' John proudly told him. 'And times and things. What do you want to know?'

'When did the party all arrive, sir?' was the chief inspector's first question.

'Well, Alfred came down from London as soon as he heard about Mother's diamonds, so he arrived on Thursday in time for lunch, in fact I remember the clock struck noon as his car pulled in. Then Basil, that's my sister's fiancé Basil Bartleby, he arrived later on Thursday.'

'What time, sir?' the policeman asked.

Cressida wished she could see John's face as he had paused for some time before answering.

'Oh, five ten, I believe, but he was looking somewhat agitated. Kept asking when the Harper-Ashes were going to arrive, which wasn't until four on Friday as they took the early afternoon train out of London and Jacob went and picked them up from the station in the Rolls. The major and Edmund came by their own cars at four forty-five and five thirty respectively, I believe. And, of course, Cressida drove herself and was terribly late. I heard Dotty go and say hello shortly after nine on Friday night, but she didn't come in and see us. Probably for the best as we were all a bit, well, *refreshed*, shall we say.'

Cressida had the good grace to feel sheepish as she sat, squashed and squat on the small footstool.

'And how do you know your guests?' the chief inspector asked.

'Well, the major's an old family friend and, like the rest of us, he's in the Mutton Pie Club, which was inaugurated in 1856, did you know?'

'I see.' Andrews pretended to write the date down. 'And the other young people?'

'Cressida is a pal of Dotty's, that's Lady Dorothy, my sister. And Basil is Dot's fiancé. They met in London and he rather attached himself to her, and his people are all right, I suppose, so Mother and Father rubber-stamped the match. The Harper-Ashes are his friends, but William's in the club when he's in England. Diamond miners, you know, all very glamorous. Did you know the world's biggest diamond is the—'

'That's all very interesting, thank you sir. And was anything said by anyone during the course of the evening that we should know?'

There was a pause while John thought again. But before he could answer, a gunshot echoed around the grounds. Cressida jumped, clasping Ruby to her a little firmly, at which point the small dog snuffled in a most aggravated way. Cressida wondered if the beating of her heart could be heard beyond the screen, reverberating around the room, but, luckily, Lord John's voice filled the short silence instead.

'Bloody hell, that Basil and his squirrels...'

For a young dog, Ruby had done exceptionally well to stay hushed and unstirring for so long, despite the tempting smell of the fish paste sandwiches, the constant grumbling of her mistress's stomach and that last sudden noise, but at the word 'squirrels', the spell was broken and Ruby jumped off her lap and trotted across the room after the imaginary prey.

Cressida sat stock-still, daring not even to change her expression, lest she make some noise. All she could hope was that if the policemen noticed the small pooch, they would think she had let herself in via the garden door. When she heard John excuse himself to go and see what the devil that soon-to-be brother-in-law of his was up to, Cressida almost allowed herself to believe that she'd got away with her eavesdropping. But as soon as John had left the room, she heard the definite and purposeful footsteps of DCI Andrews approach her hiding spot. The screen was pulled aside, and she braced herself.

'Allo, allo, allo... what have we here?' The detective looked accusingly at her.

Cressida stood up, wincing as her stiff joints told her off for the swift movement after almost two hours of being so cramped up. 'Good day, officer. I don't believe we've been formally introduced. I'm the Honourable Cressida Fawcett.' She reached out a hand and winced again at the strength of his shake. This wasn't a man who was going to let her off lightly. Still, she had to try to explain her present location and in reply to his glowering face she said, 'Can we say perhaps that I'm early for my appointment with you?'

The frown that was set across Andrews' brow suggested otherwise and Cressida had a sudden flashback to when she'd decided to decorate her dorm at school and the headmistress had taken umbrage at her appropriating the school flag to make a jaunty new quilt. That episode had ended with her doing hundreds of lines and being on early starts for a month, but she worried that this man of the law might be even more of a disciplinarian.

'Miss Fawcett...' Andrews looked at her thunderously. 'Daughter of Colonel Lord Sholto Fawcett of Mydenhyrst Place, am I correct?'

'Yes, officer. That's right.' *Gosh*, she thought, *he must have done background checks on all of us already!*

'How do you explain yourself?' He stared at her, awaiting her answer, his arms folded in the most menacing of ways.

Cressida was finding it very hard to do just that, however, and only had Dotty's warning of the illegality of her plan rushing through her mind. 'I'm terribly sorry,' she all but whispered.

'I'm sure you are, now you've been caught.'

She could see Ruby out on the terrace chasing butterflies and instantly wished she could be as free as that and not under the cosh of this scowling policeman, who questioned her again.

'Can you explain what you were doing behind that screen, Miss Fawcett?'

'I... er... I was trying to work out perhaps what had... well, what had happened. Myself. Will you... arrest me?' Cressida almost couldn't bear to ask.

Andrews made her wait for an answer, his eyes boring into her all the while. 'Not yet,' he said, finally. 'But if I catch you impeding my investigation, then you'll leave me with no choice.' He looked incredibly stern.

'Yes, Chief Inspector.' Cressida breathed a sigh of relief.

'Do you understand, Miss Fawcett? No more sleuthing from behind screens. Catching murderers is a dangerous business, so leave it to the professionals. Do you understand?'

'Yes, Chief Inspector. I'm sorry.' Cressida didn't need telling more than twice and as soon as he dismissed her, she scarpered off along the terrace, scooping up Ruby and burying her burning-red face into the soft fur of her adored pup. As she neared the end of the terrace, she slowed down and took some breaths. She'd been focusing so hard on everything the Chattertons and the major had had to say, but it was the last few words DCI Andrews had spoken that stuck with her. *Catching murderers is a dangerous business...*

There was no doubt about it then: Scotland Yard were in agreement with her. Harry Smith had been murdered. She shivered and held Ruby closer to her.

And that means only one thing, she thought. *Someone here at Chatterton Court is a killer...*

12

'Dotty!' Cressida spied her friend in the ballroom, waved madly at her and ran in from the terrace through a set of French doors, much like those of the library.

'Cressy, what's the matter?' Dotty looked at her, her brow furrowed as she turned away from the curtains lying on the trestles.

'Dot, I'm in big trouble.' Cressida put Ruby down and let her scamper off back outside, where Rollo, the spaniel, was manically chasing squirrels.

'So are those squirrels if those two hounds get their way,' Dotty mused.

Forgetting her own problems for a second, Cressida looked out to where Ruby was struggling to keep up with the more athletic spaniel. 'Ruby hasn't an ounce of hound in her really, much as she likes to pretend. Those squirrels will get nothing worse than an excited snort in their general direction, and that's if she gets anywhere close.'

'Rollo's all fur coat and no knickers too,' agreed Dotty. 'He'd sooner cuddle one than catch it. Rubbish guard dog, as it turns out. Anyway, what's up with you? What trouble are you in?'

Dotty looked concerned again and placed a gentle hand on Cressida's arm.

'DCI Andrews caught me snooping.' Cressida had the decency to look awkwardly ashamed.

'Oh Cressy.' Dotty bit her lip. 'Was he dreadfully cross?'

'Yes. Terribly. But I'm only on a warning, not cuffed and carted off yet.'

'Any juicy titbits though?'

Cressida almost laughed in shock. She'd been expecting a gentle, if much deserved, ticking-off and 'I told you so' from her friend, but this was quite the opposite reaction.

As usual, Dotty seemed to read her mind. 'What? You've done it now, so we might as well see what clues or whatever we can glean from it all. Not that I think *anyone* in this household had *anything* to do with it.' She pushed her glasses up the bridge of her nose defiantly.

'I must say, there wasn't much that could be classed as a clue.' Cressida scratched her head, trying to remember what she'd overheard. 'Might help the grey matter if I could stop looking at these ghastly curtains for a bit. What were you doing in here anyway, Dot?'

'Oh nothing. I was trying to find you, actually, but Rollo wouldn't stop barking at this door. I thought it might upset that chief inspector chap, so I opened it up and let him run in. Edmund was out on the terrace by the French doors, probably waiting to be interviewed, and Rollo shot right past him in search of those squirrels.'

'Those poor squirrels. If it's not Basil, it's the dogs.' Cressida watched the dogs running around on the lawn. Well, Rollo was running and Ruby was sort of wobbling at speed.

Turning back to look at the purple-and-gold confection that was threatening to dominate the fine old ballroom at Chatterton Court for another generation or so, she thought back to the silk she'd possibly risked her life to get. She pulled it out from her sleeve again.

'I still don't know what to make of this, Dot,' she said, turning the piece of silk over in her hands. 'I hate to say it, but it's very similar in colour to the livery the footmen and Cardew are wearing.'

'Oh Cressy!' Dotty looked at her friend aghast. 'You can't possibly think one of them... Perhaps they climbed the tower for some other reason. Harry Smith was always demanding cups of tea, maybe one of the younger lads decided to take one up to him?'

'There you go again, trying to find the best in people, Dot.' Cressida sighed and slid the piece of silk back up into her sleeve. 'And perhaps you're right. But that scaffolding tower shook like billy-o and Cardew was the first person I saw after it stopped.'

Dotty shook her head. 'Cardew had excellent references. He'd worked for the Duke of Rutland before coming to Chatterton Court, I really don't think he'd—'

'I know, I know...' Cressida didn't want to think badly of the hard-working butler either, but he had been there at exactly the right time. 'Maybe he only wanted to scare me?'

'Scare you?' Dotty looked shocked.

Cressida was about to reply when a strong, clipped man's voice answered them both instead.

'Yes, scare you.' DCI Andrews walked towards them from the other side of the ballroom. Dotty instinctively clasped Cressida's arm. 'Which is why I want no more of this hiding behind screens and climbing up dangerous structures.' His face looked like thunder.

'DCI Andrews, hello.' Cressida let Dotty drop her arm and straightened out her blouse and skirt. 'I didn't realise you knew about my adventure up the tower. But, as you can see, I'm quite well, though admittedly I do feel as if I should apologise to you again for my little indiscretion in the library. It really is a very fine Persian wooden screen and, you see, I was merely having a closer look at it when you started your interviews and then I was simply too polite to interrupt you, and—'

'Ahem.' The detective cleared his throat. 'Let's just say, least said, soonest mended, shall we, Miss Fawcett? And leave the hole-digging to the moles out there on the lawn.'

'Yes, dratted things,' Dotty agreed, looking out at the lawn. 'Basil said he'll take a potshot at one if he sees it surface, but I don't think the poor creatures really deserve that.'

DCI Andrews cleared his throat again. 'In any case, Miss Fawcett, although I've asked the whole household to stay while we investigate this death, can I reiterate that by "we" I mean Sergeant Kirby and myself, and *not* you. Stop nosing around, for your own safety.'

'Yes, Detective Chief Inspector. Roger that.' Cressida saluted him and then paused. 'But what if I *had* found something that might help?'

'Then it would be your duty to hand it over to us, Miss Fawcett.' Andrews was starting to look both frustrated and perplexed, a deep furrow forming over his brow.

'Even if we don't really know what it means?' Cressida asked.

Andrews sighed. 'As I just said, Miss Fawcett, the only "we" in this situation should be me and Sergeant Kirby. So it's even more important that you hand anything you find over to us professionals.'

'You really think Harry Smith was murdered, don't you?'

DCI Andrews scratched his head. 'Investigations are ongoing, Miss Fawcett. However, from our preliminary enquiries, yes, it seems like the victim met with misadventures unknown. At least that is what we'll have to present to the coroner.'

'And what about Mama's diamonds?' Dotty piped up. 'Do you think he was the thief too?'

'That's a separate investigation for the local constabulary to —' DCI Andrews started but was interrupted by Cressida.

'Excuse my French, Chief Inspector, but pish posh. They've got nowhere with it, which isn't their fault, they were looking for some outsider who they think opportunistically and stealthily snuck in and made a clean getaway. But it's obviously a heist that was expertly executed by someone who knew exactly who everyone was and where they would be of an evening, where the electric switch was, the sturdiness and closeness of that drainpipe to the window and not to mention they had a good idea where the diamonds were kept. It has to have been an inside job.'

'Oh... oh dear.' Dotty looked crestfallen.

Cressida noticed, but couldn't help herself from continuing her train of thought. 'And surely the murder had something to do with someone who is still here, too? If it wasn't, why would someone have shaken the blazes out of the tower when they saw me climbing it? Perhaps they didn't want me to find that...'

'Find what?' Andrews looked from Cressida, who had infuriatingly paused at the most interesting point of her story, to Dotty, who suddenly found the dogs outside exceedingly interesting. He turned again to Cressida. 'You said you'd found something. Do you have it?'

Cressida rummaged up her sleeve and pulled out the scrap of fabric. 'It's all right, Dot, I think he needs to see.'

'What have we here then?' Andrews took the small piece of silk from Cressida and turned it over in the sunlight a few times.

'Silk,' Cressida filled him in. 'And most likely dressmaker's silk, rather than upholstery grade. There's only a slight difference, but the upholstery stuff tends to be thicker and more hard-wearing, designed for countless bottoms to be sat upon it, whereas dressmaker's silk is somewhat finer.'

'A bit of silk clothing...' DCI Andrews noted it in his book. 'Gentleman's or lady's, do you think?'

Cressida shrugged. 'I don't know. But it's a clue: I found it up the tower, from which poor Harry Smith fell. Or was pushed.'

'This is an interesting find, Miss Fawcett, but you seem to want to link the two incidents and I don't see how this does?'

'I'm not sure either, but there is something I heard from the servants' quarters that might.'

'Do you often go around talking to the servants, Miss Fawcett?' Andrews looked at her and Cressida wasn't sure if his face was one of incredulity or if he was perhaps a little impressed. She chose to believe it was the latter.

'I'll talk to anyone, Chief Inspector, if they have something interesting to say.'

Andrews nodded and Cressida carried on.

'Jacob, the footman, told me that Lady Chatterton's jewellery case was taken last night... the night *before* the murder. It was the one that had always held her diamonds, the whole set. A rather lovely black velvet number with indents for all the pieces. It was left behind on the night of the robbery but then taken last night, two nights after the original theft.'

'I can ask Mama more about it,' piped up Dotty. 'Though she'll be terribly upset.'

'No need, Lady Dorothy.' Andrews was still writing notes as he spoke to her. 'Your Mama has been through enough and she did mention it actually.' He coughed, as if embarrassed that he hadn't drawn a similar conclusion.

Cressida leaned in, keen to make her point while his pencil was still poised. 'So, don't you think this links the crimes, Detective Chief Inspector? A remnant of the original burglary, taken hours before the murder of poor Harry Smith. Surely that's more than a coincidence and means you'll be investigating those missing diamonds after all?'

Silence fell over the three of them in the ballroom. It was

broken by DCI Andrews riffling through his notebook and then clearing his throat again.

'We shall see. So let me get this straight. Miss Fawcett, you travelled down here to Chatterton Court late last night.'

'Oh, this is your turn now, Cressy. Hope you don't mind me interloping,' Dotty said, and Cressida rolled her eyes at her, before turning back to DCI Andrews.

'In my little motor car, yes. It's a Bugatti – that's two Ts...' Cressida tailed off as DCI Andrews' eyebrows furrowed and his nostrils flared.

'I can spell Bugatti, thank you very much. So, at the invitation of Lady Dorothy here—'

'Yes, Cressida's my oldest friend and I'm hoping she'll get to know my fiancé Basil a little better this weekend. We're due to be wed this summer, you see, and—'

'Thank you, Lady Dorothy.' He cleared his throat. 'And congratulations, I'm sure. But back to the night in question: Miss Fawcett, you arrived yesterday?'

'That's correct,' Cressida confirmed.

'And did you meet the victim, Harry Smith, at all?'

'Yes, briefly...' Cressida closed her eyes, remembering the almost romantic nature of the flickering candlelight and the moonlit glow haloing the young man as he cleaned the chandelier late into the night. She took a breath and continued, 'You see, I was unforgivably late for dinner, but even so, Harry Smith was still hard at work. Still polishing as I went to bed too, just like Alfred told you.'

DCI Andrews cleared his throat again and Cressida duly noted that any allusion to her eavesdropping on his interviews was not to be made.

She carried on. 'Then, of course, this morning we all awoke to that horrible scene on the floor of the great hall.' Cressida shuddered, remembering the awkward angle of Harry Smith's leg and the pool of blood around his head.

'It was all so horrid,' Dotty whispered, her eyes downcast.

'Yes.' Cressida rubbed her friend's shoulder in a comforting way. 'After we'd recovered from the shock of it all and got ourselves dressed, I followed the sound of your beautiful piano playing to the drawing room, didn't I, Dot?'

'Only Schubert could take my mind off it.' Dotty forced a smile up at Cressida to show she was all right. 'You better carry on, Cressy.'

'Right. Yes. Well, in the drawing room, I was properly introduced to Edmund and the Harper-Ashes. But then I thought I really needed some air, and having spoken to Lady Chatterton late last night, I got it into my head to retrace the steps of the thief, as far as it was theorised anyway. You know, from the bottom of the drainpipe onwards. I only got as far as the icehouse in the small woods over there, where I met young Jacob, one of the footmen. He told me something very interesting, which I think you should know.'

'Yes?' DCI Andrews held his pencil poised.

'I'm sure your sergeant will report back the same thing once he's interviewed the staff too, but Jacob told me that Harry had been bragging about suddenly coming into some wealth. I thought, rather cravenly, that perhaps it was because he'd stolen the diamonds, but Jacob pointed out that Harry hadn't done a runner and was happily talking about it all and turning up to work. So I did start to wonder if perhaps he'd *hidden* them in the chandelier...'

'Oooh.' Dotty looked wide-eyed at Cressida. 'How clever. You'd never spot diamonds hanging up there.'

'But then Harry Smith was killed. So maybe he hadn't stolen the diamonds, rather he had stumbled across them, hanging in the chandelier...'

'Cripes!' Dotty exclaimed. 'Now that is clever, Cressy.'

'It's all a hypothesis at the moment, Dot, but I did notice

how sparkling some of the crystals looked and your Mama's diamonds would fit right in.'

'Hang on, Miss Fawcett, if you will...' DCI Andrews flicked back a couple of pages. 'You've made a few leaps here, but if I'm right, you *did* think that Mr Smith was the thief, and you *now* think that Mr Smith was killed by the thief, who is potentially still in this house? And the diamonds were in the chandelier?'

'Exactly. But the cunning hiding place was rumbled!' Cressida looked very pleased with herself.

'But then how does that explain the open window in Lady Chatterton's bedroom and the boot prints beneath it?' queried DCI Andrews.

'I don't know,' admitted Cressida. 'But what if the diamonds never left this house the night of the theft?'

'I think we can give the local boys a little more credit than that; they searched the place top to bottom,' Andrews gently reproached her. 'And Lady Chatterton said she most definitely hadn't left her window open.'

'Well,' Cressida shrugged, 'it was only a theory.' *If rather a good one*, she thought to herself. 'I could always ask around a bit more, you know, sniff out some more clues or—'

'Absolutely not!' DCI Andrews, who Cressida hoped had been softening towards her and Dotty, was back to his gruff and authoritarian self. He continued, his brow furrowed and his face as serious as it could get, 'No more prying, poking, climbing or, dare I say it, hiding behind screens when officers of the law are going about their business. I mean it.'

'Of course, Chief Inspector.' Cressida answered.

'As I said before, hunting down murderers can be a dangerous business and it's not a thing for a young lady such as yourself to get involved in. No more amateur sleuthing.' He had put his notebook away and was wagging a finger at her. 'That goes for you too, Lady Dorothy.'

'Y-yes, Chief Inspector,' Dotty stuttered, and Cressida felt her move a little closer to her.

'Miss Fawcett, do you understand?' Andrews demanded, his full glare aimed directly at her.

'Yes, Chief Inspector, I promise not to do any more sleuthing.' Cressida looked suitably chastened as he turned and walked away.

Looks, as we all know, however, can be deceiving, and behind her back, Cressida may have crossed her fingers as she'd made her promise. As far as she was concerned, there was a murderer on the loose and a lot more to be untangled here at Chatterton Court – and she rather thought she might be the one to unravel it.

13

The ballroom fell into a hush after DCI Andrews had left and Cressida uncrossed her fingers from behind her back. Dotty was still flushed from the policeman's stern words, but Cressida was more worried about the fact that someone in this house was a killer. The stripes on the curtains were starting to make her eyes go crazy when she looked at them and the mantelpiece clock all of a sudden ticked annoyingly loudly. She needed to get outside where the fresh air would help her think, too.

'I better find Ruby. Fancy a walk?' she asked Dotty.

'Love to, but I think I should really go and be the hostess with the mostest and see how Petronella and William are. They're here as guests of Basil, so I do hope he's entertaining them and not taking potshots into the pine trees still.'

Cressida felt like saying all sorts of things about Basil, but kept schtum for her friend's sake. At some point this weekend, she really must find time to properly talk to Dot about her intended, but now was not the time. So, instead, she bid her friend goodbye and decided that her court shoes really were too silly for a stomp around the grounds... despite being deemed perfectly safe for scaffolding tower climbing before lunch. She shook her head to herself at her idiocy in even thinking of climbing that thing and was rather pleased to see a team of decorators starting the onerous job of taking down the scaffold as she left the ballroom and headed back out to the great hall. Cardew the butler was co-ordinating the affair, with a frazzled-looking Lady Chatterton pointing out heirlooms and paintings that wouldn't be helped by having a twelve-foot metal pole accidentally driven through them.

'Oh, do look out for Sir Roger!' Lady Chatterton winced as a scaffolding board was dropped to the floor, narrowly missing an alabaster bust of a Chatterton ancestor. She turned and saw Cressida at the bottom of the stairs. 'Oh, Cressida dear, hello. Sorry about all of this. Poor Sir Roger died in the 1730s, you know, believe it or not from having a plank fall on his head as he walked under a building site in Soho. Would be terrible for history to repeat itself. Here, be a useful thing and take Lady Adelaine up to your room would you. I fear she's not as robust as Sir Roger.' Lady Chatterton passed a delicately sculpted bust to Cressida, who bowed under the weight of it but cradled Lady Adelaine as best she could as Lady Chatterton kept talking. 'Now, *she* actually died from a nasty dose of the clap, but she's clean as a whistle these days. Do pop her in your room, will you?'

'Of course, Lady Chatterton. Come on, Lady A, let's go.'

As Cressida walked up the stairs, she jumped a few times at the awful clanging that reverberated about the grand marble hall of Chatterton Court as one hefty pole after another was taken down.

Once Lady Adelaine was safely deposited on the top of her chest of drawers, she had to admit that the graceful alabaster bust of the ancestral lady did add a certain *je ne sais quoi* to the room.

Moments later and Cressida, in stout shoes and a light tweed coat, along with Ruby, who had been found sunbathing in the late-afternoon sunshine on the terrace (but now also in a light tweed coat that Cressida had found advertised in the back pages of *The Tatler*), were taking a stroll around the lawn and grounds. The molehills really were rampant, to the extent that a previously beautifully mown piece of grass that looked like it was used as a crease for when the household played cricket was now as textured and bumpy as one of Lady Chatterton's alligator-skin handbags.

Moles... Cressida wondered if there was a mole in Chatterton Court. Perhaps someone on the staff let in the thief, rather than it being one of the guests, or even family, who'd done the heinous crimes? Cressida shook her head. She couldn't fathom either Alfred or John killing someone, nor doing anything to upset their mother... well, except for how they acted in London, but that was a different thing altogether. Mothers the world over were no doubt upset by the antics of their sons when they drank a little too much at the Mutton Pie Club and then headed out to the nightclubs of London's West End afterwards. *In fact, mothers were almost made to be upset in that situation*, Cressida thought, remembering that her own mother had looked shocked when her father had given her the rather sensible advice on signing for the lease on her flat that 'if you can't be good, be careful'. Cressida smiled to herself, and for some reason thinking of her dear papa reminded her of DCI Andrews. Different men entirely, yet something about the policeman, despite his salt-of-the-earthness, brought to mind her father.

'He doesn't like me poking my nose in, Rubes,' Cressida told her dog. 'Though I wonder if it's more to do with him not wanting to share the glory of the victory. Think how wonderful it would be if the newspapers all heralded *moi*, The Hon. Cressida Fawcett, as the "brain that beat Scotland Yard". Wouldn't that be splendid?'

Ruby snuffled one of the molehills and Cressida took it as a firm agreement.

'I must say, I've given him quite the best leads so far. He'd be a numpty not to follow up on them, but where would he... or indeed I... go from here?'

Ruby looked up at her, her dark, round eyes blinking. Then she promptly sat down and started scratching her ear, getting freshly dug-up molehill soil all over her tweed coat.

'Oh Ruby. You mucky pup. You're right though. The whole idea of a mole in the house is a good one. What do we know about Cardew? Or Mrs Climpton, for that matter? Apart from the fact that she makes exceedingly good cakes. And then there's the housemaids. One doesn't want to slander, but a set of diamonds like the ones that were nabbed from Lady C would go a long way to getting oneself out of service and onto the next boat to America. Except...' Cressida bent down and flicked a worm off Ruby's coat. 'Except... Maurice hadn't heard of anything being fenced yet. I wonder if that's still the case?'

Ruby snuffled and walked a few yards until she found another molehill to play in.

'I can't imagine Alfred or John would do anything, Rubes, and I think it would test mine and Dotty's friendship to the limit if I were even to suggest her brothers could be guilty of it. That fiancé of hers, on the other hand...'

As Cressida walked, she stomped down on the molehills, like the gardener at home had taught her. She was about to walk across the lawn to another ripe batch of molehills, Ruby at her ankles with a similar, if slightly more destructive, idea, when the soil of one of them suddenly exploded in front of her.

Pffft. Another one lost its top.

'Ruby!' Cressida cried out and whirled around, looking for her dog as another shot whizzed across the lawn and hit a bullseye in the middle of a particularly ripe pile of soil. Ruby, wide-eyed and trembling, scuttled over to her mistress and all but leapt into her outstretched arms.

Holding her pup tight, Cressida stepped back and away from the molehills but followed the trajectory of the shots to a second-floor window and clearly saw the muzzle of a rifle pointing out of it. As she looked, the barrel of the gun moved slightly... was it turning on her?

'Excuse me!' She waved up at the window. Surely the shooter merely hadn't seen her. 'I say, be careful with that thing!'

Pffft. Another shot skimmed the top of a molehill a few feet away from her. Whoever was up there could no doubt clearly see her now and yet they weren't stopping...

'Jeepers, Ruby, let's seek cover!'

Cressida was pleased that her stout shoes were thus that she could hotfoot it off the lawn and under the cover of a large cypress tree. Once shielded under its swooping boughs, she dared to look back up at the house, where now, clear as day, she could see who was behind the gun.

'Basil Bartleby, you ass.' Cressida swore under her breath. 'Taking potshots at me is one thing, but at you, Ruby...' She held the small dog close to her and Ruby panted in appreciation. Cressida narrowed her eyes as she looked up towards the house again. 'What's more Rubes, with his penchant for deadly weapons, guess who's just gone to the top of my suspects list?'

14

'Basil!' Cressida knocked firmly on the bathroom door. 'Basil, I know you're in there. I can still smell gunpowder.' She rapped her knuckles on the bathroom door again. Cressida had skirted around the edge of the lawn and come back into the house via the main door, out of sight of the gunman in the bathroom. She had run up the main staircase, shutting Ruby safely into the Blue Room on her way, and then ascended another flight of stairs that led to the upper storeys of the house. She'd heard the thwack of shot pellets hitting soil as she'd left the terrace, so knew he couldn't have gone far in the time she'd taken to reach him.

And she was right. The door was pulled open and a grumpy-looking Basil greeted her from within the peach-coloured bathroom suite.

'Bloody idiot, walking across a lawn when a man's shooting. You'd have been court-martialled in my regiment. Could have taken an eye out, what?' he blustered, but Cressida knew this was offence instead of defence and stood firm.

'Basil, you could see me plain as day. Or if you couldn't, you should really give up your gun licence. Now, are you going to apologise or am I going to have to tell Dotty that you almost shot her best friend?'

Basil looked flushed and Cressida wondered if perhaps no one ever spoke to him like this. Once more, it flashed across her mind that she really couldn't fathom why Dotty was so potty about him.

Basil cleared his throat and, to Cressida's relief, opened the bathroom door wider and put the gun down. 'My apologies, Cressida,' he said, though Cressida would have put ten bob on the fact that he didn't mean it.

'Accepted. On the condition you let me ask you a couple of questions.' Cressida crossed the threshold of the bathroom, which, on closer inspection, was less peach and more a dark salmon pink in colour and not terribly fancy, unsurprising since this floor was mainly used for lower-class guests or higher-ranking visiting servants. And shotgun-wielding mole hunters it seemed. The bath was low and wide though, and she sat herself on the side of it, while Basil leaned against the sill of the still open window. Cressida was glad of the fresh air, as now she was face to face with Basil and about to ask him if he had anything to do with a theft or a murder, it was making her queasy. She was glad Ruby was probably catching the last of the afternoon sunbeams and safely away from this brute, but she missed the comforting warmth of the little dog as she braced herself for this awkward conversation.

'Go on then,' Basil urged. 'I've only got an hour or two of daylight left and I'm sure those moles are surfacing every five to ten minutes. One good shot and, bam,' he punched one hand against the open palm of the other, 'got him!'

Cressida took a deep breath. 'Basil, can you tell me anything about this morning?'

'This morning?' Basil looked confused. 'Breakfast and the like?'

'No, Basil. The early hours of this morning.' Cressida found it hard not to add 'you clod' onto the end of the sentence, and so congratulated herself on her restraint.

'Ah, you mean that cleaner chap? No.' He looked down at his hands. Now they weren't thumping each other, they hung awkwardly in front of him. 'Why?'

'I'm wondering if the death of Mr Smith had anything to do with Lady C's diamonds going missing and I thought—'

'You thought I had something to do with it?' Basil looked maddened, a red flush growing from his neck and pinking his cheeks.

Cressida wondered why he'd leapt to that conclusion so quickly and held her nerve. 'Well, did you?'

There was a moment of silence and Cressida couldn't help but glance at the shotgun that was precariously leant against the windowsill next to Basil. He could have his hands on it again in a second... but instead, he spoke and, to Cressida's surprise, he laughed.

'You silly woman.' He mocked her. 'You think that I might have something to do with stealing Honoria's diamonds?'

The fact he used Lady Chatterton's first name in such a familiar fashion rankled with Cressida more than his insult towards her. She looked blankly at him, hoping it would urge him on. It did.

'I thought you were the bright one out of that cohort of debutants, but you're missing something very obvious. Why would I want, or indeed *need*, to steal any Chatterton diamonds when I'm marrying into the family? Those are practically *my* diamonds. Once Dorothy inherits them, of course.'

'Which wouldn't have been for a while, I sincerely hope. Lady C said she'd had planned on passing them onto Dotty on her deathbed, as her dear mother had to her,' Cressida countered.

Basil, who had started kicking the side panel of the bath with the toe of his shoe, looked across at her, his eyes narrowing.

'Well, in the meantime, I would have been living very well off the cash settlement she's due to receive on marriage. It's the same amount as John's getting when he comes of age and very nicely he'll do out of it. And Dorothy will get all the rest of her mother's jewellery as they're not from the Chatterton side, so won't go with the estate to Alfred. Lucky blighter, he'll get the rest of it all.' Basil stopped talking when he noticed a flake of paint from the bath panel on the end of his shoe. He bent down to flick it off before finishing his point. 'So, me marrying Dorothy equals me in the money, understand?' He jabbed a finger against his temple. 'Hence no motive. QED.'

Cressida sighed. The brute had a point. She was about to make her excuses when he continued.

'Tell you who might know a bit more than he's letting on: that Major Elliot.'

Cressida looked up at Basil and raised an eyebrow. He took the floor again.

'Always hanging around the family, knows the ins and outs better than most guests. *And* horribly in debt.'

'Oh?' Cressida wanted to think that this was nothing more than lurid gossip, but she knew this information was more important than mere drawing-room ammunition.

'He owed money to most of us in this house.' Basil thought about it and shrugged. 'Who knows. But he's a terrible gambler, in that when he's at the Mutton Pie Club, he's all but glued to the baize and I think John took him for at least fifty guineas the other night.'

'He wasn't here the night of the burglary though,' Cressida stated, more to herself than Basil.

'Wasn't he? Just because he wasn't invited to stay... And didn't the police say that the footprints showed military-issue boots? So, as I said, QED. Job done. I don't know why these police kick up such a fuss when it only takes one sensible man, like me, to sort it all out.'

'Did you sort out Harry Smith's questions on how to cope with his windfall too?' Cressida recalled what Jacob had said. 'Apparently he'd been asking you gents how to spend it wisely.'

'Who? Never heard of the chap. Harrow? Or Eton?' Basil looked genuinely confused.

'Neither, Basil. Harry Smith, the poor man who died this morning.' Cressida shook her head, exasperated by this man's oafishness. 'Apparently he asked you and some of the other chaps about how to cope with suddenly being wealthy.'

'Who said that? Priestley?'

'No, one of the footmen.'

Basil grunted. 'All balderdash. Never said a word to the chap. Why would I? Servant? Why would I talk to a servant? Now, if you'll excuse me.' He picked up the shotgun and Cressida instinctively backed away towards the door as he spun it round, briefly letting it point right at her. 'Don't get between my cross hairs again, what?'

'Goodbye, Basil,' Cressida managed, while storing up all the other words she wanted to say for when she was alone with the bedclothes pulled well up over her head. What an oafish brute he was. There was something detestable about Basil, and for the umpteenth time she wondered what dear Dot saw in him. Despite his annoyingly good point about marrying into the Chattertons and their money, and the lead he'd given her about the major, Cressida wasn't willing to strike him off her list of suspects yet.

15

'Miss Fawcett!'

Cressida's name was barked at her and it made her jump. She couldn't see who had yelled at her, but its tone reminded her of Mr Jensen, the eternally angry science master at her school. It had been a few years now since she'd walked the halls of her educational establishment, but back then, Mr Jensen had had to reprimand her on several occasions as she snuck equipment out of the laboratories. He hadn't been terribly impressed when, caught and questioned, she'd shrugged and said, 'How else can one distil one's own gin?' The gruff, manly voice behind her sent a shiver down her spine, and as she turned to face Detective Chief Inspector Andrews, she realised shrugging of shoulders and offers of a cocktail in the common room wouldn't pass muster here.

'Miss Fawcett. Stop right there.'

'Chief Inspector?' Cressida queried, wondering what she'd done wrong. She hoped Ruby was still snoozing under the eiderdown in her room and hadn't purloined a string of sausages from the kitchen.

'Was that you I just saw dashing across the lawn, with potshots being fired at you?' Andrews asked, bluntly.

'Well... yes... but...' Cressida, as much as she disliked Basil, didn't want to get him into trouble, for Dotty's sake. 'It was all a misunderstanding, you see. All dealt with. And if you would like some information, I think I've found out something—'

'Miss Fawcett,' Andrews cut her off, 'I thought I told you clearly not to continue any sort of investigation. You gave me your word.'

Cressida was good enough to look slightly abashed.

Andrews carried on. 'And who was that firing at you?'

'No one. Well, Basil, but it was an accident and he apologised, sort of, and I was...' Cressida began, but tailed off when she saw how cross DCI Andrews looked. He wasn't an old man, but he looked like he'd been around the world and then some. Perhaps it was the grizzled grey hair, neatly cropped but obviously not the dark brown it had once been, or the wrinkles at the corners of his eyes, which Cressida couldn't decide were from age or sun. Her father, who'd served in India in the last century, had similar wrinkles and he always said each one was created during an Indian summer. The sun would beat down on them, their uniforms becoming drenched in sweat in moments in the humidity of Delhi's downtown heat. If it hadn't been for his batman – the soldier he'd tasked from his men to be the one to look after his uniform, attend to his meals and run his errands, leaving him free to work on strategy and leading his men – he said the wrinkles would have gone right down to his toes. This fond memory of her father made Cressida smile, but she quickly regained her composure as she saw Andrews' reaction to it.

'Do you think this is funny, Miss Fawcett? Because I can tell you that perverting the course of justice, and impeding a lawful investigation, can get you several years in jail.' He looked deathly serious.

'Of course. Sorry, Detective Chief Inspector.' Cressida looked down at her hands, which were clasped tightly in front of her. It seemed she would have to keep her information about Basil and his annoying lack of motive, and indeed Major Elliot and his abundance of motive, to herself.

Luckily for Cressida, the gong sounded for dressing for dinner and she used it as an excuse to skedaddle up the grand staircase to her room. A snuffling Ruby greeted her and Cressida threw herself onto the bed next to her, allowing the little pup to climb on top of her and snort and snuffle in contentment before climbing off again and heading straight for the door.

'Hmm, perhaps you would like those sausages after all,' Cressida said, and chuckled at how excited Ruby seemed to get at the mention of the word. 'Come on then, the coast is clear from grumpy old policemen.' Cressida had checked the landing and the hall below, now devoid of the scaffolding tower and back to its stunning best.

As the daylight from the cupola waned, the chandelier really came into its own. The bulbs were on – it was an electrolier, as Dotty had proclaimed, after all – and they shone through the newly cleaned crystal drops, making each one sparkle and shine like a diamond. Cressida thought about her theory that someone had hidden the diamonds in the chandelier, and that perhaps that was 'the wealth' Harry Smith had found. But then why would someone hide diamonds in a chandelier when they knew the scaffolding that they would need to retrieve them would be gone again, for a year at least?

'It doesn't make sense, Rubes,' Cressida told her dog as they went down the staircase. 'Perhaps they were never up there, and that poor cleaner did just accidentally fall to his death?'

Ruby stopped and sat down on the bottom step of the stairs, almost tripping Cressida up. Cressida wagged a finger at her pup, but as she did so, she could hear two voices, the sound of them echoing around the hallway. Cressida couldn't help but be intrigued, and despite DCI Andrews' admonishment ringing in her ears, she stopped to listen.

'Now's the time to act. You should be helping me to push the idea with Lady Chatterton,' the male voice said.

'We have to be more subtle about it,' the female voice counteracted. 'Her own diamonds have only just disappeared; if we push more on her now, she'll smell a rat.'

'Fiddlesticks. She's not exactly Sherlock Holmes. Besides, isn't this why we came to Chatterton Court in the first place?' the male voice demanded.

'You, perhaps. I've got a different game plan.'

'You have to put the family first and not let this silly notion of yours stop us from getting a foothold here. I've risked enough to be here already.'

'Fine. But don't expect me to jeopardise my happiness for your inheritance, brother.'

Cressida jumped up a few of the steps and then, as nonchalantly as possible, walked down them just as William and Petronella Harper-Ashe rounded the corner and entered the great hall.

'Hello both,' Cressida greeted them brightly, hoping that they hadn't realised that she'd been eavesdropping on their conversation. 'Quick dinner dash to the kitchen for the pup before I get my glad rags on. See you in a bit!' She indicated Ruby and nodded towards the kitchen as she spoke and let the brother and sister past.

With a smile glued to her face, she watched as they went upstairs and then let out a breath. As she headed across the hall and found the discreet door that led to the servants' quarters and kitchen, she couldn't help but process what she'd overheard. Despite a shocking lack of respect for their hostess, which made Cressida jolly cross, the pair had been talking about 'pushing more onto her'. What did that mean? And what had been the risk that William said he'd taken? Cressida remembered the conversation she'd had that morning with Petronella. *Oh*, she thought to herself, *their family diamond mines...* Perhaps William, who had only recently returned from Africa and seemed to be the driving force of the two, was trying to get Lady Chatterton to buy some diamonds? *And perhaps stealing her family heirlooms and leaving her bereft would put her in the market for buying some more?*

'Gosh, Rubes,' Cressida whispered into the ear of her beloved pug. 'I think we've just added one or two more names to our list of suspects.'

The servants' quarters, beyond the baize door, were the epitome of their type. Graciously proportioned corridors had airy and bright rooms leading off them, and although the kitchens and various pantries and housekeeper's rooms were technically on the lower ground floor, the house had been designed with large sash windows that let in as much light as possible.

The smell of cooking goose fat lured both Cressida and Ruby towards the bustle of the kitchen. With under an hour to go before dinner, Mrs Climpton and her team of maids were busy at the stove and countertops. Cressida managed to catch the eye of a young footman and beckoned him over. She couldn't help but notice the soft cream of his waistcoat, freshly pressed and looking terribly smart, but also very reminiscent of that scrap of fabric she'd found, and she fiddled around up her blouse cuff to try to find it before remembering that she'd given it to DCI Andrews. Still, even though she couldn't colour-match it exactly, it stayed in her mind as a possibility.

The genial footman, unaware of the analysis of his waist-coat, led them to one of the pantries, where Rollo the spaniel was nosing into his bowl of dinner table scraps. Ruby, despite her lowly stature, muscled her way in to join him.

'Thank you.' Cressida smiled at the footman and then

thought he might be able to answer something for her. 'Actually, excuse me...'

'Yes, miss.' He bobbed a small bow and Cressida tried hard not to wave away the formality. In some cases, it was easier to let it stand.

'Could you show me where the electric switch is?'

'The one what was flicked the night of the robbery, miss?' He looked at her quizzically and she knew it was now her turn to be analysed.

'Yes, that's the one. I want to see the lie of the land and all that.'

'Of course, miss. Don't mind your dog, miss, she'll be fine with Rollo there.'

He led her back to the passageway and walked away from the kitchen towards the baize door. They stopped just short of it and the footman opened what looked like a normal pantry door to reveal a room full of the most up-to-date circuit boards and cabling.

'Here you are, miss. Telephone cabinet, electric switch-board, the works. It's a fine addition to the house. Maybe too close to the hall, though, as someone got in here and flicked it last night.'

'Last night? Don't you mean Wednesday?'

'Well yes, but last night too, miss.' He stood straighter and clasped his hands behind his back, giving himself an air of importance. 'I had the sad duty to come in here myself to call for the police this morning and found the switch flicked off again. Very odd, if you ask me.'

'Quite. Did you hear anything in the night? Or Wednesday night, for that matter? Young Jacob said there were whispers about the scaffold wobbling the night of the robbery?'

The footman nodded. 'That's right, miss. One of the maids thought she saw someone, though there was only moonlight in the hall at that stage. Said she'd heard the scaffolding wobbling too, much like the early hours of this morning.'

'Oh, that is interesting.' Suddenly her theory about the diamonds going straight from the drawer to chandelier and never leaving the house until the cleaner was found killed looked a lot more likely, despite what the local police thought about the drainpipe and footprints. 'Would you excuse me?' Cressida thanked the footman and waited for him to leave.

She'd spied the telephone as soon as he'd pointed it out and felt an urge to call Maurice in London. He should still be at work, as the busy Saturday trade would have no doubt kept him there until closing. So as soon as the footman had left, she picked up the earpiece and spoke into the candlestick.

'Hello, operator? Liberty of London please. Upholstery and fabrics. Yes, I'll hold.'

The line fuzzed and clicked.

'Oh Maurice, hello. Cressida Fawcett here.'

'Hello, Miss Fawcett. How are the curtains?' Despite it being the end of what must have been a long trading day, he sounded pleased to hear from her.

'Simply ghastly, Maurice. A hundred times worse than feared, though beautifully made. Such a shame. I think I've got the go-ahead to choose Lady C something else though, so you will start looking out some damask, won't you? Something simple but sophisticated. Or an archive pattern perhaps. Not Morris, too busy, maybe a Sanderson?'

Cressida felt soothed talking about fabrics. Being back in a world she understood, where no one was getting killed and the worst thing that could happen was, well, those curtains, made her feel all right again. But there might well be a murderer in their midst and Cressida realised that Maurice's warning to her before she left London couldn't have been more pertinent. She told him of the tragedy that had befallen the household this morning.

'Miss Fawcett, didn't I say there'd be trouble afoot if you started pulling at loose threads?' He sounded genuinely worried about her, though the line was crackling terribly.

'I don't think Mr Smith died on my account,' Cressida reassured him, and herself. 'Though I'm getting increasingly convinced that his death is somehow linked to the disappearance of the diamonds. Have you heard anything on the grapevine?'

'Nothing, I'm afraid.' Maurice confirmed what Cressida had wondered. 'Not a trace of them fenced or broken apart into loose gems. Those diamonds have completely disappeared.'

'Disappeared, or just disappeared from sight. I'm beginning to wonder if they've even left Chatterton Court at all.'

'I did tell you—'

'Yes, you did.' Cressida paused and the line crackled. 'And another oddity, Maurice, the diamonds' box, which had been discarded in Lady C's room the night of the theft, was then stolen on the night of the murder.'

'Murder? You only said that the young man had died.'

Cressida took a deep breath, what felt like the first during the whole conversation. 'Yes. Murder. I'm pretty convinced of it anyway.'

There was a pause before Maurice concluded the call. 'In that case, heed my warning again and do be careful, Miss Fawcett. As I said, the wrong type of person will do an awful lot for two thousand pounds... and if they've killed once, as you suspect they might have done, who knows what else they might be capable of?'

Cressida put the receiver down, Maurice's warning echoing in her ears. She let herself out of the telephone cupboard and collected Ruby from the cosy dining club she was enjoying with Rollo.

'Your very own Mutton Pie Club,' she muttered, thinking things over as she pushed through the green baize door and headed up the great stone staircase to her room. Was Maurice right? Could someone here at Chatterton Court really be capable of murdering not just once, but twice? Were they all in danger?

She closed her bedroom door behind her, her mind soothed by the colours of the late-afternoon sunlight as they played across the cool blues; the peachy-orange of the setting sun turned the blue walls aqua green, while the silk curtains almost sparkled with opalescent depth.

Cressida sat down on her bed and put Ruby cosily among the extra cushions. 'I may not know much about refraction waves or spectral resonances, but I can put a darn fine room scheme together, Rubes.' She sighed, as despite trying to distract herself with decor, she was feeling unsettled and out of kilter. *Probably because someone tried to kill me earlier*, she thought, then shook her head, trying to rattle the notion out of it. She was a Fawcett, and the stiffest of upper lips was required. She stroked the folds of fur on Ruby's brow. 'I wish I knew more about what was going on here at Chat—'

Cressida was interrupted in her musings by a soft knock at the door. Leaving Ruby perkily alert on the bed, Cressida got up and crossed the room to open it. She heard a snuffling the other side of the door and was about to prepare herself for Rollo to bound in with whoever had done the knocking when she realised that it wasn't the sound of an excited spaniel at all.

'Dotty?' she asked, as her red-eyed friend slipped in past her to her room, blowing her nose and sobbing. 'What on earth's the matter?'

16

'I shouldn't get so upset, I suppose,' Dotty sniffled, sitting down on the neat little stool that sat in front of the dressing table in Cressida's room. 'Basil's just not a romantic. But thanks to those dratted fairy tales we all read when we were young, I did have this vision of courtly love and all that.'

'Wimples and veils and all?' Cressida tried to make light of it, but was finding it hard to maintain her goal of learning to like Basil Bartleby.

'Yes, and an oh-so-charming prince.' Dotty's lower lip began to tremble.

'Chum, I'm not sure any of us will get a prince. Well, Veronica Haverford-de-Croute might, but I believe Leonard is only a minor royal...'

'Basil's not even a minor *noble*,' Dotty sniffed.

Cressida wondered if this was perhaps the time to query her friend's attraction to the man she had proclaimed undying love for.

'What is it about Basil that made you fall for him, Dot?' Cressida perched on the end of her bed, facing her crestfallen friend.

'Well, he's awfully manly, don't you think?'

Cressida could at least genuinely agree with that description. Whether or not she thought his particular brand of 'manliness' was attractive was an entirely different thing.

'I'd noticed him during our debutant season and thought him frightfully good-looking. So tall! And he's confident and knows what's what. His father knows Papa, and they thought it a decent enough match.' Dotty blew her nose.

'I know family connections are important, Dotty, and a manly man is all very exciting and all that, but do you love him? Is he kind and thoughtful?'

'Cressy!' Dotty's lip properly trembled. 'Of course he's kind to me. He... well, he's here this weekend. That's something. And he's awfully impressive on horseback and can do that obstacle course the army make you do in a terribly good time. He'll be good for me, I think. Toughen me up a bit.'

'I'm not sure you need toughening up, Dot.' Cressida leaned forward and put a reassuring hand on Dotty's knee. Her mind was elsewhere though, logging Basil as being good at obstacle courses... and perhaps drainpipes or scaffold climbing... in her head.

Dotty carried on telling her best friend her feelings. 'I haven't admitted this to anyone, but I was rather hoping that Basil might bring back something shiny and sparkling from his trip to South Africa. The diamonds there are fabulous apparently. But he brought me back some sort of tribal mask and a photograph of a penguin.' Dotty sighed.

'Like I said, some men just aren't romantic, old thing. Look at Freddie Brise-Norton. He whisked Jessica off on what she thought was going to be a honeymoon on the French Riviera but turned out she'd misheard and they spent a month fishing *tench* out of the local *river*. French... tench... Riviera... river... I can see the misunderstanding. Still, men can be wholly unromantic at times, but it doesn't mean he doesn't love you.' For her friend's sake, Cressida really, really hoped that what she was saying was the truth. Though she feared with Basil Bartleby, it might not be. She clapped her hands on her thighs and changed the subject. 'Right, old fruit, what shall I wear tonight? I've brought the satin shimmery thing that Mama says is too short to be proper, or the full-length eau de Nil thing that Lord Summersbury said I looked like a delicious little pistachio in. What shall it be?'

'Oh the delicious little pistachio, I think, Cressy.' Dotty seemed cheered up. She looked rather lovely this evening herself, despite her red-rimmed eyes, in a dark green silk number that set off her chestnut hair perfectly.

Cressida made her shuffle along the dressing-table stool and started dabbing powder on her nose. She took Dotty by surprise, dabbing some loose powder on her nose too, which made her friend squeal and then laugh.

'Oh Cressy, you wag.' Dotty giggled. 'Though you're right, I should "fix my face", as Mama would say. Basil will never come hither if I don't have the eyes for it.'

Cressida smiled at her friend. The last thing *she'd* want was for Basil Bartleby to come anywhere near her, hither or no hither, but she was glad she'd managed to cheer her friend up.

Together, they patted powder on their noses and Dotty then helped Cressida slip into her silky pale green dress.

'*Shell* we go downstairs, my little pistachio?' Dotty joked when they were ready.

'*Nut* before you, old chum,' Cressida answered, and turning to check that Ruby was soundly snoring where she had left her on the bed, they went downstairs just as the gong for cocktails was sounding.

'Cheers, old girl.' Alfred clinked his glass against Cressida's, the gin cocktail sloshing around the crystal coupe as he did. 'Feels bad to be jubilant, what with everything that happened this morning, but it *is* Martini o'clock. Reminds me of that time you—'

'Shush,' Cressida scolded him, seeing Dotty and Basil approach across the room. 'Anyway, you can talk, look at that splodge on your waistcoat. Maybe it wasn't just me doing things to the trifle the other night.'

'Touché, old thing, touché.' Alfred chuckled and looked down at his frilled waistcoat and noticed for perhaps the first time a tell-tale grease stain. 'That was actually a cream puff from Madame Fifi's Hall of Delights—'

'I don't need to know, Alfred.' Cressida held her palm up and sipped her Martini, allowing her friend the briefest twinkle of her eye. He was right though. It did feel odd to be acting as if nothing had happened today, but it made sense too – to most of the guests, the death had been a tragedy that had now turned into a minor inconvenience thanks to the Scotland Yard detectives, who had obviously finished their work for the day. The English upper classes did nothing better, Cressida fancied, than brushing vexatious troubles under the Persian carpet. She looked at Alfred again. 'Fancy waistcoat though, is this the new Mutton Pie Club one?' She admired the rich buttery pastry colour of the silk, which, as the major had said, was decorated with a frill much like that of a Cornish pasty. She couldn't help but compare the colour and the texture to the scrap of fabric now languishing in police custody...

'Yes, bit gaudy, isn't it? Still, all part of the club fun. Cummerbunds too, for those of us who managed to spill whisky or jam or whatever down them last night.'

'Ah, the major, you mean? Don't worry, I gave him the number of that wonderful chap in Notting Hill who managed to get that claret out of my... well, you know the story.'

'Indeed I do, old girl. How are your—'

'They're fine thank you Alfred.' Cressida cut him off.

Alfred chuckled at her. 'Well, you might like to give Basil his number too, as the best part of Father's bottle of whisky went down his front.'

Cressida rolled her eyes.

All the young of the party were now in the drawing room. John and Edmund were playing barmen, shaking their cocktail shakers like Mexicans with maracas. William Harper-Ashe and his sister Petronella laughed at their antics and suggested more names of cocktails they wanted to try. It was as if nothing had happened today and Cressida sighed, feeling a touch let down by her class. She also remembered the hushed conversation she'd overheard earlier. William, and especially Petronella, had seemed so charming and here they were chatting and drinking, but was their presence here less than innocent?

'Alfred, how well do you know the Harper-Ashes?' Cressida asked, glad that Alfred was still by her side and hadn't yet moved over to where the others were spinning the cocktail shakers and sloshing spirits into glasses.

'Not especially. Friends of Basil's, I believe. Though William is in the Mutton Pie Club too, when he's in the country, of course. Always threatens to bring us back some wildebeest or springbok for a pie, but the chefs have so far declined. Basil spent some time with them out there recently.'

'Heard my name, what?' Basil appeared next to them, a glowing Dotty by his side.

'Just saying you're the reason the Harper-Ashes are here, Basil,' Alfred answered him.

'Well, yes. Investments and whatnot.' Basil straightened his silk waistcoat and pulled on his bow tie. He had at least now shaved, and Cressida supposed that he could be classed as handsome, though she couldn't see the attraction herself, especially with a badly dealt-with whisky stain down the front of his waistcoat. She noticed him looking over at the other guests with longing in his eyes and she could see that his glass was empty.

Alfred must have noticed too as he indicated his own empty one and guided Basil over to where the others were now creating what they were calling a Chatterton Club and also a Drawing Room Daiquiri. Both drinks sounded downright dangerous, but Basil had a look of glee as a fresh glass was thrust at him by a flushed Petronella. Cressida, no stranger to a strong tipple, held back from joining in to speak to her friend.

'You look happier, Dot,' she said, observing the glow to Dotty's cheeks.

'Oh rather, yes. I told Basil all about Freddie and Jessica and the mishap between the word French and tench, and how they spent their honeymoon by the river not the Riviera... and Basil let slip what he was planning for our honeymoon.' Dotty bit her lip, inviting Cressida to guess, but then blurting it out anyway. 'Cape Town! Isn't that marvellous?'

'How splendid! You'll get to see that penguin he so thoughtfully photographed for you.' Cressida wiggled her eyebrows and Dotty biffed her on the arm.

'They mate for life, you know. Penguins. He said that was the reason he gave me the photograph.'

Cressida had to admit that that was annoyingly romantic of Basil. 'I'm so happy for you, Dot, I really am.' She squeezed her friend's arm and, noticing Alfred beckoning them over, led her to where the other guests were now lounging across the chintz Chatterton Court sofas.

'Well, we can't stay miserable all night, can we?' Edmund raised a glass to the group. 'I propose a toast to that dead chap and then let's carry on with our weekend. To Harry Smith, poor blighter.'

'To Harry Smith.' The rest of them raised their glasses and Basil, who was already in his cups, it seemed, toasted their hosts as well, sloshing his drink around so it spilt over the rim.

'Oh, dash it all.' He rubbed the pink liquid that had spilt down his front with his handkerchief. 'Anyway, to the delights of Chatterton Court.' He raised his glass and Cressida could see Dotty blushing.

Petronella, next to him, chinked her glass with his, and then also her brother. 'It's so lovely to be back in England.' She smiled coyly, raising her glass to a few others in the group. 'Though South Africa has my heart.'

'Sweeping plains and wild, exotic animals,' agreed Edmund, adding a growl at the end for emphasis.

'Starlit desert camps with views that go on for miles...' reminisced William Harper-Ashe.

'Penguins!' Dotty enthusiastically added.

Basil snorted a laugh at her and Cressida hoped it was in an indulgent way. He turned back to Petronella. 'It's a damn fine country though, you're right.'

'And full of diamonds,' Petronella added.

'Speaking of diamonds,' Basil took the floor, 'some people round here think that poor man was killed because of Lady Chatterton's going missing.' He glared at Cressida.

Dotty stared into her cocktail, and Cressida was about to speak when John beat her to it.

'I was here the night Mother's diamonds were stolen, it was—'

'Horrible, quite horrible,' Dotty interrupted her brother. 'But I'm beginning to think the police,' she snuck a glance at Cressida, 'might have a point about poor Harry's death being linked to their disappearance.'

'It's still being ruled as an accidental death though, isn't it?' Edmund leaned into the group, from his perch on the arm of one of the sofas. 'Last thing you Chattertons need is this house to be known for a murder.'

There was a general murmur of 'ghastly thought' and 'dear God, no' from the guests.

Alfred spoke up next. 'We can weather most storms; the most important thing is that if that young man was killed, he gets justice. And if they find Mother's diamonds to boot, then that would be a good thing too.'

'Perhaps it was one of the servants?' Petronella ventured, and Cressida thought it awfully impudent to mention that when at least two footmen were in the room. It seemed the others felt the same and a hush descended.

Basil rescued her from her faux pas by speaking next, but Cressida was astounded by what he said.

'Good point, Petronella. Can't trust the underclasses. Diamonds of that value, they'd change someone's life.'

'Basil!' Cressida couldn't stop herself, despite allowing the thought to cross her mind earlier in the day. She had been convinced by Jacob's argument and said as such, finishing with, 'If Lady Chatterton was good enough to vouch for her staff here, I think we can do them the same justice.'

'Still,' Edmund joined in, 'does beg the question of who needs the diamonds the most and I hazard it's not one of us, from the line-up of Rolls-Royces, Crossleys and that natty little Bugatti of yours in the garage, Cressida.'

Cressida frowned. She didn't like having her car brought into the argument, especially to the detriment of the hard-working staff of Chatterton Court.

'Damn good point, Priestley.' Basil obviously didn't share Cressida's feelings on the matter. 'Stands to reason those diamonds were pinched by some poor person who needed the money.'

Cressida wanted to divest Basil of this snobbish notion by telling everyone about Maurice and his excellent network of informants who were adamant the diamonds hadn't been fenced yet, but as she was debating the good sense of this to herself, Edmund replied to Basil.

'Well, we're all fine for it, aren't we?' Edmund sipped his Martini. 'Allowances from mater and pater feathering our fledgling nests, what?'

'Basil's in line to get something from his aunt, aren't you, darling?' Dotty gazed up at him, an innocent look of pure adoration in her eyes. 'He's been her favourite and she thought it wholly unfair that—'

'That's enough, Dotty,' Basil snapped, softening it with an 'old girl' as Dotty, luckily a bit tipsy now herself, mimicked zipping her lips up. Cressida rolled her eyes and once more wondered what Dotty saw in him.

Petronella spoke next, saying to the group, 'Well, at least you men can earn your fortunes—'

'Earn them?' John interrupted. 'Academia aside, the only alternatives for younger brothers are some sort of speculating abroad, the church, the army... or marrying heiresses.' He said it with a straight face, as if genuinely calculating his options, but it made the other young men laugh.

Petronella shook her head. 'At least you have those options. We ladies *rely* on you to marry us.'

'What tosh,' Cressida said without thinking and then apologised. 'I'm sorry, Petronella, that was rude of me, but honestly... marry? That's the last thing I shall do!'

'Ah,' Alfred cut across them. 'The Honourable Cressida Fawcett – the ultimate heiress.' He smiled at her. 'Made even more charming by her complete lack of want or need of a husband. You should see the broken hearts shattered across London,' he swept an arm through the air in front of him. 'So many poor younger brothers, desperately in need of the Fawcett fortune and the Honourable Cressida resolute in her independence.'

'You'll get a coaster thrown at you next, Alfred,' Cressida told him, a twinkle in her eye.

'Well, here's to all of us being well off enough to not need heartless Cressida's money.' Edmund laughed.

'Very funny.' Cressida gave him a withering look. 'And I'm not heartless, thank you very much. In fact, I've made it my mission to find out what's happened to Lady C's diamonds, not to mention poor Harry Smith. I'm sure with my eye for details—'

'Your eye for design means you have an eye for a crime, eh Cressy?' Alfred interrupted her and the rest of them laughed.

'I quite like that actually, Alfred. Yes.' Cressida raised her glass to him. 'So, you see, Edmund, I do have a heart... just not the stomach for fatuous young men.'

A coaster flew past her ear and the conversation carried on around her.

Cressida looked at them all. *An eye for design means I have an eye for a crime. I do like that...*

17

Lord and Lady Chatterton and Major Elliot were the last of the party to join the younger set in the drawing room, and almost as soon as they'd had a glass of something, Cardew announced dinner. Once the party were seated and the first of several courses had been served, any onlooker to the dining room at Chatterton Court would have hardly known that there'd been a discovery of a dead body first thing that morning.

DCI Andrews and his sergeant were nowhere to be seen and Cressida assumed that they must have taken themselves off to the local inn for a slap-up meal of something hearty. It wouldn't have been right for them to have been invited to dine with the guests, unless of course DCI Andrews happened to be of noble birth too. However, anyone hearing him speak would know he was as salt of the earth as a tablespoon of Maldon's finest. In between conversations to her left with Alfred and right with Edmund, Cressida wondered to herself why she was thinking so much of the gruff policeman and his supper arrangements. She shook herself out of it, putting it all down to the fact that no one had been cross with her like he had for a while, not since that policeman in Knightsbridge had told her off for parking right in front of Harrods. How was she to know that the omnibus had priority at its own stop?

A light lemon tart had just been served and Cressida tucked in. She'd enjoyed talking to Alfred about some mutual friends of theirs during the first course of asparagus and hollandaise sauce, and despite his views on the staff at Chatterton Court, Edmund hadn't been a bad conversational neighbour either as they'd enjoyed their beef Wellington. But, all the while, Cressida had wanted to spend more time talking to the major, who was seated at the other end of the table, especially after what Basil had said about his possible motive in stealing the diamonds. He was in debt, according to Basil, and, unlike the other younger men of the party, hadn't been swilling cocktails and bragging about his inheritance. Perhaps as a career soldier he wasn't able to service his gambling debts and had needed to steal the diamonds? He would definitely be possessed of army boots, and though older and not as fit as some of the younger men, he could possibly shimmy down a drainpipe...

But as she washed down her lemon tart with a decent Sauternes wine, Cressida looked across the table at the sheer delight the major was taking in talking to Lady Chatterton. Lord Chatterton, when he wasn't having to listen to Basil, was laughing at the major's anecdotes, too. He simply didn't seem the type to steal from those who loved him.

And what of William Harper-Ashe and his whispered demands of his sister to go along with whatever plan he was hatching? Surely that was more suspicious than some gossip from Basil, who was chewing Lord Chatterton's ear off about investments, it seemed.

Cressida put her spoon and fork together and sat back. She wanted to find out what had happened here at Chatterton Court, but she knew she mustn't let it stop her from being a good guest, and despite her determination, she couldn't help but notice the sumptuous decor of the dining room, with its silk-lined walls and elegant paintings of cornucopias and game birds. The guests, too, looked decorous, in flowing gowns and smart black tie – even if most of the gentlemen had some sort of stain down their waistcoat. *I really must give them my chap in Notting Hill's card*, she thought, noticing jam, whisky and now cocktail stains on several of the men's Mutton Pie Club waistcoats, not to mention Alfred's greasy spot from Madame Fifi's.

Edmund, next to her, seemed to take more pride in his appearance than most of the others and was wearing one of the club's cummerbunds instead. Perhaps his astute dress sense meant he paid attention to other things too? Cressida decided to find out.

'How well do you know William Harper-Ashe?' she asked, waiting for him to finish his mouthful.

'Fellow clubman, when he's here.' Edmund wasn't as elucidatory as she'd hoped. 'Why do you ask?'

Cressida blanched. She hadn't come up with a reason for being so inquisitive. *Darn it...* She thought on her feet and came up with the only excuse she could think of, as much as it grated on her to even suggest it.

'Oh, you know, Mama's been on at me to find a suitor.' She clenched her jaw, shuddering inwardly at the thought of it.

'Indeed? The legendarily single Hon. Cressida Fawcett finally in need of a husband?' Edmund raised an eyebrow at her, but luckily kept his voice low. 'I always had you pegged for Alfred.'

Cressida blushed, which took even her by surprise, and she fought every fibre of her being in order to keep the pretence up. 'Yes, but all those diamonds... One can't help but think...'

'Magpie eye yourself then?'

Cressida frowned, not liking the comparison to a garden bird renowned for its avaricious love of shiny things.

Edmund carried on, getting into the conversation. 'He may be set to inherit a carat or two, but I heard a bit of club gossip that the mine is running at exceedingly high costs and the family needs a bit of cash flow, you know what I mean. Not enough liquidity.' He winked as he picked up his glass and took a swig of Lord Chatterton's very good Burgundy.

Cressida abhorred a winker, as a wink usually meant something distasteful was about to follow, but then she only usually got winked at in the small hours after many cocktails and by those not within her inner circle. Anyway, she wanted to hear more from Edmund about the Harper-Ashes' diamond mine, however distasteful discussing other people's finances was.

'So, by selling gems that were already mined and cut, it would help their cash flow?' Cressida asked.

'Know a bit about finances then, eh?' He took another swig. 'The heartless heiress that you are.'

Cressida braced herself for another wink and received it with grace when it came.

'But,' Edmund carried on, 'you could do worse. Add some English nobility to their New World money. They'll both be rich enough if they can get over this cash flow crisis. I'd hold off for a year or two, if I were you.'

Cressida, now feeling thoroughly sordid about the whole thing, thought herself in for a penny, in for a pound...

'And what about you, Edmund? Would you be a suitable suitor for a young lady?'

He turned to look at her, an enquiring look in his eye. She realised he must think that this was a proposition of sorts and she stuck her chin out a touch, hoping it made her look aloof.

'I'm well provided for, for now at any rate,' he said and Cressida was convinced she saw his eyes dart down across her body, before alighting back on her face. 'Trust fund until I come of age, then I'll make my own way in the world.'

Cressida was about to blow her cover and admit she had no intention to marry at all, when she was rescued by Alfred to her left.

'So, Mother tells me you have her curtains in your sights.'

Cressida almost fell on him in her relief to be out of her tawdry conversation with Edmund. 'Yes, though I'm afraid you'll have to put up with those travesties for a while. They have to be hung now the scaffolding tower has moved into the ballroom, but I'm working on it. I have a wonderful friend at Liberty of London who will no doubt come up trumps with something much more apt for Chatterton Court, by midsummer at the latest, I promise.'

'More apt than deckchair stripes? I should hope so!' Alfred laughed and Edmund nodded, seemingly approving of the plan, too.

'Those bloody ugly things in the ballroom not your work then? Glad to hear it.' Edmund leaned over to join the conversation. 'It seems no one in your family has a good word to say about those curtains, Delafield.'

Cressida, not enjoying Edmund's lean over her, had to admit he was right and wondered what Lady Chatterton must have been drinking when she ordered them.

'Still,' Edmund chipped in again. 'Gone by midsummer, eh?'

'It'll be a stretch, what with fabric to be ordered and, of course, curtain makers are always frightfully busy, but I have faith in my friend.'

'Glad some replacements are on the cards, however long it takes.' Alfred smiled at Cressida.

'Someone say cards?' Major Elliott asked across the table. 'Damn fine idea.'

Cressida sat back and listened as the men started reliving the game from a recent night at the club and made bets and speculations about what tonight's games might bring.

Lady Chatterton, hearing this as well, sighed and suggested the ladies retire to the drawing room, allowing the gentlemen their sport.

'I don't suppose fortunes will be won or lost tonight, but I for one would prefer a nice cup of coffee and a chance to read my journals. Ladies, shall we?'

The ladies nodded and stood up, leaving the men to take the proffered cigars that Jacob, the footman, had been asked to pass around. Despite her best efforts to ignore the mysteries that abounded at Chatterton Court, Cressida couldn't help but glance across at the red-cheeked, braying gentlemen, puffing away on their fine cigars and accepting balloon glasses of brandy. Could one of them be a thief... or worse, a murderer?

18

Lady Chatterton led the ladies into the drawing room, where one of the maids was pouring coffee.

'I won't, thank you,' Petronella refused the fine china cup being passed to her by the maid, who handed it to Cressida instead.

'Thank you,' Cressida mouthed to the maid, recognising her as Mildred, the one who had found the poor body of the cleaner only that morning.

'I find it keeps me up all night,' Petronella explained. 'And after today, I do need a good night's sleep.'

'I do understand, dear,' Lady Chatterton said, but Cressida disagreed.

'I've had a shot of coffee before in a vodka, shaken with a sort of coffee liqueur. Delicious and, I must say, kept me going til dawn that time Lady Rivers had a ball.'

'Cressida, dear, you do seem to have a lot of fun,' Lady Chatterton said, indulgently. She turned to Petronella. 'Now you're back from South Africa, do you think you'll be joining these two during the season?' Lady Chatterton was of course referring to the summer of parties and balls that was held in

London and various country houses for the young debutantes and unmarried women of society.

Cressida realised that this new angle of questioning was a double-edged sword, for although 'the season' was familiar ground, it usually came round to talk of her finding a husband, which was rather irksome. But, in this case, at least that might stop Petronella collaring Lady C and flogging her some diamonds. She really must get to the bottom of that conversation she'd overheard earlier between the Harper-Ashe siblings, she pondered.

'I'm not one for large parties, or late nights. And I don't know how long I'll be in England for.'

'Aren't you keen to find a husband, dear?' Lady Chatterton asked. 'Like Dotty. Knowing she's got someone by her side is such a comfort to me and her father. I'm sure your parents would feel the same. And yours, Cressida.' Lady Chatterton raised an eyebrow in her direction. She knew Lady Chatterton and her own mother, Lady Fawcett, had discussed her 'prospects' many times before, in fact *who* the Honourable Cressida Fawcett was going to marry, *if ever*, was often a subject of motherly conversations around the edges of Mayfair ballrooms. But before Cressida could counteract with any of her perfectly good reasons why the last thing she wanted was a husband, Petronella replied.

'Oh, I have a beau already, Lady Chatterton.'

'Oh yes?' Dotty leaned forward. 'Who is he? Do tell!'

Petronella straightened her back and paused before answering. 'No one you'd know.'

Cressida thought she looked awkward and Lady Chatterton seemed thoroughly unimpressed.

'But we know *everyone*, dear. What's his name?' Lady Chatterton pressed.

'I met him in South Africa, Lady Chatterton, a far cry from the drawing rooms of Berkshire.' Petronella relaxed a little and spoke again. 'One of those practical, outdoorsy types. Rather be shooting something than playing madrigals to it. I very much hope to be back out there with him again soon.'

'Oh splendid,' Lady Chatterton said, letting the subject of the beau's name drop.

'He sounds a bit like Basil. Never far from his shotgun, that one. Still, you're more of a sportswoman than us two, aren't you, Petronella?' Dotty asked. 'Get your energy out of your system on the playing field, and whatnot?'

'Yes. And the gymnasium. Did you know that some very simple calisthenics can do so much to prolong your suppleness and fitness?'

Cressida thought that as long as she could climb onto the American Bar at The Savoy, she was quite fit enough, but she managed a smile and an encouraging nod in Petronella's direction. The mental image of Petronella shimmying down the drainpipe outside Lady Chatterton's room, however, played over in her mind. Could the South African diamond heiress have been so bold as to steal Lady Chatterton's diamonds in order to sell her some of her own? And worse, kill Harry Smith to cover her tracks?

The ladies discussed a few things from the articles in *Time and Tide* magazine, a publication that espoused feminist rights, but also had some exceedingly good tips on overwintering hyacinth bulbs. Eventually, Petronella decided to call it a night. Having accepted another cup of coffee, Cressida bid her goodnight with the triumphant feeling that she hadn't let either Petronella or her brother William get any alone time with Lady Chatterton all evening, whether it was to flog her diamonds or not. Her bladder may not thank her later, however, for her selflessness now.

Once a few more minutes had passed and Lady Chatterton

herself had yawned a few times, Cressida drained her cup and placed it back on its saucer.

'Bedfordshire for me, I think.' She stretched her arms up and yawned.

'Bedtime for me too,' Dotty agreed. 'Up the wooden hill and all that.'

'Or stone in this case,' Cressida joked.

As the two young women left the drawing room, they passed the door to the library, where it was clear that, coffee or no coffee, the gentlemen of the house were well settled in for the night. Snippets of conversation carried into the dome of the hallway.

'Diamonds are trumps,' Edmund's voice reverberated.

'And dangerous in the wrong hands,' the major quipped.

'Aha, an ace,' Basil triumphantly declared, and Dotty looked up at Cressida with a look of pride in her eyes.

'Where were you hiding that three of diamonds, Major?' Alfred asked.

'It was hemmed in by my pie of clubs.'

'You've had too much to drink, old boy, speaking gibberish like that,' one of the chaps said, but the major's voice came out to the hallway clear as a bell.

'You know what I meant, young man.'

'Dammit, another ace, John! How do you... Oh, there, take my king.'

Cressida shook her head. The voices had started to merge into one and the game had moved on. Someone else's gambling debts weren't her problem, she thought to herself... *Unless those debts made you desperate enough to kill...*

19

Those two cups of coffee, like the cocktail at Lady Rivers' ball, did keep Cressida up, but, sadly, instead of dancing the night away, she was lying in bed wondering about the events of the last day or two. It was terribly, terribly sad that someone had actually died here at Chatterton Court, that very morning. Yet as she'd undressed and brushed out her shingled hair earlier, she'd heard the hoots of laughter and petty squabbles of the gentlemen playing cards. Even she, Cressida Fawcett, no stranger to a good time, thought it didn't seem right.

Ruby snuffled and snorted at the foot of the bed, reminding her of how waiting for the pup earlier had meant she'd over-heard Petronella and William's scheme. They'd both recently returned from South Africa, perhaps with a suitcase full of diamonds. Would either of them really steal those of Lady Chatterton in order to sell her a new set? And then kill Harry Smith because he'd found their hiding place?

Her heart raced, thanks to the caffeine, as she recounted a few other options. Alfred and John, Dotty's brothers, should be above suspicion surely? Alfred, already a viscount, would inherit the estate from his father. But John...? Cressida remembered the conversation about being younger sons earlier that evening, and that it was only really academia, the church, finding some sort of employment abroad or the military that were viable options for those not inheriting a living from their parents. The army... she was pretty sure that John, Edmund, Basil and Major Elliot had all been through the Royal Military Academy. Edmund and Basil had served a year or two as commissioned officers, the major had made a career of it. Did that mean they could each be the owner of the mysterious 'army boot' print in the flower bed beneath Lady Chatterton's window?

Were the household servants as innocent as they seemed? Cardew had appeared beneath the scaffolding tower immediately after it had been violently shaken, and according to Lady Chatterton, John had come upon him by the electric main switch on the night of the theft. Not that old Greystoke was much to compare to, but Cardew was definitely a fitter and more vigorous man, capable of climbing scaffolds and sliding down drainpipes...

The ticking of the carriage clock on the mantelpiece of her bedroom seemed to be louder tonight than before, each measured and mechanical tock and tick mocking the speed of her heart rate. If only DCI Andrews would accept her help, and in turn let her in on what he was thinking. Yet he seemed to be doing just the opposite and wasn't at all interested in her discoveries. The piece of silk she had found on the scaffold, for example... she needed to check exactly which shade of cream it was again. Golden like the Chatterton livery? Or pale like a silver-skin cocktail onion, the colour Petronella said her dress had been on Friday evening? Or, as Cressida had thought tonight, buttery cream like the Mutton Pie Club waistcoats and cummerbunds? And if it was from one of them, who was missing a piece from their prized waistcoat? If she wasn't worried that the gentlemen would be sleeping fitfully after bellies full of coffee and spirits, she would launch a midnight flit into their rooms to check... though the risk of being caught put her off. If she was, then her reputation, already on thin ice, might be ruined forever.

Her mind flitted back to the gruff detective from Scotland Yard. Was he perhaps hindering her on purpose? No... he had a sense of goodness about him. Under that gruff exterior, and annoying habit of excluding her from this investigation, she felt strangely familiar with him, as if he had been part of the family for years.

The clock ticked on and Cressida tossed and turned. The coffee took its toll on her bladder and she finally admitted that she would have to slip out from under the cosy covers of her bed and venture out into the cold landing to find a bathroom. Each bedroom did have its own 'facilities', but now she was used to a proper flushing lavatory, she didn't much fancy the 'gazunder' – named as such due to the fact that it was a bowl that 'goes under' the bed, ready for the housemaids to deal with in the morning.

Braced for the cool of the floorboards, Cressida put her feet down and patted Ruby on the head, reassuring her that she wouldn't be long.

'Nature calls, Rubes, back in a jiffy.'

She found her dressing gown and firmly tied it around her with the cord, and she grasped the big brass doorknob of her bedroom door and gently turned it, trying not to make a sound. She wasn't so much afraid of waking the family and other guests as being caught by anyone already awake. It wasn't so many years ago, before large houses had such things as bathrooms, that any lady caught leaving her bedroom in the night would be assumed to be 'bed hopping' and instantly labelled some sort of scarlet woman. *Thank heavens the world is more liberal now*, she thought. But still, she didn't want tongues to wag needlessly. She pulled the door open silently and peered out into the landing. There were no oil lamps burning and the electricity had either failed or all the lights had been turned off for the night. The moon was high in the sky, though, and from her vantage point by her door near the top of the stairs, Cressida could see it shining through the glass of the cupola.

She was about to step out of her room when a noise caught her attention. It sounded like footsteps, but she could have been mistaken. She carefully pushed her door to, allowing just a crack for her to peer through. There was definitely somebody on the landing, and what was that...? A doorknob being turned? There was the familiar clunk-click of a latch sliding back into the door jamb and then silence.

Probably someone else needing a tinkle in the night, thought Cressida as she ventured out into the moonlit landing. She could easily see her way to the bathroom and opened the door almost silently. It was only when she was back under her covers, staring at the upholstered canopy of her four-poster bed with sleep still evading her, that she realised that the lavatory cistern, a wall-hung affair with a long chain, had been silent as the grave when she'd entered the bathroom. No one had been in before her.

20

The small hours had turned into slightly larger hours, but Cressida had finally nodded off, with a snuffling pup beside her. Her dreams had been full of moustachioed army officers with boots for hands, and drainpipes with chandeliers at the end of them. The ace of diamonds had fluttered through with a waist-coat on... Surreal didn't even begin to describe it. It was almost a relief to wake up, except that the mode of awakening was as nightmarish as anything she could dream of.

'Cressy! Wake up! Oh, Cressy, he's dead!'

The voice, hollow and mournful, the words chilling. Was she still dreaming?

Hands shook her shoulders, but Cressida's eye mask meant she was still swathed in pitch-black darkness.

'Cressy... I can't bear it...'

Cressida pulled her eye mask down and saw Dotty's face close to hers, her eyes full of tears, her cheeks puffy from sobbing. Cressida's heart broke for her friend as she repeated again. 'Dead, Cressy. He's dead.'

'Who, Dotty? Who's dead?' Cressida sat bolt upright, pulling Ruby close to her.

Dotty looked as pale as an alabaster bust, all the colour drained from her face.

Cressida almost dared not repeat her question for fear of the answer. She mustered the courage, however and asked again. 'Who is it, Dotty? Not your father? Or Alfred?' She had the most un-Christian thought in hoping it was Basil, then bit her lip for fear of saying that out loud.

'It's the major, Cressy. They found him dead this morning. Just lying there in his bed,' Dotty sobbed, and crumpled into the bedclothes.

'Major Elliot?' Cressida couldn't believe it, and she felt a chill come over her as the news sank in. Death had stalked the halls of Chatterton Court again. She shivered. This time, he had taken one of the party. A guest, just like her.

'He was quite well last night, wasn't he?' Dotty looked up from the quilt, her eyes pleading with Cressida.

'Yes. Yes, I think so.' For what else could she say? But Cressida threw her mind back to hearing the men playing cards, Major Elliot's voice clear and strong, despite perhaps being in his cups somewhat. 'Was he...' she paused, catching herself before uttering the unmentionable. 'I mean, did he die in his sleep?'

'We don't know yet, but I think so.' Dotty's brow creased. 'Cressy, surely you don't think he was... done away with too? Not here? Not the major?'

'No... no. Sorry, Dot. I didn't sleep at all well and my dreams were all a confusion. I'm so terribly sorry for your loss, Dotty. He seemed such a nice man.' Cressida placed a hand on one of Dotty's, hoping it would be of some comfort. 'He was an old friend of the family, wasn't he?'

'Yes. His uncle was one of Papa's best friends and Papa helped Major Elliot get his commission and into the right regiment and all of that.' Dotty wiped her nose and eyes with her pyjama sleeve as she spoke. 'He ended up coming to Chatterton

Court when on leave and was always so useful, a real mentor for Alfred and John. I think when we were all too young to be interesting, Mama and Papa liked having someone around to talk to.'

'Because he's... *was* older than you three, wasn't he?' Cressida hoped her self-correction didn't upset Dotty too much. *Another death at Chatterton Court... surely this is no coincidence?* Cressida pulled Ruby closer to her and Dotty carried on.

'Yes. Alfred is twenty-eight, but Major Elliot was in his forties. So when we were all ugly ducklings, he was the handsome swan who delighted Mama and Papa with his stories of India and London. He was quite the man about town. I know he looked older than his years. All that foreign travel and military service took it out of him, I think.'

'Still, far too young to simply die for no apparent reason...' Cressida couldn't help putting the thought into words, but regretted it when she saw the last vestiges of colour blanch from Dotty's face.

'How can...? How could anyone here be a murderer? I... I refused to believe it possible about poor Harry Smith, but now the major too. Oh Cressy.' Dotty burst into tears anew and Cressida did what she thought was the kindest thing and handed the warm and comforting body of her pup over to her weeping friend. Cressida thought she could see a look of reproach in the young dog's eyes as she apologised.

'I'm so sorry, Dotty. I shouldn't have said that. Only, it's such a lot to take in: the theft, and the death of young Harry Smith and now Major Elliot. I am so sorry, Dot. This is all rather ghastly. How are your parents? Are they coping all right?'

Dotty pulled a very compliant Ruby to her chest, proving that dogs really were the best comforters, before saying, 'Mama's not up yet. I presume Cardew let her and Papa know first thing. Papa then came in and told me, after he'd been in to see Alfred and John of course.'

'Of course.' Primogeniture meant more than just the eldest

son inheriting the estate; it meant there was always an unsaid pecking order in the family, too.

'That's the official channel anyway. I should imagine the servants all knew hours before us. Apparently it was Cardew himself who found the major this morning.'

'Oh really?' Time and again, Cardew popped up in Cressida's thoughts. She was sure he was a most sensible fellow, and no doubt came to the family with the best references, but then, of course, he could also be classed as someone who not only knew the family, their routines, the whereabouts of where the now-stolen diamonds were usually kept and... Cressida shook her head, she must really stop suspecting everyone of these crimes, and Lady Chatterton had vouched for the staff.

'Yes. And of course he told Papa and then DCI Andrews, who was about to catch the early train back to London.'

'Andrews is still here?' For some reason, this made Cressida properly sit up and pay attention. If DCI Andrews had decided to stay on and investigate, then he too surely thought there must be something suspicious about Major Elliot's death. And this time, Cressida was determined that he was going to let her help him solve the case.

21

Dotty, terribly upset and sniffling into her handkerchief, had left Cressida to wash and dress. Standing in front of the looking glass in her bedroom, Cressida put the final touches to her Sunday best – as a church-going family, the Chattertons would expect their guests to join them at the parish church of St Giles in the village. Cressida remembered that the church was an easy walk across the lawns and park and so although she chose a rather lovely cream silk blouse and smart ankle-length skirt, she decided her stout walking shoes would be more apt for the morning. Elevating the outfit with a stunning pearl and aquamarine brooch that kept her cashmere shawl from falling off her shoulders and deciding that now was the time for her new feathered hat to get its first outing meant that she was dressed properly for church... but there was something rather more unholy that she was set upon doing before she joined the grieving family in the pews.

She regretted upsetting Dotty while they'd been talking this morning. But there it was... she didn't think the major, a man who had appeared to be in the rudest of health last night, would die in his sleep. And if it wasn't a death by natural causes, then perhaps last night she had been a whisker from witnessing Major Elliot's murderer on the landing. If she had opened her door with more gusto or decided to act on her bladder's request a little earlier, she might have rumbled the whole thing – saving Major Elliot, but conceivably putting herself in danger instead. She shivered at the thought, and the echo of Maurice's words still stuck in her head... *the truth of it all lies closer to home...* If DCI Andrews still refused to parlay later this morning, she might have to bring something to the table. Something that would force him to accept her into his confidences.

With this in mind, and Ruby eagerly tagging along in her wake, Cressida quietly crept out of her bedroom and tiptoed along the landing, keeping to the boards she hoped would be the less creaky ones. She passed Dotty's bedroom door, which was opposite hers, and she had to scoop up Ruby, who had made a beeline to it hoping for more cuddles. Then there were John's and Alfred's rooms. The other guests – the Harper-Ashes, Basil and Edmund – were in the opposite wing, along the landing that led the other way from the top of the stairs, but old family friend Major Elliot had been this side of the house.

Cressida looked around as she approached his bedroom door. As with many country houses of this ilk, each bedroom door had a brass name card holder attached to it, and Cressida could see that this was the right room. Could the murderer have misread it in the night, though? Accidentally killed the major instead of... who?

Cressida shook her head again. Her lack of sleep and confused dreams had left her in a most befuddled state. *Clear your head, Cressy*, she told herself. *You're going to need every wit about you...*

Checking once more that no one was about, and holding Ruby tight, she gently gripped the large brass doorknob and turned it until she felt the latch unhook itself from the door frame. She pushed the door open and slipped inside.

Putting Ruby down on the floor with the instruction to stay put and keep watch, Cressida tiptoed her way towards the bed. Unlike hers, this one wasn't a fancy four-poster with an upholstered canopy, it was more masculine, a grand mahogany sleigh bed, with strong curved head and footboards in a colour that looked like freshly fallen conkers. As she approached it, her breath caught in her throat. She hadn't thought about the reality of seeing the dead body of the major himself, but there it was, lying in his bed, and Cressida had to steel herself to move forward. Death itself held no fear for her. The afterlife, in whatever form it came, would surely be a jolly party of some sort. Or, if not, then at least she knew she'd had enough parties here on earth to see her through an eternity of fluffy clouds and white tunics. But she had never been this close to a dead body before. She'd briefly seen poor Harry Smith, of course, but she hadn't had a proper look at him, as he'd had Cardew and Lord Chatterton fussing over his body and she'd been comforting Dotty from the landing above. But here, not another soul was with them, excepting Ruby, who gave a low growl every so often.

'Shush, Rubes,' Cressida whispered. 'We're not meant to be in here, remember?'

Ruby panted a bit, but remained quiet, so Cressida turned her attention back to the major's deathbed. He looked serene, if pale. His hair was messy, something she'd never seen in life, being the sort to spit on his boots before entering a room to ensure they were polished enough. She'd even heard Dotty once giggle about the fact that he slept with a net over his moustache so that it stayed in place and didn't get all haywire in the night. There was no sign of the net now, if indeed that had ever really happened. His eyelids were closed though, thank heavens, as Cressida wasn't sure she could cope with seeing his glassy eyes questioning her presence in his bedroom.

'I'm sorry, Major,' she whispered, then took a deep breath and focused her attention on what she could see. There was a bottle of pills by his bedside and Cressida picked them up. A full glass of water stood next to the bottle and she noticed a fleck of dust floating on the surface of the liquid. It might have been there for a night or two then, rather than fresh last night. In any case, no swig large enough to help down a pill had been taken from it recently, as it was still full. She tried to open the pill bottle and couldn't at first, the lid was so tight. So, the major hadn't reached for any pills in the night and popped a few down with a big sip of water. She looked at the label. *Quinidine. To be taken during an attack of arrhythmia or atrial fibrillation.*

'Strange for someone in their forties to need heart medicine, Rubes,' Cressida thought out loud on seeing the semi-familiar terms on the label. When Ruby snuffled in agreement, she replied, 'Yes, yes. I know, I should be quiet.'

She put the pill bottle down and looked at the major. His head was resting on just one pillow, yet next to him, on the other side of the bed, there were two.

'That's odd,' Cressida whispered to herself. 'Why have two on one side and only one on the other? No one would make a bed like that. There must have been a fourth pillow...' She crept around the other side of the bed and then stopped in her tracks. There was the fourth pillow all right, flung to the floor and lying in an odd heap next to the bed.

Ruby gave a low growl and Cressida was about to turn on her heel and creep out of the room when something else caught her eye. It looked like one of the pockets of the billiards table, or a net bag for a doll.

'Of course, Ruby!' Cressida quickly picked up her dog before chancing one more look at the other side of the bed and the item she'd spied. 'It must be the major's moustache net. Now why would he fling *that* off in the night?' He'd been wearing it for years, if Dotty's giggles as a schoolgirl had been correct. 'Something to ponder, Rubes.'

A creak from the landing outside made Cressida jump and

she placed her finger on her lips to shush the low growl coming from Ruby. She tiptoed around the bed away from the discarded pillow and moustache net and back towards the door. As she passed the fireplace, something else caught her eye. She held her finger up to her dog and mouthed 'one more minute' at her. Ruby flopped down on the floor and started licking her back leg in response.

The fire had been used recently. Very recently, if the warmth of the ashes was anything to go by. The odd thing about it was that the spring had been unseasonably warm so far, yet the major had obviously asked for his fire to be lit. *Perhaps it wasn't so odd for someone who had a weak heart and poor circulation*, Cressida thought to herself.

This morning's bleak discovery of his body must have disrupted the maid's usual efficiency in clearing away the ashes and relaying the fire, as the grey dust still lined the grate and embers gently smoked at the back of the basket. Cressida could see a piece of paper, though, charred and burnt at one end, but still clean and in good condition – at least the end that hadn't made it into the coals. She bent down and pulled it out, blowing on it to rid it of ash and stop the damage. It flared a little red and she cursed herself for her stupidity – her breath merely acted as an accelerant to the dying glow.

She glanced around and saw the major's washbowl on the vanity by the window and in three steps she was next to it and carefully dunking the piece of charred paper in the clean water just enough to make sure any flame was doused. Once satisfied that it was no longer in danger of spontaneously combusting on her, she held it up to the light of the window.

'That's the Chatterton's crest at the top of the writing paper, dark blue and gold like the livery, Rubes.' Cressida tilted the angle of the paper so she could see the faint and badly charred words that were left visible, if only just. 'I know you... the diamo... chand... at six... and... your...'

Cressida read it over another couple of times, desperately altering the angle of the scrap to see if she could read any more words under the blackened soot. Was that the word *great*? And maybe *I'll make*?

'What on earth is this, Rubes?' Cressida looked over at her dog, who gave a low growl. 'I know, I know, I'm done.' Cressida carefully held the paper by its corner letting it air out as much as possible. 'This is some sort of rendezvous though, Rubes, surely? A note from the thief to... Or was it from Harry Smith to the thief?' She looked at it. The writing was assured, legible... an educated hand. And the notepaper from the house itself; even she had several leaves of it on her dressing table in case she should feel the need to write while she was a guest. 'This is from a guest, Rubes... it's from one of us.'

Cressida gingerly held the note, and with Ruby at her heels, she slipped out of the major's room and onto the landing. No one was about, so Cressida stole back along the carpeted corridor to her own bedroom, and deposited the charred note, a clue no less, in the closest drawer she could find. Then, once out on the landing again, with Ruby by her side, she upped her pace and, with her more usual lightness of foot, traipsed down the stairs, where Dotty and her brothers were waiting for their parents in order to all walk together to the local church.

Cressida was under no illusion as to what she'd found. It was a note organising a meet, here in the great hall. Chandeliers and diamonds were mentioned... it must have been what had drawn poor Harry Smith to his final rendezvous. A rendezvous among the crystals and diamonds that had ended with him plummeting to his death. But who had written it? And how had it ended up in the still-burning embers of the major's fireplace? The major who was himself now dead by nefarious means, she was sure of it.

22

'I'm so terribly sorry for all of you,' Cressida said to Alfred as they walked companionably across the lawn in the direction of the church. 'Such a shock, as he really wasn't an old man, was he?'

'No, not in the grand scheme of things,' agreed Alfred. 'Mid-forties, I think. Should have been in his prime.'

'Should have been?' Cressida picked up on Alfred's choice of words.

'Dicky ticker since a bad bout of malaria picked up in India. Had to be shipped home pretty pronto and in some sort of feverish state. Made a good recovery once back in Blighty, but it meant he spent the last war behind a desk. Think that saddened him really. I caught him talking to Andrews, that detective chap, yesterday about his service and old Spike looked almost wistful. Both he and the inspector fought the Boers apparently and knew people in common despite Andrews not having a commission.' Alfred talked and walked at a good pace, and Cressida could comfortably keep up with the walking, though she had to admit to being slightly confused by what he was saying.

'Sorry, so Major Elliot and DCI Andrews served in the Boer War together?' she asked, wondering if perhaps either of them had known her father, who had been an officer out there too.

'Not together, different ranks of course, but yes, Andrews was in South Africa, whereas Spike made it back from South Africa and then onto India, where he got the lurgy. Then, heart not up to the regimental drills, he dedicated the rest of his career to the recruits at Sandhurst and desk jobs in Whitehall. Not such a bad place to end your career.' Alfred walked, his back straight, his hands clasped behind.

'Being in London meant he could join you at the Mutton Pie Club,' Cressida noted and, as she did so, cursed the fact that she hadn't taken the opportunity this morning of checking through the major's clothes. *If he had the rendezvous letter and a tear in his waistcoat...*

Alfred puffed out his cheeks. 'I suppose I better be the one to tell the club.'

They walked on in silence for a little while before Cressida posed another question.

'So, do you think it was his heart that gave out then? Last night?'

Alfred thought about it. 'I suppose it must have been. He had pills to take when he was feeling queasy, though, and he was in fine fettle last night at the table.'

'Cards?' Cressida remembered hearing them play while she struggled to sleep.

'Yes, poker and baccarat.' Alfred chuckled to himself in a fond recollection. 'More of a social player than a real gambler at heart. Terrible with cards, but always enthusiastic.' The chuckle turned into a mirthless sigh. 'He'll be missed.'

Cressida remembered what Basil had said about the major, about how his debts had been crippling and that it gave him a motive to steal Lady Chatterton's diamonds. After what she'd found in the major's bedroom this morning, she couldn't not ask

Alfred his thoughts on it – now she could never ask the major himself.

'Alfred, did you know much about the state of the major's finances? I know it's tawdry to ask, but I've heard, well, rumours, that he owed a fair amount of money.'

Alfred shook his head. 'The major was all right. What makes you ask?'

Her pause was long enough for Alfred to clutch at the correct straw.

'Cressida, no.' He turned to look at her. 'There's no way the major would have even thought of stealing Mother's diamonds. He was the most honest and thoroughly decent chap a man could know. One of those who'd give you a chance to right your own wrong, if you know what I mean. If anything, he'd die to protect this family, rather than steal from it. Any gambling debts he had, Father would have paid off in a blink of an eye. And if not Father, then any of us would have.' Alfred strode purposefully, his confident steps mirroring his certainty.

Cressida, despite what she'd found in his bedroom just now to incriminate him, believed Alfred's conviction and couldn't imagine the kindly major as a thief, let alone a cold-blooded murderer. She really did feel sorry for him.

'I'm sorry if he was having a bad game of cards, on his last night on earth and everything.' She changed tack, hoping Alfred would forgive her blunt question about the major's finances.

'Yes, it was a run of rum luck. We did drink rather heavily, which, come to think of it, probably wasn't the wisest thing for a chap in his condition.'

Alfred fell silent, and Cressida decided not to bother him with more questions. She had a feeling that Alfred himself had only just realised that as a group of friends and acquaintances they all should have been looking out more for the man they knew to have a heart condition. She only hoped that the solace and comfort of the church service they were about to attend would help his grief.

The church service was a simple affair, a time for mindful worship, and more poignant for the Chatterton family in that the vicar very kindly alerted the organist to Major Elliot's recent passing and changed the hymns to reflect those that the family knew were his favourites. That one of them had been the cheerful 'All Things Bright and Beautiful' had at least brought a cheering end to the otherwise sombre service, and the family, guests and villagers had filed out from the thirteenth-century church of St Giles with the tune still on their lips.

Cressida was humming it as she walked along the old stone setts of the pathway. The churchyard was neatly hemmed in by a drystone wall and the lychgate had been covered in flowers from a local wedding the last weekend. The villagers, some of whom had greeted and spoken to the Chattertons, turned one way back towards the pretty hamlet of Chatterford and the family walked along the lane towards the parkland of Chatterton Court. Dotty was just ahead of her, linked arm in arm with Basil. Cressida sighed. At least he was able to bring her some comfort this morning, even if she herself had upset her in being so single-minded about these murders...

Yes, murders, she thought to herself, *plural*. She'd been thinking about it during the reverend's sermon and decided that the flung-off pillow and moustache net simply couldn't have been a natural act. Of course, people had nightmares, and tossed and turned, but to peel off one's own moustache net and throw a pillow over the other side of the bed? Plus, his pill bottle had been untouched, at least as far she could tell. It was tightly screwed shut and the water in the glass almost to the rim. She couldn't say that there was *no doubt* in her mind, but she had a strong suspicion that the major had been suffocated by a pillow. As he'd fought off the assailant, he must have loosened his moustache net, with the whole thing coming away with the pillow once the attacker's lethal mission was done.

'But who would it have been, Ruby?' Cressida asked her little pup, who had been as good as gold in church, if you didn't count the unprovoked snapping at the verger's ankles. Perhaps he reminded Rubes of Jacob, the footman who had tried to take her below stairs when they'd arrived, and Cressida made a mental note to ask Dotty if they were related.

'What ho, Cressida.' John ambled up next to her.

'Hallo there, John. Terribly sorry about Major Elliot. I know he was somewhat of a mentor for you.' Cressida placed a comforting hand on John's arm and took a little pride in seeing him blush.

'Yes, safe pair of hands. Saw me through basic training in the army. I still don't believe in the power of threes. This must have been a coincidence, much like the other two, well, accidents. It's statistically unlikely, of course, but then so are a good many things. I'd need to do some mathematical modelling, of course, but, well... All in good time.' He paused, not usually able to stop himself when he got excited about mathematics, but obviously realising that now was not the time nor place for data sets and analytical observations. He thrust his hands into the pockets of his tweed trousers and spoke about the major again. 'Good chap was Spike.'

'Why do you boys call him Spike? That can't be his real name.'

'Haha, no. Do you know what, I have no idea. Something about his hair perhaps.'

Cressida remembered the messy mop of the dead man she'd seen this morning and how it was usually so well-kempt. *Another sign a pillow had been forced onto him...* she shuddered.

'I say, Cressida, do you think you might like to step out with

me once we're back in London and out of mourning and all
that?'

John's request roused Cressida from her thoughts. One
moment she was contemplating murder by suffocation, and the
next, the Honourable John Chatterton was propositioning her.
She couldn't help but think that marriage to a member of the
Mutton Pie Club might be a sort of suffocation of another kind,
but she put her reply more kindly than that.

'Let's enjoy each other's friendship a while longer, shall we,
John?' She squeezed his arm and let him 'harrumph' and 'aha' a
few times before he nodded her a farewell and paced ahead.
She felt sorry for him, and was flattered; a young woman could
do a lot worse than John Chatterton, even with his peculiar
obsession with figures and fractions and whatnot. But now,
more than ever, was not the time for courtship. Now was the
time to try to find that policeman.

'Detective Chief Inspector!' Cressida called across the marble
hallway of Chatterton Court, catching him and Sergeant Kirby
as they made their way into the library. 'Please wait one
second!'

Cressida walked across the hall towards where the tired-
looking policeman stood, his sergeant rocking from one foot to
the other next to him.

'What can I do you for, Miss Fawcett?' he asked.

'Please may we have a chat?' Cressida asked, hoping a
flicker of her eyelashes, not to mention the baleful, if panting
face of Ruby, would work their magic.

DCI Andrews sighed and then gestured for Cressida to
head into the library. He followed her in and Sergeant Kirby
shut the door behind them.

'Yes?' DCI Andrews stood, his back ramrod straight and his
hands behind his back.

At ease... Cressida thought to herself and remembered what Alfred had said about Andrews' military service.

'I really, really would appreciate your help with something,' Cressida managed, suddenly feeling a bit tongue-tied and wondering how to approach the subject she'd been roundly told off for pursuing before. 'Something rather serious.'

'Which is? No, let me guess... you've discovered *whodunnit* and need me to make the arrest?' DCI Andrews looked at her and she wasn't sure if he was joking and that was a twinkle in his eye, or if he was joking and that was a look of 'stop wasting my time' in his eye...

'Actually, I do have some more information for you. But I also need your help.'

'Yes?'

'I think Major Elliot was murdered. I can't prove it, and I shouldn't really admit to you why I think it, as you'll possibly invoke some sort of perverting the cause of justice accusation at me again, but I think you should know that I think he was murdered.'

Andrews stayed silent and Cressida was forced to continue talking.

'I also think that the Harper-Ashes are using the loss of Lady Chatterton's diamonds, while she's vulnerable, so to speak, to flog her some of theirs. I'm not suggesting they had anything to do with the theft of course...'

'Of course...' DCI Andrews narrowed his eyes as he took in what Cressida was saying, but she could sense his body relax slightly. 'They're South African, aren't they?'

'English father, I think, but yes. They grew up there and Petronella even has a beau waiting for her back there apparently.'

'Indeed? Are you writing this down, Kirby? Headline news that pretty young woman with good family and prospects has a beau...'

'Yessir.' The perplexed sergeant hurriedly got his pencil and notepad out and started writing what he could remember of what his boss and Cressida had just said.

Cressida, however, pursed her lips and was tempted to set Ruby on the vexatious policeman, if she wasn't convinced that the small dog would merely lick him rather than bite his ankles.

'You're teasing me, Detective Chief Inspector.' Cressida pulled herself up to her full height to take him on. 'And you've hindered my own investigations into the tragedies that are happening under my good friend's roof. I know you're a professional, but I think you could have been, and could still be, a bit more courteous.'

'Hindered *your* investigations?' Andrews crossed his arms as he replied. 'You have done nothing but tamper with evidence and eavesdrop on private police interviews. Not to mention almost get yourself killed by climbing a piece of equipment you had no right to climb.'

'I was... well, I mean I gave you the proceeds of that little adventure.'

'This isn't some adventure, Miss Fawcett.' Andrews rubbed his hand over his brow.

It was Sunday morning and Cressida suddenly realised that this gruff policeman might actually have a wife and children at home who were now without their father for Sunday lunch or a trip to the park, or whatever people like him did on a Sunday. Kirby too, and Cressida had a fleeting impression of him being the star of his local football team, playing the Sunday league and—

'Miss Fawcett?' Andrews clicked his fingers in front of her eyes. 'Did you hear what I said?'

'Sorry, Inspector. I was quite away with the fairies.'

'Well, fairies you can play with, fine by me. But, for heaven's sake, can you keep out of police business!'

23

Feeling slightly bruised, ego-wise at least, from her run-in with Andrews, Cressida decided to investigate something completely different for a bit. Namely, the noise she could hear coming from the ballroom. It was a cacophony of shouts, crashes and 'ooohs', and Cressida rightly surmised that it was all due to the curtains, ghastly as they were, being hung.

'Ruby, t'is a sad day indeed, and not just because Major Elliot has died. Those curtains really should never have seen the light of day, let alone be responsible for dressing this beautiful room once the light of the day is over,' Cressida whispered to her pup as she entered the room.

'Cressida dear, thank goodness you're here,' Lady Chatterton beckoned her over. 'These chaps are doing their best, but the curtains – and I know you'll have something to say about them – simply will not hang correctly.'

Cressida put Ruby down and let her waddle off to sit by the fireplace. 'I can't blame the pattern of the fabric for the way they hang though, however much I'd like to. Who made them up for you?'

'The usual people. They did a splendid job of the ones in

the drawing room and the silk drapes in your Blue Room. I can't imagine what might be making these ones crinkle and catch.'

Cressida nodded in agreement. The curtains in her bedroom here at Chatterton Court, The Blue Room, and the ones in the drawing room, were made perfectly, not a stitch out of place. But Lady Chatterton was right; the curtains that the workmen were currently struggling to hang from the high rails above the great sash windows didn't sit right at all as they skimmed the wooden parquet floor. Cressida, careful of the scaffolding tower and the workmen leaning off it in order to access the rail above her, ran her hand down the silk. The lining felt luxurious and well stitched in, the inside hem of the curtains bearing no sign of sloppy workmanship or poor stitching. The pattern of the garish purple and gold stripes seemed to hang straight, it was only at the bottom that they dipped and crinkled.

'Well, I suppose it's another reason, if one were needed, to make sure that they're taken down as soon as possible and replaced. Speaking of which, I telephoned my friend Maurice Sauvage at Liberty and have asked him to look out for something suitable. Damask perhaps? Or a touch of florals?'

'Yes, dear, do what you can.' Lady Chatterton, pale-faced against the black woollen skirt suit she was wearing, looked thoroughly spent, exhausted by the whole thing, and Cressida paused to consider what the poor lady had been through over the last few days. Not only had she coped with the horror of having two deaths in the household, one of which was of a very dear friend, but she'd also had her bedroom ransacked, her jewellery stolen, her guests questioned and her home taken over by policemen.

Cressida placed a hand at Lady Chatterton's elbow and guided her over to the chairs by the fireplace. 'Shall we take some tea, Lady Chatterton? Something to revive us a little after the terrible events of today.'

'Yes, let's. Where's Dotty? I do hope Basil is consoling her. She's taken the major's death worse than any of us, but then she is a sensitive soul.'

Cressida thought of her dear friend, always so thoughtful and kind towards others and a true romantic at heart too. She'd wept during the sermon, and Cressida had had to pass her more than one clean hanky. She *really* hoped that Basil was looking after her now.

'She was terribly upset at church this morning, which is understandable. He was a big part of your family, wasn't he?'

'Part of the furniture, you could say. Major E was here for almost every holiday and festivity as the children were growing up and Francis and I rather relied on him to keep an eye on the boys.'

'Alfred said as much, on the way to church. And John.'

'Of course it was Dotty he was most fond of,' Lady Chatterton said with wistful remorse. 'Could never show it though. The army trains young men wonderfully in discipline, courage and morals. Leaves them as emotionally stunted as house plants though.'

Cressida realised that Lady Chatterton hadn't meant to be funny, not so soon after the major's death. This was new information though. The major fond of Dotty?

'I didn't think they had an understanding?'

'Oh, they didn't. That's what I meant. The dear major would never have assumed she'd be interested in him, what with his career cut short by his weakened heart. He was upset when Basil came on the scene though. Frightfully miffed about it. Francis and I tried to ask his opinion, but he said he had faith in Dorothy.'

'That's an odd thing to say.' Cressida thought back to Basil pointing the finger so obviously towards the major. No love lost there, and perhaps it was all due to the affections of Dotty.

'As I said, dear, emotional spectrum of an aspidistra. Poor

Major. He seemed not quite himself last night. We laughed and he told some wonderful stories over dinner, but it also felt like he had the weight of the world on his shoulders. He was distracted, I thought. Maybe he could sense his heart was about to give out.' Lady Chatterton got up. 'Now, do excuse me, dear. It has been lovely to talk to you about dear Major E, but I fear talking won't go far towards organising his funeral and telling his nearest and dearest. I must write to his uncle, who will be terribly upset, as are we.' Lady Chatterton squeezed Cressida's shoulder as she walked past her. 'Do look in on Dorothy, won't you, dear? I thought I saw Basil marching off across the lawn with one of those guns of his just now.'

'I will, Lady Chatterton, of course.' Cressida touched her hand and then let her go, her next mission of the day in clear sight – operation cheer up Dotty.

Dotty, however, was not making herself easy to cheer up, being that she couldn't be found. Cressida had scooped up Ruby and left the curtain hangers to it in the ballroom. Lady Chatterton had been right, there was most certainly something amiss with the curtains, and it wasn't just their repugnant fabric. But there were more important things than worrying about hemlines and Cressida had looked high and low for Dotty but to no avail. She popped her head around the drawing-room door and found William Harper-Ashe reading the papers. Before she could silently back out without being noticed, he called over to her.

'Good morning.' He put down the paper he was reading and beckoned her in.

Cressida let Ruby scamper down from her arms and snuffle her way under the coffee table in search of crumbs. William Harper-Ashe... perhaps it was lucky that she came across him. There were a few questions she'd been burning to ask since she'd overheard him under the cupola the evening before.

Having risked causing offence to Alfred with her questions about the major this morning, she kept her tone breezy. 'Have you seen Dotty at all?'

William gestured towards the door. 'She's in with that Andrews chap.'

'At least it won't be a grilling, not for Dotty.' Cressida was relieved that Dotty was being occupied, though she hoped it wasn't all too raw and gruesome for her, so soon after losing the major.

'She was close to him then?' he asked, rather impertinently in Cressida's view. But with her conversation with Lady Chatterton still fresh in her mind, she replied.

'Yes, he was a family friend. He was fond of all the Chatterton children, I believe, a mentor to them.' She paused for thought; this was not the route she wanted the conversation to go down.

But William carried on regardless. 'Yes, their very own British bulldog.'

'What do you mean?' Her questions over the diamonds would have to wait.

'Only that the major seemed to be very protective of the Chattertons.'

Cressida nodded. Alfred and Lady Chatterton had said very much the same thing. 'He was a good friend to them, and they to him, I believe. Now, William, tell me—'

'He was in love with Dorothy, wasn't he?' William interrupted her.

'I... I don't know. Dotty's never spoken of him in that way.' Cressida once again had to put her questions over the mine's cash flow problems to the side as she sat down on the arm of the chintz sofa. Where were all these allegations of the major loving Dotty suddenly coming from? She was intrigued. 'What makes you say that?'

'He and Basil almost came to blows at the club a few weeks

back. Basil had just invited me to stay here, along with Petronella. Thought it would be pleasant for us, a good introduction to English society while we're over.'

'That was very thoughtful of him.' Cressida couldn't imagine Basil being thoughtful, unless, despite his protestations of lack of motive, he had stolen Lady Chatterton's diamonds so that his friend William could sell her some of his? Perhaps there was something in it for him? she wondered ruefully, before turning the conversation back to the major. 'Why did he and the major fight though?'

William leaned forward. 'There's been some talk of Basil not being exactly above the law himself.' He winked at Cressida, which made her cringe, but she gave him the benefit of the doubt and cocked her head, inviting him to carry on. 'Have you heard of Boris Berkley? No? Nor had any one, yet his name appeared on several share certificates and whatnot. Turns out Basil had made a "slip of the hand" clerically, so to speak. Basil Bartleby... Boris Berkley... but there were rumours of money laundering and tax evasion. Hush-hush though, nothing ever proven. Didn't stop my father from letting him invest that small inheritance of his in our mine.'

'Gosh. So the major accused Basil of all this?'

'Hinted at. The bulldog baring his teeth perhaps.'

'And protecting Dotty...' Cressida sighed. 'He didn't like the thought of her marrying such a chump. I'm with him there.'

William's face clouded over and he got up, throwing the folded newspaper down on the sofa. He made his excuses and left Cressida to ponder this new avenue of the investigation, and indeed William's own reaction to it all. Had the major been in love with Dotty? And had he been killed by a rival for her affections? Was William worried about Basil's investment and involvement in their family business? She'd had a bad feeling about Basil Bartleby from the start, and William's suggestion that he'd traipsed over to the wrong side of the law confirmed other things she'd heard about him.

But it was Dotty who she really felt for. Despite never hearing her speak much of the major, save the schoolgirl giggles they'd shared over hot chocolate in their dorms, her friend had obviously had some sort of connection to the older man. And his death had shocked her to the core this morning. She had to find Dotty and see if she was all right – and Cressida hoped DCI Andrews was being as gentle with her as he could be.

24

Cressida hovered outside the closed door of the library. She had raised her arm and was about to knock, when an 'ahem' behind her stopped her in her tracks.

She turned and saw Cardew standing there, smart in his dark blue tailcoat and cream waistcoat. She hadn't realised how tall he was, though his high forehead and bald pate emphasised his height.

He spoke to her, looking down over his beaked nose, in that calm manner that butlers seem to have. 'I'm afraid that room is not to be disturbed, madam. Mr Andrews is interviewing Lady Dorothy and has asked not to be interrupted.'

'I see. Yes, of course.' Cressida lowered her arm. Investigations were going on inside the library, but now might be the time, she thought, for her own investigation to carry on here in the hallway. She'd been meaning to catch Cardew on his own so she could ask him one or two things, so called him back as he began to turn away. 'I say, Cardew.' She paused while he turned to face her. 'Thank you again for helping me down from the scaffolding tower yesterday. I don't know what came over me to climb it.'

Cardew, the epitome of discretion, merely nodded.

Darn, thought Cressida, *I'll have to be more direct.* 'Lucky you were there, it was shaking like billy-o.'

Cardew, in the politest possible way, looked at her disbelievingly. 'Shaking, madam?'

'Yes, Cardew. Like a cocktail shaker.'

'I'm afraid I didn't see that, madam. No wonder you were so shocked when I sounded the lunch gong.' Cardew kept his hands clasped behind his back and although he was responding perfectly politely to her, he had the look of someone harassed who had other places to be.

She cut to the chase. 'Cardew, did you see anyone in the hallway? Moments before you came in to sound the gong?'

'No, madam. Though we were very quickly joined by the Honourable John and Mr Priestley, followed by Lady Dorothy and Mr Bartleby.'

'Yes, Edmund and John followed me into the dining room, didn't they,' Cressida remembered. 'And, Cardew, on the night of the diamonds being stolen, did you see anyone in the house?'

'The police have asked us all these questions already, madam.' He sighed. 'But no, I had realised the electrics had been thrown at the same point that the Honourable John came to see what was happening.'

'I see. Thank you, Cardew.' He was being less than helpful.

'Is there anything else, madam?'

Cressida sighed. She couldn't interrupt Dotty and her mind was as scrambled as a kitten's ball of yarn trying to think through all the motives and opportunities... She needed some fresh air. 'Thank you, Cardew, but no. I'm heading out for a walk.'

'The weather is fine, madam, though you may wish to take a coat. They're predicting wind and rain tonight after this warm weather.'

'Typical. Thank you, Cardew.'

Cressida headed away from the library. She did need some air, and despite the sunlight currently coursing in through the cupola, she heeded Cardew's warning about imminent rain and wind. She also remembered Basil's appalling aim when she ventured out to the lawn yesterday, so went via the Chatterton Court boot room and picked herself out a sturdy wax jacket. Although she wasn't convinced it would save her life from a point-blank shot, she had heard that Lord Rupert, one of the chaps from her inner circle, had taken a blast from the other end of a field and his faithful wax jacket had saved the day. She smiled at the fun they'd had that raucous evening at Claridge's when Lord Rupert had showed off where the pesky pellets had penetrated his countryside clothing, a white smattering of scars across his chest. The other good thing about these oversized, sailcloth-smelling coats was the size of the pockets and although they were designed for cartridges, they were almost big enough for a pug.

'I think you can walk though, Rubes, it'll be good for you. I have an inkling the crumbs under Lady C's table have been both plentiful and frequent.' She raised an eyebrow at the little dog, who snuffled but obediently trotted out of the side door of Chatterton Court with her.

Cressida breathed in the fresh air as she walked across the lawn, Ruby padding along by her side. She would have liked to have upped the pace a bit, but little legs could only do what little legs could do, so she used the time it took her to cross the lawn to think about what William had said about Basil and how she might broach the subject with him. Especially bearing in mind the last run-in she'd had with Basil Bartleby in the upstairs bathroom.

'Oh Rubes, how foolish of me!' Cressida exclaimed to her small companion. 'Last time I spoke to him, Basil was pointing the finger at Major Elliot. And now I've had William pointing the finger at Basil... Oh, what ho, Edmund!' Cressida called across the lawn and received a jovial wave from her fellow guest. 'Have you seen Basil?' she called out to him, but Edmund gave an exaggerated gesture to show he could not hear her, so she waved him off with a dismissive flap of her hand. 'Never mind, Rubes, we can find him ourselves. And when we do, I will forge ahead and ask him about this Boris Berkley business. He's the sort of man that only responds to confident, blunt questioning, I feel. And to think he pointed the finger at the poor major! The cheek of it. Sounds to me as if the major never did anything wrong, he was merely fond of Dotty and looked out for the Chatterton boys.'

Ruby snorted and sat down, panting.

'Tired, pup? This is what constant eating and not enough exercise does for you.' Cressida wagged her finger at the small dog, who gazed at her adoringly and wagged her tail. 'Come on then, up you come.' Cressida picked Ruby up and walked at a faster pace across the vast lawn. 'He must be around here somewhere, though I haven't heard any potshots and you certainly haven't been tempted to chase any scarpering squirrels.'

Ruby squirmed at the mention of her favourite nut-loving rodents, but then decided the crook of Cressida's arms was better than a fruitless chase.

Cressida walked on until the edge of the lawn came close and with it the start of the wooded copse that she'd walked through yesterday, when she'd spoken to Jacob the footman as he was chipping the ice for the kitchen. The woods would be a rich hunting ground for Basil, and Cressida started to worry that the earthy brown of her wax jacket might camouflage her rather too well in Basil's less-than-discerning gun sights. She shivered, but that could have been the change in temperature as she left the sunshine of the lawn and stepped into the shade of the woodland.

The path to the icehouse was well-trodden and obviously used frequently by the kitchen staff. The Chattertons would no doubt invest in one of those modern refrigerators soon, but for now they relied on ice deliveries, or harvesting their own blocks of the stuff from the lake the other side of the wood. A well-insulated and below-ground icehouse could keep ice frozen for up to eighteen months she'd heard, though busy houses like Chatterton Court had more regular deliveries. They'd already used it in countless cocktails this weekend, as well as in the kitchen making parfaits, sorbets and iced creams.

Well-trodden, then, this path through the woods, and it was soft underfoot, so much so that given her unintentionally camouflaging coat, Cressida wondered if she should be making some more noise during her approach; something to alert Basil to the fact there was a non-brush-tailed animal that he really shouldn't shoot coming towards him.

In a bid to make her presence felt, Cressida released Ruby onto the ground and only hoped that in so doing she wasn't putting her in harm's way. In fact, she suddenly panicked about it and called out to Rubes, but to no avail, the little pup with her short curled tail bobbing along behind her was off as fast as her stumpy legs could carry her and for once it was Cressida who skipped a little to keep up.

'Ruby, Ruby!' she called, but then stopped as she approached the icehouse. Cressida had seen her pup run off in this direction and then disappear the other side of the brick dome. She couldn't see her pug, but she did see something else that stopped her in her tracks. It was a shotgun, leaning up against the side of the dome.

Basil's? Cressida thought to herself and approached it cautiously. She knew Basil wasn't a particularly careful gun-owner, but she also knew it wasn't the done thing to leave your weapon lying around. She was almost upon it when she let out a gasp in terrified shock. For there, revealed just around the edge of the icehouse, was a pair of legs – a man's, judging by the tweed trousers and brown brogues, lying motionless on the ground.

'Oh no...' Cressida bit her lip and mustered all of her courage to approach the lifeless-looking legs. Suddenly one of them twitched and she bolstered herself in case first aid was needed. 'Basil... Basil, is that you?'

The legs twitched again and as Cressida rounded the icehouse fully, she saw the reason for Basil – for it *was* him – lying on the floor.

'Basil!' she cried out, her hands flying to her face in shock. It was a sight she wished she could erase from her memory, but once seen it was not to be forgotten. And in that moment of horror all she could think of was how was she going to explain this to dear, innocent Dotty, who would be utterly, utterly heartbroken.

25

'Basil Bartleby! You....' Cressida balled up her fists and gulped in air like a beached goldfish. Ruby ran towards her, yelping with excitement, and Cressida scooped her up and buried her face for a moment in the young pup's fur, just as Dotty had done that morning when she was grieving for her poor friend Major Elliot.

Now Dotty would be heartbroken again, and not because someone else dear to her had died, but because the scene that had greeted Cressida as she had rounded the corner of the icehouse, so worried that she'd find her friend's fiancé dead, was one of Basil lying on the ground, his legs twitching with excitement as a flushed Petronella Harper-Ashe looked up at Cressida from astride him.

'Both of you! You should be ashamed of yourselves,' Cressida blustered at them. 'How could you? How could you do this to Dotty?'

Basil pushed himself up on his elbows as Petronella rolled off him and then stood up, brushing moss and twigs off her skirt. Cressida could only thank her guardian angels that at least they had been fully clothed; that she'd interrupted the beginnings of a fumble on the forest floor rather than anything more sordid.

'It's not what you think...' Basil tried to clear his throat and his name at the same time.

This cowardly defence received glares from both Cressida and Petronella, and the latter now finished dusting herself off and turned to face her lover with her hands on her hips.

'What do you mean it's not what she thinks?' she asked him. Then, before he could bluster out more of an answer, she turned to Cressida. 'I'm afraid this is exactly what you think.'

Cressida was shocked by Petronella's bravado and would have planted her hands on her hips too, if she hadn't been holding onto Ruby.

'You won't tell Dorothy, will you?' Basil asked, and for the first time since she'd known him, Cressida thought he sounded sheepish. He stood up and dusted the dry soil and dirt from the seat of his tweeds.

'Give me one good reason why I shouldn't?' Cressida demanded.

'Because it will break her heart.' The voice was Petronella's, and at least this time she sounded more contrite and aware of the heartbreak that they'd caused. 'It should come from him. He needs to end it with her, don't you, darling? And we'd appreciate it if you didn't tell her about this...' She waved her hand in the direction of the ground where they'd been found. 'It would only make things worse for her. Harder to get over and all that.'

Annoyingly, Petronella had a point.

Basil nodded. 'I need to be the one to tell Dorothy. Cressida, can you give me the time to do it?'

Cressida was suddenly feeling like a part of their sordid plan and she didn't like it. Plus, there was something else niggling at her.

'You should count yourself lucky that I'm not pals with your

South African beau, Petronella, else you'd be begging me not to tell him either.'

'Oh, Cressida.' Petronella laughed, and any goodwill Cressida had once felt towards this woman disappeared like the puff of a dandelion clock. Her tone changed too. 'Don't be a fool. I made him up. I couldn't have sat there in Lady Chatterton's drawing room and admitted to carrying on an affair with her daughter's fiancé, could I?' She shook her head as if talking to a simpleton.

Cressida was infuriated... and furious. 'How could you both do this to Dotty? Basil, when were you going to tell her? Before or after your marriage?'

'Before, of course...' He cleared his throat. 'I was going to tell her. I was.'

'Oh really? You weren't going to introduce your mistress here to her on your honeymoon to – where was it again... Cape Town?' Cressida let that sink in. 'I knew I didn't like you for a reason.' She narrowed her eyes at him. 'I will give you twenty-four hours to let Dotty down in the most gentle of ways, and if you haven't done it by then, I will do it myself.'

For the first time in her life, Cressida witnessed Ruby do something she'd never seen before. The little dog growled at both Basil and Petronella and struggled to be let down. As soon as she was, the small dog purposefully walked over to where Basil was standing and peed on his leg.

'Good girl, come on.' Cressida beckoned Ruby over to her and scooped her up. 'Twenty-four hours, Basil, and if you don't let Dotty out of your engagement in the nicest possible way by then, by Jove I will make life exceedingly difficult for you. And don't think I won't.' She threw a look over to Petronella and then stalked away from them both, along the path to the sunlight of the lawn.

Cressida wasn't usually one to let her emotions get the better of her, but Basil's betrayal of Dotty made her so angry.

Stupid penguins... she huffed, thinking back to the things Basil had said to Dotty. And those looks he'd given Petronella... 'That wasn't the cocktail bar he was looking at yearningly the other night, it was Petronella standing next to it.' Cressida stamped her feet with every step. 'And his investment in the diamond mine... he's the outdoorsy type that Petronella fell in love with. And poor Dotty even said her beau sounded like Basil!' Cressida was fuming. Ruby was padding along next to her, panting, but Cressida was sure she could see an angry look in her eye too. 'Well done for peeing on his leg, Rubes, that was the least he deserved. And Petronella! Can you believe it? Perhaps she's the one capable of murder round here, with her calisthenics and athletic prowess. Not to mention the fact she's a proven liar. I bet she *did* steal Lady C's diamonds, coming here to sell her replacements and then stealing Dotty's fiancé to boot, all in one fell sweep. Oh, keep up, Ruby!'

Cressida stopped her stomping and let her dog catch up. She picked her up and nuzzled her into the crook of her arm, feeling her heartbeat thirteen to the dozen.

Cressida softened. 'I'm sorry, Rubes. I'm just so angry at him. At her. At both of them. And it's darling Dotty who will suffer and that's jolly unfair. I wonder if perhaps the major knew about this affair of Basil's? William must do too, hence his finger-pointing at Basil. Maybe he doesn't want the same bad egg marrying his sister. Oh, it's all too confusing, Ruby. I don't know about you, but I think we need to get out of here for a bit.'

26

Still fuming as she approached the house, and unsure if she could keep her oath to Basil about not telling Dotty everything if she came upon her right this moment, Cressida veered away from the front door of Chatterton Court and stomped round towards the old stables and newer garages. A ride in her sporty motor would blow away a few cobwebs and hopefully clear her head of all the confusing things within... or help her keep them all in her head. She wasn't sure which way round she wanted it, but she knew that right now, with the sun high in the sky, she wanted very much to be scooting around the pretty lanes of Berkshire with the roof down and the wind in her hair.

'You'd like a run out in the countryside, wouldn't you, Rubes?' Cressida nuzzled her pup, accidentally using the pug's warm fur to wipe away a tear of frustration that had crept out of her eye.

The garages were situated next to the old stable courtyard and there was the reassuring noise of neighing and whinnying from the horses. Cressida knew that crossing through the court-yard was the quickest way to the garages, where not only her Bugatti was being kept but also the family cars. She remembered John listing off who had arrived and at what time and by what means to DCI Andrews in his interview, and as she walked under the main arch to the stable blocks, Cressida mulled over the fact that Edmund and the poor major must have cars in the garage too.

The stables were fine Regency buildings, each horse cosseted in a large box with a stable door. A few of the handsome beasts had their heads poking over the closed bottom half of the doors, nodding at each other and watching the world go by. Grooms were busying themselves mucking out and brushing down a couple of the beautiful bays and chestnut-brown racehorses that Lord Chatterton intended to race at Newbury this coming season.

The garages, unlike the Regency stables, were more modern and built of brick and concrete. Though not unattractive, they didn't have the style of the old architecture, but they were solid, weatherproof and secure, perfect for housing the family's and guests' cars. Lord Chatterton had decided against employing a mechanic, saying something about all his spare guineas being spent on the horses, but it wasn't a problem; Cressida's Bugatti was as reliable as an old carthorse and as fast as a mustang – and as long as she didn't do anything silly like bust a tyre or hit a wall, she'd be fine without mechanical help.

Still, the thought of who else might have a car garaged here pricked her mind. Would there be a clue at all in anyone's glovebox? Would the cars be unlocked?

Cressida tried the side door to the garage and was relieved to find it open. Although Jacob had acted as valet when she arrived, there was no one manning the garage full-time and she was pleased it had been left unlocked. In accordance with the building's modernity, it too had electric lights and Cressida flicked the large brown Bakelite switch, flooding the vast space with a warm orange-tinged glow. There were the cars. The Chattertons' Rolls-Royce was nearest her, its beautiful curving wheel arches and well-polished running boards delighting her sense of design. It was silver and the yellow light of the bulbs hanging above made it almost sparkle like a glass of champagne.

'Now there's a car, Rubes,' Cressida said appreciatively, putting Ruby down and letting her scamper around as she ran a hand over the curvaceous bonnet of the Rolls. Next to it was a Crossley Tourer and Cressida wondered if that had been the major's...

She peered inside through the open windows, but as with most car owners, whoever's this was hadn't left much on display.

· 'Suggests it's a Londoner,' Cressida said to Ruby, though she doubted the little dog was listening. 'I never leave so much as a playbill on view in case someone fancies it.'

Next to the Crossley Tourer was a four-seater Standard with a spare coat of Lady Chatterton's in the passenger seat, along with several novels and a catalogue of hats from Debenham & Freebody. Another sportier Crossley was next to it, again with items left on the passenger seat; this time a flat cap and up-to-date *Automobile Association Gazetteer*. Cressida leaned in and picked them up.

'E. Priestly. Huh.' Cressida read the name tape inside the flat cap. 'He must have had it since Sandhurst. I hear you have to label everything in that place.' She dropped it back onto the seat and opened the gazetteer, flicking through a few pages until she got to where a bookmark had been left. It was a rather clever design, a bookmark that was integral to the road map, secured by a silk ribbon to the spine of the book, but left plain so that one could write one's route or directions on it. A miniature pencil was attached to it too. She saw Edmund had scribbled the name of one of the local public houses, a place well-known for selling a decent pint of beer and with rooms to put up those in no condition to make it safely home behind the wheel.

Cressida carefully placed the road atlas back into Edmund's

car and moved on to where her own, beautiful Bugatti was sitting.

'Ruby!' she called, wondering where her pug had got to. 'Time for a drive. Where are you, Rubes?' Cressida poked around under the workbenches lined with spanners and various other tools calling for her dog.

Shaking her head at the infuriating hound, she set about opening the large garage doors, in order to get her car out. Sunlight flooded the garage, trumping the orange glow of the electric bulbs and Cressida had to blink a couple of times to acclimatise.

She ran a hand along the long bonnet of her car and pulled the handle. It would need starting, but she could do that herself easily enough. As soon as she'd found Ruby...

Cressida stood still, using her ears to locate the familiar snorting or snuffling that tended to come from her dearest canine friend. And, sure enough, she heard it.

'What are you doing over there, Rubes?' Cressida wound her way back through the tightly parked cars to where she could hear her pup.

She stopped, silencing her footsteps so she could pinpoint where the sounds were coming from again. It sounded very much like Ruby was inside one of the cars, the Crossley Tourer to be exact. Cressida moved towards it, and now the daylight was streaming in through the garage doors, she could see the pale mushroom colour of Ruby's tail, excitedly waggling in the footwell of the driver's seat of the Tourer. She was like a duck that had dived down, but all Cressida could wonder was how she'd managed to get up to the open window in the first place. It was only seeing the scratch marks on the wheel arch that must have come from Ruby's claws as she reached over to unlatch the car door that she worked it out, the realisation coming with a certain amount of guilt.

'Oh dear pup, what are we going to say to the owner of this

smart vehicle when he, or she, finds out you've scratched their paintwork?' Cressida secretly hoped it was Basil's. She picked Ruby up, bum first, and then noticed what the little dog had been so excited about. A brown paper bag was lodged under the foot pedals of the car. 'How odd,' Cressida said, and with Ruby now the right way up and safely in the crook of one arm, Cressida used the other to dislodge the paper bag and bring it to the light. 'I missed this when I was being nosy earlier,' Cressida told Ruby, though she thought to herself that it was little wonder with the light not being so good before she opened the garage door.

Temptation and nosiness got the better of her and she opened the crumpled-up paper bag to have a look inside.

'Dear me!' Cressida plopped Ruby down into the passenger seat of Lady Chatterton's car among the catalogues and coats. With both hands now free, she pulled out the item that had given her the third biggest shock of the day... a cream-coloured silk waistcoat with a pie-frilled edge to the inner seam. She turned it over, for once not worrying about how someone could treat a fabric so badly by scrunching it and... ripping it. 'Oh Ruby. I think you might have found our biggest clue yet.'

Ruby looked up, her eyes inquisitive.

Cressida showed her the waistcoat and explained, 'Look, see here, pup. A tear, but this is no simple rip. A whole piece of the silk has come away, and I bet that if I showed this right now to DCI Andrews it would match the piece that I found on the scaffolding tower.'

Ruby panted, as if that was an appropriate reply to Cressida's big reveal, but Cressida didn't mind. Her thoughts were now going hell for leather with more suppositions and theories. Carefully folding the waistcoat back into the bag, for even in times of stress, she wouldn't mistreat a fabric as fine as that, she scooped up Ruby again and headed over to her Bugatti.

Yes, DCI Andrews needed to see this, but he was still being

a grump and a half to her, and she was still, despite this recent excitement, seething and upset about finding out about Basil and Petronella. A drive out and away from this place for an hour or so would be no bad thing and it would help her think. As, surely, the owner of that Crossley Tourer could be the thief... and the murderer.

27

Cressida pushed her accelerator pedal down harder and felt the Bugatti's power kick into gear. She loved driving, the sense of being so free and independent, while also being in control of something so beautiful. It was like riding a stallion or, if those dreams she sometimes had after too many shots of good rum were anything to go by, like flying.

She was pleased she still had the tough wax jacket on, and wished she could fashion a smaller version for Ruby, making a mental note to ask Maurice next time they spoke if he could find her some waxed material and a willing seamstress. She'd not had a hat with her when she'd left the garage, and thought it a bit much to steal Edmund's, so she truly did have the wind in her hair and it felt refreshing and invigorating, the way a country drive should.

But although her outside was receiving a good refreshing, on the inside she was still churning about what to do. And not just about Dotty and Basil, although that took up most of her heart, but also the waistcoat she'd found and now had firmly wedged into the footwell of her own passenger seat. She glanced down at it occasionally when the road was straight and she could reliably look away from any oncoming traffic, be they car or cart.

Whose car was it? she wondered to herself, drumming her fingers on the steering wheel as she thought about it. She had assumed it might have been the major's, but it could have been Basil's. Or even Alfred or John's. Or even Lord Chatterton's second motor for days when the Rolls was simply too posh.

Cressida huffed out a deep breath, then sounded her horn when a family of ducks had the temerity to try to cross the road in front of her.

'Shoo!' she shouted at the flock but did release the pressure on the accelerator a tad in concession to them all. She'd been driving for a while, but the ducks reminded her that she wasn't too far away from the back lane into Chatterton Court, the one that wound around the far side of the lake.

That might be a good place to stop and have a real think, she decided, so steered the car around the necessary bends and junctions to get there.

The approach to the lake tested the suspension of the Bugatti, and Cressida had to put a reassuring hand out to Ruby, who was bouncing up and down in the passenger seat next to her like a chubby mushroom on a trampoline.

'Almost there, Rubes,' Cressida said as she swung around the last corner and the vista of the lake was revealed. She brought the car to a stop and killed the engine.

It was one of those still and bright days and the lake was as quiet as a millpond. Cardew had warned of winds coming during the night... *So this must be the calm before the storm*, Cressida thought. The trees of the wood in which the icehouse was situated reflected off the still surface and now the engine was silent, the only sounds Cressida could hear were the chirping of the birds and the occasional quack from the nesting ducks in the reeds this side of the lake.

She opened her car door and stretched as she got out.

There's nothing more sublime than the English countryside, especially on a day like today, she thought as a dragonfly buzzed past her ear.

Then she remembered the murders, and murderer, who lurked back up at the house. The house that she could now make out in the distance, beyond the lake, woods and lawns.

Cressida walked around to the passenger side of the car and picked up Ruby from the leather seat. She caught sight of the brown paper bag nestled in her footwell and tried to work out who the waistcoat inside of it could possibly belong to. Whoever it was knew that they had ripped it on the scaffold tower... she thought to herself, letting Ruby down so she could scurry among the water birds and dip in the cool of the lake. *But they might not have needed to hide that fact until I found the scrap when I climbed up it...*

This was an interesting thread to pull. Perhaps it was her own intervention that put a chain of events in order. If she hadn't publicly climbed the scaffold... then whoever had been up the tower, whether it was to kill Harry Smith or hide the diamonds, wouldn't have had to cover the fact their waistcoat was torn. *The torn waistcoat then had to be hidden, in case I found the scrap... which I did...*

Cressida plodded around the lake, taking a path that was more used to the traffic of the local wildlife than a lady in a wax jacket with a serious furrow to her brow and a panting pug behind her. She could hear the cautionary quacks of the ducks as Ruby no doubt bounded in a little close to their nest, but she knew the small dog wouldn't hurt them.

Someone's been doing a lot of hurting though... Initially thinking of the murderer, her brain also snapped back to Basil and Petronella up to no good by the icehouse. *Oh, I ought to have socked him on the nose as soon as looked at him!* Cressida balled her hands into fists as she thought about it. This idea of hers to drive out in the country lanes was meant to have helped calm her down, but now, more than ever, she was thinking about poor Dotty and how heartbroken she was going to be when she found out. She didn't deserve this, sweet, kind Dotty.

Some ducks flew up from the lake and an excited Ruby suddenly appeared by Cressida's side, her black eyes shining with what Cressida could only assume was pure delight.

'Having fun with the ducks?' Cressida asked her and assumed the wag of her curly tail was an admission in the affirmative. Cressida sighed. 'At least one of us is having fun this weekend. So far, I've all but witnessed two murders, almost done myself an injury up a scaffold, annoyed Scotland Yard to the extent that I might be leaving this house under caution, discovered my best friend is being cheated on and failed to stop the hanging of the most ghastly curtains in Christendom.'

Ruby panted as she tried to keep up with her mistress. Cressida slowed, and not just for the young pup to gain some headway. She realised she was walking in the direction of the copse of woodland in which the icehouse was situated and although she could as easily turn around and walk away, there was something drawing her to it.

'Perhaps I need to see it without Basil and Petronella spoiling the view? Try to erase that vision and all that,' Cressida said to Ruby.

She walked on, her hands behind her back helping her posture and giving her the confidence to face the scene again. As before, the temperature changed as she entered the woodland, and the path became softer underfoot as the years of fallen leaves and pine needles created a mattress-like effect.

Mattress, huh. Too apt... she thought, but pressed on to where she knew the icehouse was. This time, to her relief, the scene she found there was quite different. No discarded shotgun, no Basil in a state of repose and no flushed Petronella on top of him. Instead, the icehouse was open and that familiar *chink, chink* sound greeted her.

'Hello again, miss,' the friendly footman greeted her as she approached.

'Hello, Jacob.' She wondered if he thought it odd, her always appearing when he was trying to hack out chunks of ice for the kitchen, but decided that he probably spent his life thinking the upper classes were odd, and he wouldn't be wrong. *If we're not killing each other, we're lurking in woodlands with impossibly small dogs*, she thought to herself, and clicked her fingers to try to get Ruby to heel. She didn't want her canine chum getting too close to that ice pick, or annoying the poor lad as he went about his duties. He certainly didn't deserve Ruby relieving herself on his leg...

But Ruby wouldn't come and she stayed resolutely pawing away at the ground by the icehouse door. Cressida clicked her fingers again and when Jacob caught her eye, she shrugged, as if to say, 'You try getting this one to do anything you want her to do.'

'Come on, Ruby, leave whatever it is. Jacob needs space around him to wield that pick of his.' Cressida had noticed that Jacob had stopped chipping away at the ice.

'Miss,' he called over to her. 'Begging your pardon, but I think your dog has found something.'

'Oh dear. It's not a dead pigeon again, is it? She was ill for a fortnight after she found one in Mount Street Gardens last month.' Cressida gave in and walked around the dome of the icehouse towards the igloo-like door to join Ruby and Jacob.

'I don't think it's a pigeon, miss,' Jacob deduced. 'What with there being no feathers and blood or that.'

'Oh good.' Cressida sent a thanks up for small mercies but was intrigued as to what Ruby was persistently pawing at. 'What is it, Rubes? Let it be.' She leaned down and pulled Ruby off the patch of ground she was so interested in. The forest floor was damp beneath her – ice must have melted here after the last time Jacob, or someone from the household staff, had hacked off a chunk for the kitchen. But it wasn't only the wet ground that Cressida noticed. Where Ruby had been pawing, she saw a black velvet box, about the size of a decent hardback book.

'Anything interesting, miss?' Jacob asked, leaning on his ice pick and peering over at where Cressida was crouched down.

'Oh yes, Jacob,' Cressida replied, picking up the black velvet box and turning it over in her hand. 'Something very interesting indeed.'

28

Cressida turned the black velvet box over in her hands a few times. It was damp and a bit muddy, but there was no mistaking what it was. It was a jewellery case, the sort of thing that very expensive necklaces were kept in. It was extraordinarily heavy too, much heavier than Cressida had expected when she picked it up, and as she turned it, she heard the faint and cosseted clunk of something moving around inside. Could she have just found Lady Chatterton's stolen jewels? This was no empty box, but were diamonds really that heavy? Cressida glanced up and saw Jacob looking at her, a sense of great anticipation on his face. Ruby too was looking at her and panting, so Cressida found the catch and carefully opened the box.

'Oh.'

'What is it, miss? Is it the diamonds, miss?'

To say Cressida was disappointed was an understatement.

'No, Jacob, sadly not.' She let the box snap shut again. 'But I shall take it back to the house and show it to the police in any case. Cheerio then.'

'Cheerio, miss. Sorry, miss.' Jacob swung his ice pick up and

continued with his work and Cressida trudged back along the
pathway out of the woods and towards her car.

Lead... why was lead in the box? Cressida shook her head as
she ran through it in her mind. There was no doubting that it
was indeed the box that *had* had the diamonds in, what with the
embossed gold emblem on the inside silk lining from the smart
London jeweller, and the spaces inside the box in the shape of a
necklace, a pair of earrings and a bracelet. But instead of
dazzlingly bright diamonds, the box had contained coin-sized
discs, dull as proverbial ditch water and obviously, judging by
the weight of them, made from lead.

'Well, well done you, Rubes, for making the discovery, but
I'm jam roly-polyed if I know what it means.' Cressida tucked
the velvet box into one of the capacious wax jacket pockets and
then crossed her arms as she strode back to the car. There was
no doubting that she would have to show this, and the torn
waistcoat and the burnt piece of paper from the major's fireplace, to DCI Andrews as soon as she got back to Chatterton
Court. But quite what he'd make of it, or indeed what he'd say
to her, bearing in mind she'd hardly stopped investigating after
his warning, she didn't know.

Back at the car, with pug, paper bag full of silk waistcoat
and weirdly heavy jewellery case on the seat next to her, Cressida reversed away from the lake and back onto the lane. The
drive to the house was short, and the twisting country lanes
soon met up with the driveway to Chatterton Court.

Cressida eased the Bugatti into the garage, grateful that no
one had come along to close the door after she'd taken the car
out an hour or so before.

'The door wide open does show that anyone could gain
access though,' she told Ruby, who panted at her.

'I suppose it does,' a voice replied to her, and it made Cressida jump, as although she was as convinced as any dog owner

of her own hound's intelligence, she did think that *actually talking* was beyond Ruby. Especially in a posh male voice.

Cressida turned to find Alfred tinkering with something on the workbench.

'Oh Alfred. I didn't see you there.' Cressida was relieved it was only him. She hadn't seen him lurking in the darkness back there at the depths of the garage. 'Sorry. Talking to myself again.'

'Only way to have a sensible conversation at times, as they say.' Alfred emerged from the back of the garage and walked towards Cressida. He was holding a large spanner and his hands looked dirty.

'Indeed,' Cressida agreed with him. She was aware that the paper bag that contained the waistcoat wasn't exactly well hidden next to her, and neither was the jewellery case, and the problem with open-top cars was that people could see right in. She hoped Ruby was obscuring them somewhat, though why she should hide any of this from Alfred, she didn't know. He was, after all, not just her friend (and brother to her very best friend) but set to inherit the whole of Chatterton Court... he had no motive whatsoever to do harm or steal from anyone in the household, and yet Cressida felt there was something in the way he held that spanner, lightly tapping it against the palm of one hand as he walked towards her.

Cressida shook her head. Her worries must only be stemming from her anxiety in facing up to DCI Andrews again.

She put on her brightest smile and kept talking as she clicked open her car door and stepped out, further obscuring Alfred's view of what was in the passenger seat. 'And what are you tinkering with? I know your father doesn't keep a mechanic – are you the next best thing?'

'Oh, I'm not above a bit of tinkering, as you put it. I always think that if there's a problem, then sometimes you simply have to take the matter and fix it yourself, no matter how dirty your own hands get.' Alfred smiled at her. 'Pa's Rolls was making a knocking sound last time he took it to the racecourse, so I thought I'd have a go at the carburettor myself.'

'Good for you, Alfred.' Cressida smiled, relieved that Alfred had turned away from her and was heading back to the workbench. She hoped he hadn't seen what was in her car, but his words did strike her as possibly having a deeper meaning. What other problems could possibly have been solved recently at Chatterton Court? And whose hands were dirty because of it? She shuddered, and shook her head.

Still, she walked around to the back of the car, where she had stashed a woven French country basket that dear Isobel, her old French tutor, had given her one summer. It was supple with years of use, its long leather handles meaning it could be carried over one shoulder, while the basket was deep enough to hold the paper bag and jewellery case. It had been in her car since she'd motored out to Guildford's pretty high street a few weeks back, but now she was grateful that she'd found nothing to buy at that Saturday market, so the basket was still there and unused. While Alfred's back was turned, Cressida quickly put the paper bag and jewellery case into the basket, and then picked up Ruby too.

Confident now that her contraband was well hidden, she walked past Alfred and the workbench to the side door of the garage. Then a thought occurred to her.

'Alfred?'

'Yes, Cressy?'

'Do you know who that Crossley Tourer belongs to? I've been thinking of investing in something larger for longer journeys – Scotland and the like. I'd like to know if the owner would recommend it.' It was a lie. She loved her Bugatti, but she wanted to know who owned the car she'd found the waistcoat in.

Alfred's face fell. He breathed out a sigh. 'That's... that was Spike's car.'

'Major Elliot?' Cressida's query was confirmed with a nod from Alfred. 'I'm sorry. Gosh, I wonder what... Never mind.'

Alfred nodded again, as if accepting more condolences from her.

She gave him a little wave and left the garage. Once properly out of anyone's earshot, and convinced that no surprising voices would answer back instead of Ruby, she spoke to her dog again. 'If that was the major's car, then does that mean this is his waistcoat? I'm sure he was wearing his last night, long after I found the scrap that matches this one. So was this one planted in his car so that we assumed it's the major's? Or was it a spare of his? And was it put there before or after he died? Ruby...' Cressida paused to think, a hand on her brow. 'Have I found a clue, or just made the whole thing a lot worse?'

29

Cressida dropped the wax jacket off in the boot room at Chatterton Court and, with Ruby padding along next to her, walked back into the beautifully lit hallway, her French country basket clenched tightly under her arm. She was on a mission to find DCI Andrews, braced for a telling-off, and if she was to suffer that, she might as well have all the clues with her that she'd found.

'Stay here, Ruby, there's a dear. I'm just popping back upstairs.' Cressida ran in a less-than-ladylike way up the wide stone staircase, not even stopping to appreciate the glorious light that flooded the grey and speckled marble of the hall's interior now that the scaffolding tower had gone. 'Ghastly thing it was,' she muttered to herself as she opened the door to her bedroom and retrieved the now dry piece of burnt headed notepaper. She looked at it again, knowing the words meant something but not being able to fathom quite what yet. Carefully putting it in her straw basket, she went back downstairs, hoping that DCI Andrews might be in a more collaborative mood and would be able to shed some light on it.

'Hallo, Cressy!' Dotty seemed to spring from nowhere.

'Where have you been? Mama thought you'd gone home as Cardew said he'd seen you zooming off in your car. Are you all right? You look rather flushed?'

'Oh Dotty...' Cressida reached out for her friend's hand. She wanted desperately to tell her about Basil, while also so desperately wanting her friend to be protected from ever hearing of it. She knew it would be better for Dotty in the long run to be rid of him, but for some reason, she was totally enamoured with him. In any case, now was not the time to do it. As important as the issues of her friend's heart were, there was something more pressing to attend to.

'What is it, Cressy? What's wrong?' Dotty looked concerned for her friend and grasped her arm in return.

Cressida took a deep breath. 'Do you know where DCI Andrews is? I have something I need to confess.'

'Confess? Cressy... what do you mean?' Dotty held on tighter and Cressida couldn't help but think of what a wonderful person she was, not to pull away from a friend when they said something like that.

'Oh, nothing sinister. I haven't played by his rules though. I've been doing some digging.' She indicated the basket under her arm.

'Cressy, what have you found?' Dotty let go of Cressida's arm, but only so that she could push her spectacles back up the bridge of her nose.

'Clues. I think. Or red herrings. I don't know. But I think I need to own up to DCI Andrews that I haven't exactly "let things be". I think he might be terribly cross with me, but let's hope for a suspended sentence, or perhaps just a night or two in the cells at the very worst.' Cressida gulped, the thought that Andrews might follow through on this threat of charging her for obstructing the investigation tightening her throat.

Dotty frowned too. 'Cressy, I'm sure if you've found something, he'll want to know. And I'm sure he won't arrest you for... for helping.' She shrugged. 'Come on, I'll come with you for moral support. I think he's still in the library having been interviewing all the staff after my grilling this morning.'

Cressida looked at Dotty and felt ashamed that she'd failed to ask how that interview had gone. 'Dotty, he wasn't mean to you, was he? Not about the major?'

'Not *mean* exactly, but he did want to know all about our... well, our relationship.' Dotty flushed.

'But you didn't... I mean, he was a family friend, nothing more or less.' Cressida remembered what Lady Chatterton and William had said earlier about the major being fond of Dotty.

'Well exactly. But I think Andrews was only exploring all possibilities. The poor man's heart did give out, after all.'

Both of the young ladies flushed at the image Dotty had alluded to.

'Gosh,' was all Cressida could say, however, before Dotty knocked on the library door and a gruff voice invited them in.

DCI Andrews looked tired. Cressida wasn't surprised, as having been barking up the wrong tree with Dotty and the major, he had had an afternoon of the footmen and housemaids with all their opinions and views. Still, what other leads could he follow, there being so little in the way of anything to go on? Not to mention the toll that two mysterious deaths in the house two nights running was taking on all of them. Hopefully he would look kindly on her. As, surely, her basket of clues should help.

'Miss Fawcett,' he greeted her, his tone severe, and Cressida had a sudden image of a cold, grey prison cell enter her mind as she approached him, basket still firmly clamped under her arm. The library, usually so draughty, what with the French doors so often open onto the terrace, felt airless and still and Cressida battled with the urge to run away.

She breathed in deeply and was about to show her inner

fortitude a thing or two when Dotty, usually so timid, or at least polite, spoke up for her.

'Now, Detective Chief Inspector, I don't want you to be horrid to my friend. She comes in the spirit of peace and good-will and tells me, though I don't know exact details, that she has some more information for you. Please listen to her with-out... well, without shouting at her.'

Cressida beamed at her friend as the atmosphere in the library lightened. To have someone as good-natured and coura-geous as Dotty by her side strengthened her own resolve to tell Andrews everything she'd recently found out – well, almost everything. He didn't need to know about Basil's moral lapse, especially not in front of Dotty.

Andrews, himself unused to being addressed in such a manner by a young lady, looked to Cressida as if he'd lost some of his puff. He even admitted as much himself. 'Well, that knocked the wind out of my sails, didn't it?' And then in a move that surprised both Cressida and Dotty, he hitched up the fabric at the knees of his woollen trousers, sat himself down on one of the easy chairs and waved over his sergeant. 'Kirby, would you go and ask Mrs Climpton for a tray of tea?'

Kirby stepped towards his boss but looked baffled. 'Sir? Wouldn't you like me to stay and make notes, sir?'

'And cake, Kirby. I think we might need some of her excel-lent cake, if she'd be so kind.'

Kirby furrowed his brow but took his orders and slipped his notebook back into his pocket. Still, Cressida thought she heard some mumbling and grumbling as he let himself out of the library, leaving the two young ladies alone with his commanding officer. Once he had closed the door behind him, Andrews indicated that both Cressida and Dotty should sit with him.

'Come on, ladies, I won't bite.'

Cressida couldn't work out what was going on. The last few

times she'd spoken to Andrews he'd done nothing *but* bite her head off, and possibly with good reason, especially when she'd hidden behind the screen in this very room and listened in on his private interviews with her fellow house guests.

'It's the barking I was more worried about, DCI Andrews,' Cressida managed, hoping that his new, softer demeanour meant he could take the joke.

It seemed he could, and as Dotty sat down on the sofa next to Cressida, he chuckled to himself.

'Biting or barking... I knew there'd be a time when I'd have to change how I approached you, Miss Fawcett.'

Cressida put her basket down on the floor by her feet, then looked up at Andrews. He met her gaze and there was a look in his eyes that once again seemed so familiar to her.

'Brandwater Basin, 1900. General Hunter led us into battle, routing out the Boers and sending them west, but not before we'd captured equipment and supplies that saved...'

'... My father's life.' Cressida closed her eyes briefly as she recalled the familiar story that her father had told ever since she could remember. 'Typhoid had taken out so many of his regiment, but along with Hunter, he'd led the British Army into the basin, surrounding and capturing about four thousand Boer soldiers. He'd been hiding an injury though...' She paused, and Andrews took over the rest of the story.

'... To his side. A stray bullet had got him in Pretoria and if it hadn't been for his batman—'

'His what?' Dotty asked, leaning into the story.

'His batman. Someone chosen from the ranks to aide senior officers in their chores and non-leadership duties. Running messages, cleaning uniforms, preparing food and...' Cressida looked up at Andrews. 'Sometimes saving their lives too when they'd given their own medicine to the junior officers.'

Andrews smiled, and the creases around his eyes crinkled. That's why they in particular had looked so familiar. There was a photograph in her father's study, faded now and not particularly well focused to begin with, but it was of him in full military uniform and a young man by his side, grinning so much that his eyes crinkled at the sides – Andrews.

'Thanks to your father choosing me as his batman, I rose through the ranks faster than any soldier from the wrong side of the tracks had the right to do.'

'If you were to hear Papa speak, he'd say you were an equal to General Hunter himself. "Double the man for half the pay," he used to say about you.' Cressida could see Andrews blushing and wondered if perhaps that had been embarrassing to him. But he was smiling, not a big grin, but a knowing smile, as if the words she'd quoted to him were as familiar to him as an old pair of slippers.

'He was a good officer, your father, and it was my pleasure to serve under him. That it did me no harm on Civvy Street to have his letters of reference, I have to put my hand up to, but Scotland Yard looked kindly on a former soldier who had served under Colonel Fawcett of the King's Own Royals.'

'There's a photograph of you on Papa's desk,' Cressida told him. 'Whenever I was in his study being told off for whatever misdemeanour I'd committed, he'd say, "Next time, Cressida, I'll be calling Andrews. He's a policeman now, you know." I think he's very fond of you, Chief Inspector. Of course, I haven't been called into my father's study for a fair few years now and I'm sorry I didn't recognise you straight away from that old picture.'

'Taken at Cape Town before we left to return home. With him gone, I was left to do regimental work until I retired out before the last war. Policework now. Easier on the knees.'

Cressida and Dotty laughed along with him, the atmosphere in the room entirely different now to how it had been when they'd entered.

'So, you see, Miss Fawcett, how could I have let the

daughter of my most trusted mentor run around getting herself into danger when there might very well be a murderer loose in this house? I had to stop you, for your own sake. But, like your father at Bergendal, you led your own charge and seem to have come out unscathed and victorious.' He nodded at the basket. 'Come on then, show me your own spoils of war, or clues, or whatever it is you've been hiding from me.'

30

Kirby pushed open the library door with his shoulder and brought in a tray of teacups and a steaming hot teapot. Mildred, the housemaid, followed him with a tray of cake and plates, her face a little flushed. Looking at Kirby, the consternation he'd shown at being sent out to fetch tea by Andrews a few minutes ago was gone, replaced by a rosy glow in his cheeks too. *Perhaps heading down to the kitchens hadn't been such a chore after all,* thought Cressida.

Dotty accepted the cake and tea from the young policeman and housemaid and poured out the cups. Once passed round and generous slices of cake handed out too, even to Kirby, who looked more and more like the cat who had got the cream (and sponge cake underneath it), Cressida opened up her basket and pulled out the first of her finds.

'I found this in the garage,' she said, opening the brown paper bag and pulling out the torn waistcoat. 'More specifically under the pedals of the major's motor car.'

'I won't ask why you were searching through cars in the garage,' Andrews said, the gruffness in his voice now coming across as long-suffering rather than angry.

'Well, Ruby was the one who found it really.' Cressida looked down to where Rubes was enjoying her own slice of cake from a china plate under the table. 'She sniffed it out and I just had to see what she was snuffling at.'

'And what do you think it shows... Ah,' said Andrews, having turned it over in his hand enough to see the torn section. 'Kirby, fetch the small piece of silk Miss Fawcett gave us.'

Cressida felt more gratified than perhaps she ought that he'd kept it. There had been a moment when she'd been worried that he'd tossed it away, so uninterested in her help she'd thought him to be.

Kirby dutifully put down his slice of cake and, licking the cream off his fingers, walked over to where the two of them had commandeered a desk to work from.

'Evidence bag 001, sir.' He passed it over and Andrews opened it up and removed the scrap.

'Perfect fit.' He smacked his lips together. 'This is definitely the waistcoat from which that scrap of fabric came.'

'And it was bundled up in the major's car. But it might not be his,' Cressida hurriedly added.

Andrews studied it intently. 'Any reason to believe it's not?' he asked.

'Only that it could have been planted. To incriminate him after, or even before, he was murdered,' Cressida said, while she reached a hand over to where Dotty's own were trembling in her lap. 'I'm sorry, Dotty, I know you think it was his heart.'

'He had a weak heart, though a large one too,' Dotty mumbled miserably, her face downcast. Cressida pulled her hand away and passed Dotty back her steaming cup of tea.

'You think the major was murdered?' Andrews asked her, his fingers criss-crossed together, his elbows resting on the arms of the easy chair.

'You obviously do too, else you would have caught that train this morning.'

Andrews nodded in acceptance of Cressida's theory. 'But why do you think so?'

Oh dear... Cressida gulped. *Here goes nothing...* 'Because I searched his room this morning and noticed a few things.'

'Cressy!' Dotty turned in her chair to look at her friend, her eyes as round as the frames of her spectacles. Even Ruby stopped snuffling for crumbs and turned her dark brown marble-like eyes towards her mistress.

'I'm sorry, Dotty, you know what a hothead I am. And I'm sorry, DCI Andrews, I know you told me not to meddle. And I'm sorry, Ruby, though I don't know what for in your case.' Cressida shrugged at her dog, who stared for a moment more before concentrating on her crumbs again.

Andrews raised his eyebrows at her, and Cressida carried on.

'You see, I drank a lot of coffee yesterday evening before bed and I needed to go to the bathroom in the night and when I opened my bedroom door, I heard someone else on the landing. Of course, I didn't want an awkward *passez-vous* between us, so I let whoever it was do their business and, moments later, when the corridor was clear, I went about mine. The thing is, once I was back in bed, I realised that there had been no sign, no gurgling cistern or whatever, of the lavatory having being used. So, come the next morning, with the terrible news that it brought, I started thinking that perhaps I'd almost stumbled across the murderer in the night.'

'Oh Cressy!' Dotty reached over and grasped her friend's arm. 'That's a horrible thought. Not from you, I mean, I don't blame you for thinking that, but... oh it's all so horrid.' Dotty looked pale and Cressida leaned forward and poured her another cup of tea and stirred in a spoonful of sugar this time.

'Here you go, Dot, drink this. And I'm sorry, but I'm afraid my story is about to get a whole lot worse. You see, before church this morning, I snuck into the major's room.'

'Miss Fawcett...' Andrews shook his head. 'I really should be cautioning you here about tampering with police crime scenes.' He sighed, but gestured for her to continue.

'I noticed something. About the major's bed.'

'Oh dear.' Dotty almost swooned.

'Stay with me, Dotty, this is interesting, if a little macabre, I'll admit. But I noticed that the major was only lying on one pillow and there were two next to him. So where was the fourth?'

'On the floor beside the bed. Even Kirby and I had noted that, Miss Fawcett.' Andrews furrowed his brow, clearly getting rather exasperated.

'Yes, but why? Did you think of that?'

Kirby and Andrews looked at each other.

Andrews cleared his throat. 'Well, we were waiting for more evidence from the post-mortem.'

'Well, I can tell you what it'll conclude. That the major was suffocated in the night by that pillow, the force of the struggle pulling off the small moustache net he always slept in.'

'He did do that, I told you that, didn't I, Cressy?' Dotty had perked up, thanks to the sweet tea and second slice of cake she had just demolished.

'Yes, we'd giggled about it as schoolgirls. And I now know he had a dicky heart, but those pills next to his bed were screwed shut tight as you like and no water had been sipped. So I don't think he woke up having an atrial fibrillation and disturbed his pillow reaching for his pills – if he had done so, he wouldn't have shaken off his moustache net.'

'I see.' Andrews nodded at Kirby, who put down his cup of tea and took out his notepad.

'I found something else too.' Cressida bit her lip. Dotty was not going to like this.

'Yes?' Andrews encouraged her.

'I found this.' She reached into her bag and pulled out the

charred piece of paper with the confusingly obscured words on it that she'd found in the fireplace.

'What does it say? Where did you find it?' Dotty stretched her neck peering at the note as Cressida passed it over to Andrews.

'Both excellent questions, Lady Dorothy,' Andrews agreed, looking at the paper more properly. 'Where did you find it, Miss Fawcett?'

'In the still-smouldering fireplace of the major's bedroom. And it looks to me like some sort of invitation to meet – you see the figure six there...' She pointed to an uncharred bit of the notelet.

Andrews nodded a 'hmm'.

'Why would the major burn an invitation? I don't understand.' Dotty tried to see more of what was written on the paper.

'I don't think it's an invitation as we know them, Dot,' Cressida replied. 'There's clearly the word diamond or diamonds. And chand... that looks like chandelier to me, surely? There's a few more you can't really make out, but it looks like a scrawled note that someone would send if they were trying to organise a meet-up beneath the chandelier to talk about the diamonds. Look, it starts with "I know", surely that's someone arranging to meet the thief?'

Andrews thought about it. 'Or someone blackmailing the thief. "I know you took the diamonds..." sort of thing. "Meet me at six under the chandelier..." et cetera.'

'Oh, DCI Andrews.' Cressida pressed her hand to her lips as she thought. 'Don't you perhaps think that the six refers to roughly just before young Harry's time of death? And he was found under the chandelier. Could this be the note that brought him to the scaffold at that early hour, and ultimately to his death?'

Andrews pulled the note in closer to his face so he could try to make out more words. Cressida's theory wasn't falling on deaf ears and he nodded encouragingly at her. 'I think you might be right, Miss Fawcett. The only question we need to ask ourselves is whether this note was written by Major Elliot, or if the killer – and I do believe there is a killer – planted this in his room?'

The three of them sat in silence, while Kirby frantically scratched his pencil lead across his notebook taking down all that he'd heard.

'And what else have you got in there? Baguette and cheese?' Andrews tried to lighten the mood after the revelations about the major.

'No,' Cressida tutted and shook her head, knowing he was joking. 'Something much more exciting...' She pulled out the black velvet box, much to the shock and surprise of Dotty, Andrews and Kirby, who gave a gasp when he saw it. Dotty was first to exclaim though.

'Mama's diamonds! Oh Cressy, you've found them? Why on earth didn't you say this sooner?' Dotty grasped her friend's arm again and Cressida felt terrible that she now had to let Dotty down.

'Sorry, Dot, not the actual diamonds, only the case.' She passed it over to Andrews.

'Oh.' Dotty pulled back and crossed her arms as she sank further into the sofa. 'Bother.'

'The box is heavy enough.' Andrews weighed it up and down in his hand a few times.

'Open it and you'll see why.' As he did so, Cressida could see the same confusion on his face as she had felt. 'I found it like that. Full of lead. And tossed on the ground by the icehouse, which ties in with what the local police assumed in the first place, that someone took the box from the drawer, slid down the drainpipe and ran across the lawn to the woods and from there to the icehouse and out the other side to the lane. I drove there myself earlier, it's perfectly doable even in my sporty little motor. Someone could well have left a car idling there while they crept into the house.'

'Hmm.' Andrews snapped the lid shut on the box. 'I must admit, I thought you finding clues...' Ruby nibbled his trouser leg and he corrected himself. 'Sorry, with Ruby finding the clues and you bringing them to me, well, I thought it would help. But I hate to say it, I'm as clueless as ever.' Andrews put the velvet box down and sat back in the chintz armchair. 'Two deaths and a robbery. Dear, oh dear.'

'And nothing from the staff this afternoon?' Cressida leaned forward and pressed him to respond.

'Idle gossip and personal vendettas mainly.' Andrews shrugged. 'What did that maid say, Kirby? Something about hoping it was her they'd use in the Pathé news reel rather than Mildred? And Mrs Climpton is convinced Cardew is skimming off the meat budget and ordering cheaper cuts from the butcher than he's taking housekeeping money for. That sort of thing.'

'Surely these must help in some way.' Cressida indicated her basket. 'I know you don't want me snooping about, but you now have good reason to talk to everyone again. Ask them if they recognise the waistcoat or—'

'We'll investigate, Miss Fawcett. Of course we will.' Andrews sighed. 'Kirby, will you go to the major's bedroom and make sure it's sealed properly this time.' He raised an eyebrow at Cressida, who had the decency to look a bit sheepish. 'But thank you, Miss Fawcett. This is all very interesting and no doubt we'll get to the bottom of it. For now, though, it's probably best to act as if you know nothing and haven't spoken to us. And do what you can to enjoy your Sunday evening.'

With that, Andrews and Kirby said their goodbyes and left Dotty and Cressida, and Ruby still eyeing up the cake plate, to the rest of their weekend.

31

The atmosphere at Chatterton Court that evening was a sombre one. Dotty's maid had helped Cressida into a long black dress that she'd brought with her by chance, usually preferring more brightly coloured silks and things with tassels and sequins. But tonight it seemed appropriate to be wearing black.

Dotty popped into her bedroom before the gong sounded for dinner and sat herself down on the bed. Ruby settled herself on Dotty's lap and Cressida turned around on the dressing-table stool to face her friend.

'How are you feeling, Dot?' she asked, while fastening an earring at the back of her lobe. 'Has Basil said anything?'

'About what?' Dotty asked, absent-mindedly stroking Ruby's wrinkled brow.

'Oh, you know. The major... or, I don't know, wedding plans.' Cressida cursed herself for being so clumsy in her choice of words, but Dotty didn't seem to notice.

'He doesn't really mention the wedding. You know, we haven't even decided on a date yet. Mama was keen for midsummer. Which is only a month or so away now, come to think of it. No point in waiting though.'

'Not when you know he's the right one, but if...' Cressida paused. She didn't want to labour the point with Dotty, and Basil had sworn on his honour to let Dotty down gently, which he obviously hadn't done yet. She changed the subject. 'If, like me, you don't think you ever will, then...' Cressida shrugged as she put the other earring in.

Dotty looked up at her, a mischievous look in her eye. 'I heard a rumour that my brother was rather fond of you, Cressy?' She let the comment hang there and Cressida flushed.

'Alfred and I get into some scrapes, it's true, but—'

'Not Alf.' Dotty raised an eyebrow. 'I heard that John propositioned you this morning. After church, no less.'

Cressida could see the delight on Dotty's face. Not the delight of a dear friend who would love her brother to marry her, but the delight of a schoolgirl who had the most delicious bit of gossip with which to tease said dear friend.

'Dotty!' Cressida looked around for something to throw at her, but settled for pulling a face instead. 'Who told you that? Was it John himself?'

'Yes.' Dotty's shoulders shook with laughter. 'I knew you'd spurn him—'

'I was super nice about it actually, chum,' Cressida said indignantly but then could see Dotty grinning and rolled her eyes in return. 'But I was flattered.'

'Oh Cressy, imagine, you could be Cressida Chatterton.' Dotty all but squealed. 'Though I had always imagined it might be Alf you'd go for... Viscountess Delafield in that case!'

Cressida shot her friend a look. Talk of marriage always put her on the back foot. 'You know my views on holy matrimony, Dorothy Chatterton. And I can tell you now that I won't be falling for either of your brothers' charms, thanks very much.'

'Oh Cressy.' Dotty sighed, her fit of giggles over. 'I just want you to be happy.'

Cressida stood up and walked over to the bed, where she

picked up Ruby from Dotty's lap. 'Don't you worry about that, old thing. I am happy. I have my pug, my flat in Chelsea and my rather wonderful sports car. What else could I possibly want in life?'

'The support of a husband, the hope of a family of your own. A partner in life?'

'Partner in crime more like,' Cressida mumbled, thinking of Basil and his 'clerical slip' William had mentioned. She turned and looked at Dotty. 'All those things are very important, Dot, I'll give you that. But so is independence, freedom... and a super smart sports car.'

If winking weren't deplorable, she'd have whipped one out for her friend, but instead she gave Dotty a quick kiss on the cheek and led her out of the bedroom and onto the landing, ready for drinks in the drawing room just as Cardew sounded the gong.

Dinner was a more sombre affair that night, with Lady Chatterton arriving in the drawing room in full black mourning dress, complete with onyx beads and a large obsidian brooch. She set the tone and everyone seemed to be acting with suitable decorum. Drinks were had, though the cocktail shaker stood unshaken and the champagne bottles were unpopped.

Cressida took to watching those around her, all the time thinking through motives and opportunities they may have had. She couldn't detect anything murderous among the muted conversations but did notice that when the guests and family were called through to the dining room, Basil slipped up and placed his hand against the small of Petronella's back, rather than Dotty's. Dotty, luckily, didn't notice, making conversation as she was with Edmund about his plans to invest money in racehorses next year.

The strangest thing, though, was that Cressida caught

herself looking at Alfred several times during the evening. She spoke to him, of course, as one would as a guest in his parents' home, but she really looked at him, too. Unlike his sister and mother, Alfred was tall. He took after the Chatterton side of the family, and there was a likeness to the bust of Sir Roger and, of course, his father, Francis. His hair was the same dark chestnut brown as his sister, but less wild than John's, and his eyes were kind like Dotty's.

Focus, Fawcett... Cressida berated herself for getting distracted. Her mission was to find the murderer, and hopefully the diamonds... and definitely try to stop Dotty from getting too broken a heart. And she truly felt that, however advantageous the match, marriage wasn't for her. The conversation around the table seemed to keep coming back to it, however, and Cressida tuned back in.

'Don't you think midsummer would be splendid, Dorothy?' Lady Chatterton asked. 'If those moles have gone by then, we could have the wedding the same time as the Chatterford village fete. How jolly would that be? Something to look forward to and cheer us all up.'

'Splendid thought, Mama,' Dotty agreed and waited expectantly for Basil to agree too.

'I find high summer can be unpredictable.' Petronella spoke instead and all eyes, especially Cressida's, fell upon her. 'The weather... it can be so changeable.'

Dotty didn't seem perturbed by this and answered, 'The weather can be changeable at any time of the year. You forget, this is England. Four seasons in one day. Look at it today.'

Alfred agreed with his sister. 'There's rain on the way now but earlier the lake was as flat as a—'

'Millpond.' Cressida, who'd been thinking about her drive out earlier and how calm the lake had looked, realised she'd interrupted and spoken over him and blushed what she thought must be a deep red. 'Sorry, Alfred,' she apologised, but noticed

Dotty beaming at her... Still, this was not to be borne, so Cressida kept talking. 'Wind's getting up though. Cardew said as much earlier.'

Alfred nodded and the rest of the table murmured their own thoughts on the English weather. 'It'll blow through by the morning, though, I'm sure.'

Cressida popped some green beans in her mouth and helped them down with a good swig of Lord Chatterton's finest Chablis, hoping it would help her keep her mouth shut and prevent any other awkward moments with Alfred. Dotty, unaware of the looks passing between her fiancé and his lover, was still beaming at Cressida, who suddenly found the tines of her fork fascinating.

'As I said,' Dotty looked across at her mother, 'a midsummer wedding would be splendid. Especially with the village fete and everyone there to celebrate with us. And you never know, Mama, you might just find another couple to join in the fun too...'

Cressida, who had at that moment forked another mouthful in, almost choked on a bean. She was on the hunt for a murderer and a thief at Chatterton Court this weekend, not a husband. And the sooner her dear friend understood that, the better...

'Darling, the only thing I shall be wedded to at Chatterton Court is getting those curtains changed for your mother.' She managed to say, once she'd swallowed her mouthful.

'Oh, Cressida dear, do you still think you might be able to change them by midsummer?' Lady Chatterton asked. 'I know you all think they're better suited for the tea tent anyway.' She looked at Alfred, Dotty and Edmund, who were all smirking, letting them know she had the measure of them and their opinions on her curtains.

Cressida, despite knowing that there would be no summer wedding, nodded enthusiastically. Talk of curtains, however ghastly they were, was preferable to talk of marriage. 'I promise you, Lady Chatterton, I'll be on the telephone to Liberty first thing tomorrow morning and have those curtains swapped for something far more suitable by midsummer. The fete committee will be overjoyed at so much silk for their coconut shy.'

'Cheek of it!' Lady Chatterton said, but as Alfred and Dotty collapsed with laughter, Edmund spluttered into his wine and Lord Chatterton himself grinned from behind a decanter, Cressida knew she was forgiven.

32

Once again, a scream shattered the peace of Chatterton Court.

Cressida sat bolt upright in bed, pushing her eye mask up onto her forehead, and blinking into the morning light. Ruby, agitated by the noise and sudden movement, yelped and snuffled until Cressida pulled her close.

'Bad things come in threes, Ruby,' she whispered. 'No matter what John thinks.'

She settled Ruby back onto her cushion at the end of the bed and pulled back the covers, ready to find out what on earth had happened. All of a sudden, her bedroom door burst open and Dotty ran in, tears streaming down her face.

'Oh Dotty!' Cressida reached over to her friend. *That scream must have been Dotty, meaning Basil must has finally done the deed*, she thought, pulling Dotty into a hug. 'He's a rat, Dot, but—'

Dotty pulled away. 'Who? What are you on about? Haven't you seen, Cressy? There's been another attack!'

'Pardon?' Relieved as she was that Dotty was as yet spared heartbreak, this was not good news at all.

'Come and have a look. Don't tell me you couldn't hear what's been going on?'

'It had just woken me actually.' Cressida was led over to the window by Dotty. 'I had a terrible night with that wind howling. Oh cripes...' Cressida gasped when she saw the commotion below them on the terrace. She pulled her eye mask off from her forehead and threw it back onto the bed. She couldn't believe what she was seeing on the ground beneath them.

Cressida could hear Cardew's stern, authoritative voice as well as the more high-pitched wailing of the housemaids. But it was what they could *see* that horrified them both so much. Petronella Harper-Ashe was lying very still on the York stone slabs in nothing but her nightdress, her hair a mess and her limbs limp. Even from this height, Cressida could see a red bloom of blood in Petronella's blonde hair, matted in with the curls that usually bounced around in such a lively manner.

'Oh dear.' Whatever misgivings Cressida had had about the girl since finding her in flagrante with Basil, she didn't deserve this.

Dotty was trembling next to her and Cressida put her arm around her friend, who in turn peeled her hand away from her mouth and managed to say something.

'Poor Petronella. Why though, Cressy, why would anyone kill her?' Dotty looked at Cressida and her eyes were filling up with tears.

Cressida merely shook her head, shocked at yet another Chatterton Court death. *Bad things come in threes... or fours...*

She braced herself and stared down at the terrace, her heart beating loudly in her chest. Was this really another murder? And if so, could the killer have left any clues... Or perhaps...

'Dotty...' Cressida slipped her arm off her friend and pressed her whole body close to the glass of the window to get a better look. 'Oh Dotty, I don't think she's dead. Look!' Cressida pointed down to where Cardew was gently raising Petronella's head and placing a cushion under it. One of the housemaids then handed him a blanket and he wrapped that around the body, but didn't cover her face. 'I don't think they'd do that if it... well, if it was fatal.' Cressida squeezed her friend's arm. 'Thank heavens for that, eh Dot?'

'Poor Petronella though.' Dotty bit at her fingernails, but she did peer back out of the window at the grisly scene below. 'We must go and help, Cressy, come on!' Dotty suddenly seemed spurred into action.

As the two of them left the bedroom, Cressida grabbed her dressing gown and wrapped it around her tightly. Each step of the stone staircase felt cold under her bare feet and with each one she wondered who could have a motive to try to kill Petronella. Could someone else have known about the affair and been out to avenge Dotty? Or had Basil grown tired of his mistress and wanted her out of the way? Or was this attack connected to the other deaths and the diamond robbery? With Petronella's links to diamonds in South Africa and a family mine struggling, perhaps she was responsible all along?

Cressida was relieved to get to the bottom of the stairs, yet the thoughts still crowded her brain as they entered the library... Someone had attacked Petronella, and she *had* to find out who.

Cressida and Dotty joined the group assembled next to the large French doors that led from the library to the terrace.

'Mama,' Dotty rushed over to Lady Chatterton, who looked done in. 'What happened? Is Petronella all right?'

'Dorothy, dear.' Lady Chatterton reached out for her only daughter and pulled her into a hug. 'I don't know what's happening in this house at the moment, I just don't.' She wept into her daughter's shoulder.

Cressida looked around. William, Petronella's brother, and Basil looked ashen-faced but were talking to Cardew. Lord Chatterton was sitting very still in one of the chintz easy chairs, being attended to by Mildred. He, too, looked like someone who had had one too many shocks over the last few days and Cressida wasn't surprised that, despite the early hour, he was being poured something from one of the cut-glass decanters on the library desk. She was tempted to join him. A look from Alfred, though, the frown cutting across his forehead and reminded her this was no party.

'What happened?' she asked him. She pulled her robe around her and crossed her arms as she asked him. 'And where's Andrews? And Sergeant Kirby? Shouldn't they be here?'

'They're on their way. The doctor's been called too. One of the maids, Tilly I think, found Petronella. She thought she was dead.'

'But she's not?'

'No, badly concussed and lost a lot of blood—'

'Head wounds always do that,' Cressida said, and Alfred gave her a look as if to ask what sort of expert she was on head wounds. 'I saw it from my window, that's all. There seemed a lot of blood around her hair.'

Alfred nodded, then continued. 'Working theory is that someone attacked her first thing this morning. She's an early riser so might have disturbed someone doing something nefarious.'

'Your mother's worst nightmare.' Cressida sighed, remembering Lady Chatterton's fears the night of the burglary. 'Imagine if it had been Dotty.'

'Not an early riser, luckily.' Alfred looked kindly over to where his sister, hair dishevelled, was still comforting their mother. 'But yes, one wouldn't want to think about what might have happened a few nights ago if one of the family had come across the thief.'

'Has anything else gone missing?' Cressida wondered if perhaps that very thief was back. Hadn't Andrews mentioned yesterday that Cardew was 'skimming' off the housekeeping budget. Maybe he'd been the one to eye up a lot more than a few pennies on a pound of beef...

'No, not that we can see.' Alfred looked about him as if to emphasise the point. 'And anyway, this happened outside. What was she doing on the terrace?'

Cressida shrugged and looked back at where Petronella was now being carefully lifted onto a stretcher by two of the footmen. She excused herself from Alfred, pulled her robe tight around her again and headed towards the French doors that led out to the terrace. William and Basil were helping the footmen, but turned when they noticed Cressida coming towards them.

'Stop!' William called out, holding out a firm upturned palm towards her. 'Don't come any closer. The police haven't gathered the evidence yet.'

Cressida wanted to ask why, then, were he and Basil standing so close to the scene of the crime, but bit her tongue in deference to the fact that William was about to see his sister carted off in an ambulance. 'I'm so sorry, William. I hope Petronella isn't too badly hurt?'

Cressida could see a scowl play across Basil's face. Surely he didn't suspect her of knocking his lover over the head with... *With a what?* That was the question.

While William filled her in on his suspicions about blunt instruments, Cressida scanned the pathway around where Petronella had been found. She couldn't see much out of place, except for one of the large terracotta flowerpots that had once housed a rather fine hydrangea, which was now lying in pieces. It had been that way since she'd arrived, but it did look even more forlorn now. There were small shards of terracotta lying around it and several large chunks, their edges sharp as knives, lying in the herbaceous border.

'... Opportunist perhaps, making use of some of that broken pot,' William finished his recap of what he suspected.

'That makes sense,' Cressida said, agreeing with him.

'The only thing that doesn't is why someone would want to hurt Petronella,' Basil replied, his face still stone-like in its distemper.

'Indeed,' agreed Cressida, but, inside, her mind was churning. She glanced back towards the open doors of the library to where Dotty and her mother were now being comforted by Alfred and John. If either of them had known of Basil and Petronella's affair... well... perhaps someone hurting Petronella Harper-Ashe made a lot more sense.

A breeze whipped around the terrace and sent a shiver down Cressida's spine as the next thought occurred to her. If Petronella had been attacked to avenge Dotty in some way, would Basil, who was equally to blame for her heartbreak, be next?

33

As Cressida dressed, she thought about Dotty. She was sure that she didn't know about Petronella and Basil, but she couldn't be sure that one of her brothers didn't. Hadn't she passed Edmund on the lawn yesterday shortly before she'd come across them herself? Could he have told John? And wasn't Alfred wielding a rather large spanner in the garage yesterday? Perhaps he had seen Basil and Petronella together just as she had? Cressida had known the Chattertons for years, however, and couldn't calibrate her mind to imagining any of them doing something as violent as attacking a defenceless woman, whoever's heart she'd had a hand in breaking.

'Not Alfred, I'm sure.' She shook her head and Ruby panted in agreement. 'You think so too, don't you, Rubes. Good. John though? Edmund could have told him?' Ruby looked at her with her bulging black-brown eyes and panted some more. Cressida took this as Ruby's vote in favour of John's innocence. 'Exactly. And they'd go for Basil as a matter of honour, not Petronella, surely. And Lady C herself, she's surely beyond reproach.'

The matter was settled then in Cressida's mind that the Chattertons couldn't have had anything to do with Petronella's attack. But somebody had clonked her over the head, possibly with some of that plant pot.

'Ruby, you to me are perfect... but I do wish at this moment that you were a bloodhound. It would be awfully useful to see if there was any trace of Petronella's blood on any of the shards of that pot.' Cressida thought about it. She'd seen the wound from all the way up here. Surely a wound like that would have left more than an imperceptible trace of blood on whatever had been used as a weapon.

'Come on, Rubes, before I start sniffing around, there's other work to do.' She lifted the dog off the dressing-table stool and made her way back downstairs, passing the massive crystal chandelier that hung in the hallway, sparkling in the morning sunlight. It really would have been so easy to hide diamonds in it...

Cressida crossed the great hall, stopping only briefly to check to see if Petronella had been taken away to hospital yet. The sound of hard tyres on gravel and the sight of the ambulance disappearing off down the driveway confirmed the fact that Petronella was now out of harm's way.

Cressida carried on with her mission, which was to place another call through to Maurice Sauvage. She'd been thinking about those pieces of lead and it had struck her that they looked familiar for a reason – and she had an inkling Maurice could confirm her suspicions. She pushed open the green baize door, let Ruby scurry off in search of sausages or Rollo's breakfast and found the room in the servants' hall that housed the electrics and telephone. In a matter of moments, she was hooked up to the exchange.

'Hello, operator? Liberty of London please, upholstery department. Thank you.' Cressida held the telephone receiver to her ear and the candlestick-like base up to her mouth as she spoke. She heard the familiar, if grating sound of yet another mispronunciation of his name being called across the department before Maurice came on the line.

'Miss Fawcett, how splendid to hear from you. I was starting to worry.'

'And so you might, Maurice, but that's a story or two for another day. I'm so glad I've caught you though. I have a small favour to ask of you.'

'Fire away.'

'I've finally found something here at Chatterton Court—'

'Connected to the death?'

'I'm afraid it's deaths now.' She told him about the major and her suspicions on that front, ending her account of it all with a long sigh. 'So, you see, it's all been rather frightful here. Not to mention the diamonds are still missing.'

'Miss Fawcett...' Maurice seemed lost for words. 'I do hope you're staying safe—'

'Yes, I'm fine, Maurice, though Scotland Yard may say otherwise. Still, it's them, or more specifically DCI Andrews, who I want to help, and I need your expertise to do that. Now, promise me not to say a sausage to anyone about what's going on, but I found these strange discs...' Cressida went on to describe the button-shaped pieces of lead.

'I think I might know exactly what they are,' Maurice answered. 'But could you possibly send me one or two so I can check? You can promise Scotland Yard I'll take the best care of them and send them back with those swatches you wanted for Lady Chatterton, yes?'

'Perfect, thank you, Maurice. I'll ask Inspector Andrews if I can poach one or two back and parcel them up for you. And I assume you've heard nothing on the grapevine about them? The diamonds, I mean. Nothing been fenced yet?'

'No, nothing. It's a bit "yesterday's news" now that they've launched that enquiry into the dead dancing girl with the missing leg and that's all those porters and dyers can talk about now. Still, fancy that – her twin in disguise!'

'It's *always* the twin, Maurice. Still, thank you for your help. I'll be in touch.'

Cressida disconnected the call and left the former pantry that now housed the telephone. For the first time this weekend, she felt like she was getting somewhere and was sure Maurice could confirm her suspicions over those lead discs.

'Ruby,' she greeted her little dog, who was panting contentedly by Rollo's empty food bowl. 'You look satiated and scrumptious all in one. But useless to me unless you can find a housemaid who might be able to package up a few bits and bobs for London. If only—'

'May I be of help, Miss Fawcett?' Cardew had loomed out of nowhere and now stood, his hands clasped behind his back, his head cocked on one side, waiting for instruction.

'Cardew.' Cressida disliked the fact that her voice betrayed her surprise in seeing him. Her surprise *and* her mounting suspicion. *Creeping up on people like that...* 'Very good, yes, you may be able to help me actually.' She was concocting a plan as she spoke.

'Of course, miss. How can I be of service?'

'I need to parcel up some evidence and send it to London pronto. By car, if necessary. This is all above board with the chief inspector, so no need to worry about checking with him.' She hoped Cardew wouldn't call her out on her bluff before she really had had time to ask DCI Andrews.

'Of course, miss.' He gave a small bow. 'If you let me have the parcel and the name and address of the recipient... I assume it's going to Scotland Yard.'

'No... Liberty.' Cressida looked at the butler, waiting for any sort of sign of objection on his part to the extraordinary request, but there was none.

'Very good, miss.' He turned as if to leave her.

'Thank you, Cardew. You really do turn up at exactly the right moments.'

The butler paused and turned back to face her. 'As is my role in life, miss.'

'You were there when the scaffold shook so violently under me. And when the electric switch was thrown the night of the robbery. And you were one of the first on scene this morning, too.'

'Indeed, I was passing when Tilly screamed and was able to console the poor young woman and administer primary aid to Miss Harper-Ashe.'

He's not getting what I'm driving at... Cressida kept smiling as she thought. *Or maybe he's just very, very good at getting away with murder...*

Then Cardew spoke again: 'I'm proud to serve in this household, Miss Fawcett, and feel the family's agonies as my own. The theft and the two deaths, not to mention the attack on Miss Harper-Ashe this morning and various indiscretions this weekend—'

'Indiscretions?' Cressida interrupted him.

Cardew merely nodded, his head leaning to one side as he did. The family's secrets would indeed stay safe with him and as he left Cressida with her instruction to find some brown paper and string, she felt sure he knew more than he was letting on. She was grateful therefore to find Jacob in the scullery and she asked him to do her the same service as Cardew was set to perform, emphasising again that speed was of the highest necessity as soon as he was given the package. If Cardew's parcel never reached Maurice, and Jacob's did, then she'd know the butler had something to hide...

Housemaids went about their business, skirting the sides of the hallway as Cressida strode across it, Ruby nestled in the crook of her arm. The library door was open and, to Cressida's delight, DCI Andrews was once again in position at the desk, with Sergeant Kirby standing behind him, helping him make notes.

'Oh, DCI Andrews. Sergeant Kirby,' Cressida greeted them and let Ruby down to run around and snuffle out any crumbs she could from the biscuits that had been served with sweet tea to help with everyone's shock after Petronella was found.

'Miss Fawcett.' Andrews stood up to greet her, this time a smile crossing his face rather than the frown she'd become accustomed to.

Cressida beamed back at him. 'Any news, Andrews?' she asked, hoping he might be a bit loose-tongued about whatever the servants had revealed to him this morning.

'Not much to report, Miss Fawcett.' He looked at his notebook on the desk. 'Tilly Longwood found the victim at about seven twenty-five this morning when she opened the curtains here in the library and was about to lay the fire. She says: "I gasped with horror, so I did, to see another body so soon after the major and that cleaner chappie."'

'I'm sure she did. Did she go and help?'

'Apparently, she "flung open the doors" and "dashed to her side".' Andrews quoted from his notes, then carried on paraphrasing the maid in less hyperbolic language. 'She said she was pleased to see the young lady wasn't dead, and then called Mr Cardew to help her, who in turn called the doctor and alerted the young woman's brother.'

'Did they find a weapon at all? I was on my way through to go and nose about in the flower bed.' Cressida nodded in the direction of the doors, hoping that Andrews might give his blessing, or even his or Kirby's help.

'Nothing solid, if you'll excuse the choice of words. There were several shards of pot, but there was light rain earlier this morning, along with the promised wind in the night, and none of the pieces were obviously wet with blood rather than rain.'

'Poor Petronella. Lying there unconscious in the cold and rain. No one deserves that.' Cressida bit the inside of her lip in thought.

Andrews, on the other hand, was two steps ahead. 'You say that as if she *did* deserve something though?'

Cressida jerked her head up to look at him and felt the blush rising in her cheeks. 'No. Not at all. Well, maybe there's something, but no, I...' Cressida was lost for words and cursed herself for letting Andrews trip her up like that.

'Please, Miss Fawcett,' Andrews' tone was gentle with her. 'A young woman has been seriously injured. If you know anything about anyone who might want to do her harm, then you must tell me. Justice should never be replaced by vengeance.'

Cressida looked up at her father's former right-hand man. She felt the sting of betrayal towards the Chattertons at even contemplating telling him her worries about Dotty's brothers, but she also knew that if there was anyone who could be trusted not to charge off in the manner of the Light Brigade, then it would be Andrews. She took a deep breath and admitted what she knew.

'I recently found out that Petronella had been having an affair with Basil. That's Mr Bartleby.' She confirmed his name for the note-scrawling sergeant. 'Apparently, Basil was going to leave Dotty, Lady Dorothy, for Miss Harper-Ashe, horribly close to aisle-walking time. Petronella had boasted to us the other night that she had a beau, but she refused to say who it was. Then I found them, let's say in flagrante, by the icehouse, so they had to come clean to me. I agreed with their cowardly plan not to tell Dotty until Basil could find the right time, and it's been weighing on my mind, but I promise you, I have not told her. I know that if I had, it might be construed as motive for attacking her love rival, but Dotty wouldn't hurt a fly.' Cressida hoped she was getting her point across. She could almost see the

thought crossing Andrews' mind as it had done with hers earlier
– *Dotty might not hurt anyone, but her brothers might…*

'So you didn't tell her—'

'No,' Cressida interrupted. 'I'm ashamed to say I gave in to
their plan to let them have twenty-four hours to tell Dot about it
themselves. That would be at about 3 p.m. today.'

'I see. I believe you when you say you didn't tell Lady
Dorothy, but did you tell anyone else?' Andrews asked her.

'Certainly not! And risk Dotty being further hurt by gossip?
Never. I'm only telling you now as you're a trusted aide and an
officer of the law.' Cressida pulled herself up in righteous
dignity. She slumped again though when she thought of Dotty.
'Poor Dotty will be so hurt when this comes to light. I'd hate for
her to feel humiliated as well as heartbroken.'

Andrews nodded. 'I understand. Still, it makes as good a
motive as any.'

'I know,' Cressida agreed begrudgingly.

'And despite you saying nothing, is there anyone else you
think might know about it? Her parents? Her brothers?'

'I have to admit to having the same thought, but no, I don't
think they do. If John and Alfred knew about it, it would be
Basil they'd clonk over the head; they'd never hit a woman. And
Lord and Lady Chatterton would merely call off the marriage.'
She paused. 'I did see Edmund around the same time I found
them, but I can't see any motive on his part for hurting Petronella… And then there's Cardew.'

'The butler?'

'Yes. I know it's not done to point the finger at the servants,
but he's always there when something happens. Still,' she
brushed some imaginary crumbs off her skirt, 'I've devised a
plan that I need your or Kirby's help with to settle that one.'

Andrews looked concerned and somewhat apprehensive.
'Miss Fawcett, what have you—'

'Fear not, Andrews, it's simply a matter of two parcels

heading off to Liberty and seeing if both arrive.' She filled them in on her scheme and Kirby, possibly pleased of an excuse to head into the servants' quarters again in case a certain maid was present, hastened off with several of the lead discs and his instructions to find both Cardew and Jacob separately and send them on their urgent journeys.

'Well, that's a solid morning's work then.' Andrews made to stand up when Cressida raised her finger, as if poised to speak, then lowered it again. 'What is it, Miss Fawcett?' Andrews asked. 'If you've thought of anything else...'

'I have.' Cressida paused. 'But it doesn't paint me in Monet's finest.'

'I'm sorry?' Andrews looked at her quizzically.

'The best of lights,' Cressida illuminated him. 'You see, there is another reason why someone might attack Petronella.'

Andrews raised an eyebrow and Cressida knew that if Kirby were still present, he'd be licking the end of his pencil in anticipation.

'If you think you know anything, Miss Fawcett...'

Cressida sighed. 'Do you remember I told you that I think Petronella and William were hatching a plan to try to sell Lady Chatterton another set of diamonds? You laughed at me, I seem to recall, and the subject was dropped. Well, their family own a mine or two out in South Africa, and as I understand it, they have what's known as "cash flow issues". I overheard them talking about "pushing some more onto" Lady Chatterton and did wonder if perhaps they'd been responsible for stealing the old diamonds in the first place. In order to sell her some more, but...' Cressida trailed off.

'But what?' Andrews asked.

'But I think perhaps I was the only one who knew about it.'

'And you haven't mentioned it to anyone else?' Andrews asked her, leaning forward.

'No, not a word. Not even to Dot. Especially not to Dot.'

'I'll have to make note of it,' he said, getting his own note-book out.

'Please, Andrews... I'd never hurt the Chattertons. And ruining a pretty decent weekend party by killing several guests goes right under that remit. In fact, my only motive for coming was to see if I could *find* the diamonds... not to mention solving the biggest challenge of all...'

'Which is?' Andrews looked at her keenly.

Cressida hoped the twinkle in Andrews' eye was one of fondness, not that of a police officer who could see the solution to his puzzle and the noose in sight.

'Well,' she answered matter-of-factly, 'working out what to replace those ghastly curtains with, of course!'

34

To Cressida's relief, Andrews burst out laughing.

'Honestly, Miss Fawcett.' He shook his head with mirth. 'You played me there. I thought you were about to reveal a whole other conundrum here at Chatterton Court.' His tone changed to one of self-reflection. 'One that perhaps I could actually get my head around and solve.'

'I'm sure you're doing a valiant job with all your interviews and whatnot. But do let me help you if I can.' Cressida hoped she didn't sound like she was pleading.

Luckily, Andrews huffed out a sigh of resignation and stood up.

'Come on then, you said you wanted to have a look outside. Let's see what you can notice that Kirby and I have missed.' He gestured for her to go first across the library to the French doors and followed her out onto the terrace.

'I'm definitely not insinuating that you and Sergeant Kirby would have missed anything, Andrews.' Cressida was at pains to point that out. 'I just want to see for myself.'

'Of course, Miss Fawcett, and here you go.' Andrews led her to where Petronella had been found. The plant pot was still smashed, and pieces lay around the border and under the drainpipe.

'That's the drainpipe, isn't it? The one the diamond thief used?' Cressida put her hands on her hips and looked up at it.

Andrews consulted his notebook. 'Nothing noted here about the pot being smashed the night of the robbery.'

'I think one of the staff or family would have said so if it was,' Cressida agreed with him. 'And look at how green the edges of some of the shards are. They've been like that for weeks growing algae and whatnot. I'm afraid that's the fault of the Chatterton Court gardeners not clearing up an old pot for a while. Or perhaps Lady C is attempting some modern horticultural au naturel and leaving broken things in situ on purpose?' She shrugged but let her eyes scan up the windows to her own bedroom, from where she'd looked down on this terrace only a few hours ago when she had seen Petronella lying on this very spot. She shivered as a cool breeze rounded the house and fluttered down the terrace.

Pulling her cashmere shawl around her, she turned her head back to the ground and took a closer look at the smashed terracotta. Some shards were trodden into the soil of the flower border, while some lay across the York stone slabs, disintegrating at the edges.

Cressida looked at Andrews, who nodded to her, and she reached out and picked up one of the larger shards. It was heavy and solid, but crumbling around the edge due to being exposed now to rain and damp soil. She turned it over. No sign of blood or damage on it, but it certainly could have been used to give someone a nasty injury. There were other smaller pieces around too, but Cressida discounted them as being not nearly vicious enough to do what had been done to Petronella's head. Some darker, smaller shards caught her eye, but they too were too small to do anyone any more of an injury than a small cut.

Cressida stood up and shrugged again at Andrews, who nodded.

'Not much to go on, is there, Miss Fawcett?' he said, gesturing them back into the library.

'No, not much at all. But perhaps that's almost as important as finding something,' Cressida theorised as they returned to the library through the French doors.

'How so?' Andrews asked as he sat himself back down at the desk. This case was obviously taking its toll on him, and Cressida was worried her thoughts, unformed and slowly emerging from her brain, might sound silly and annoy him. However, he was looking at her expectantly, so she ploughed on.

'I was wondering. I mean, if we'd found a brick covered in blood or whatever, yes that would have been useful, but why would a would-be killer leave that for us, or anyone, to find? They'd be extraordinarily inept.'

'True enough,' Andrews conceded, leaning back in his chair. Cressida perched on the arm of one of the chintz easy chairs. Andrews gave her some of the benefit of his experience. 'The thing is, Miss Fawcett, that murderers aren't always cool and calculating. Many are hot-headed, thoughtless. Careless even. Or, in some cases, in the moment of their most violent urge,' he mimicked raising an arm to strike a victim, 'they repent, they regret. They fail to follow through and they drop everything, literally, and almost wish to be found out so that they can be brought to justice.'

'Justice rather than vengeance.' Cressida repeated his words from earlier back to him. 'Still, the lack of a murder weapon – and I know it's not murder per se, but let's say it was attempted... well, perhaps it's still somewhere on the grounds.'

'The local boys are onto it, ma'am.' Kirby, who had let himself back into the room moments before, advised. 'They're checking the grounds as we speak, and we instructed a house-wide check too.'

Andrews nodded.

'And will you interview any of the guests again? William and Basil at the very least?' Cressida asked.

'Yes.' Andrews looked at his watch. 'I'm one ahead of you there and expecting Mr Harper-Ashe presently.'

'Oh, good.' Cressida looked at her watch, not registering the time but using it as an excuse to leave. 'Anyway, better toddle on. Must go and see if Dotty is all right after yet another wake-up call at scream o'clock.'

Cressida made her goodbyes and closed the door of the library behind her. She had no intention of going to find Dotty. A thought had struck her and, as much as she respected Andrews and believed in his abilities, she knew that hiding behind a screen again wasn't going to be possible this time, and she had to know what William, and Basil, had to say. Andrews might have let her into his investigation now she knew who he was, but she knew that she'd always be playing second fiddle to him if she let him lead the questioning. She had to find William herself and ask him what she needed to know before his rendezvous with Andrews.

'William!' Cressida hadn't had to wait long to find him. He was coming down the grand stone stairs, a valise in his hand. He looked drained, far paler than before, his natural tan lost in the depths of worry. 'Any news?'

'She's at the hospital now. I only came back to pick these things up for her, but apparently that dratted policeman wants a word.'

'What's the prognosis?' Cressida did genuinely feel sorry for Petronella, despite the looseness of her morals.

'She'll wake up, which is the good news.' He sighed. 'I'll pass on your best. But I better dash—'

'I wish her a full and speedy recovery.' Cressida reached out and laid a hand on his arm, as much to make him stay as to display her concern. 'Can I just ask though, do you know who might have done this to her?'

'Cressida.' He closed his eyes, wearied, it seemed, by everything. On opening them, he carried on. 'I don't have time for your amateur sleuthing. That policeman wants to talk to me, and all I can say to either of you is that I have no idea who might have hit her over the head. No one in this house anyway.'

'So you think it was a stranger? A random attack from a person unknown to any of us, who happened upon your sister early in the morning?'

'Well, I...' William seemed less sure of himself. 'But it can't have been anyone here at Chatterton Court. Could it?'

Cressida rather thought it could be.

'I beg to differ, William. Think about it – she was found in her nightdress, early in the morning. Much like Lady Chatterton's diamonds being stolen, what are the chances that a stranger would be in the right place at the right time to commit a seemingly unprovoked attack?'

'Now you put it like that...' William put the valise down.

'Do *you* know why she was out in her nightdress so early in the morning?' Cressida waited for his reply, knowing it could confirm her suspicions about who might have tried to kill her, namely her lover, Basil Bartleby. William's face went from looking tired and drained, to being consumed by conflict. 'William?' She reached out to touch his arm again, but he flinched it away. 'William, was she meeting someone?'

'She may have been,' William admitted, his face looking like one of pure resignation now. Cressida hoped it meant he'd decided to tell her everything he knew.

'And you know who it was?'

William looked up at her and cocked his head to one side. 'You know, don't you?'

'I have my suspicions.' Cressida crossed her arms. She might not be the one worried about her sister, but she was still fuming about Basil and wary of letting any emotions get in the way of this conversation.

'She was having an affair.' William sighed. 'Well, *she* wasn't. He was. Basil.' William confirmed what Cressida already knew.

'And they agreed to meet this morning?'

'They had to find somewhere to talk where no one in the house would hear them, I suppose. They're both morning people and up with the lark. It's one of the things they bonded over in South Africa.'

Cressida was always suspicious of people who could spring out of bed so early in the morning, but kept this misgiving to herself. 'Is that when this all started?'

'Yes. I knew Basil of course from the Mutton Pie Club; we'd played a few hands of cards together before. He'd shown an interest in our diamonds, thought it was a sound investment. I told you all this yesterday.'

'Yes, you did... and very much pointed at Basil as being someone I should look into in the case of the major's death.' Cressida thought back to that conversation. 'Why didn't you mention then that...'

'That my sister was involved in a scandal? With your best friend's fiancé? Wasn't the sort of thing I wanted to slip into conversation.' William looked peeved.

'But you wanted Basil out of her life?'

'Wouldn't you? A man of dubious repute, cheating on his fiancé with my sister? I pleaded with her to call it off, but to my horror, she was determined that he was the one for her.'

'Did he invite you both here?'

'In a sense. When Father found out that Basil was already engaged, he threatened to renege on the deal they'd made about buying the shares. Basil wrote and said it was out of his hands, and his family had insisted he marry Lady Dorothy. Father was having none of it, but Basil was obviously desperate for those shares, so asked us to join him here, of all places. He said the

Chattertons were rich and we could no doubt flog a few sets of earrings while we were here.'

'He's such an oaf.'

'Yes, I could never see what Lady Dorothy saw in him.' William reached down to pick up the valise.

Cressida, though no fan of Basil, still remembered William's own determination to sell his diamonds to the Chattertons and decided to quiz him further. 'Seems like it was perfect timing for you both to arrive here just as Lady Chatterton's diamonds went missing.'

William stared at her. 'What are you implying? I don't have to stand here and take this from you.' He moved down a step, and Cressida had to quickly back down to get out of his way. She caught his arm as he was passing her and snatched one last question.

'But do you think, truly, that Basil will choose your sister over Dotty? Has he said anything?'

William turned to look at her. 'Sadly, I think he will. His underhand financial dealings aside, they're well suited, outdoorsy types. You should have seen them riding across the plains together, stalking antelope and shimmying up trees to get better views of the elephants and zebra. We accepted his invitation here because the fact is, we need to sell diamonds to the rich people of England and my sister came to see if the man she loved could be won over. And it looks like he has been. But the last thing our company needs is drawing-room scandals and suspicions of thefts hovering over us. I know our timing is unfortunate, but we didn't do anything wrong.' With that, he stormed off, leaving Cressida, with Ruby still waiting patiently by her side, thinking about what he said.

'Rubes, it seems Petronella was still very keen on Basil, as incomprehensible as that is to you or me. But perhaps, despite what we saw by the icehouse, he isn't as keen on her as all that. What if their early-morning tryst was Basil's attempt to call it off with her, knowing how well his bread is spread with Chatterton butter, as it were? Well, don't you think, Rubes, that he might feel the need to clonk her over the head if she threatened to tell Dotty?'

Ruby panted and, as usual, Cressida took this as a solid agreement.

'Ruby, we need to find Basil.' The small dog growled. 'I know, me neither, Rubes. But I have to ask him outright if he wanted to stop seeing Petronella and stop her from talking. Perhaps for good.'

35

'Miss Fawcett!' Her name thundered around the great hall.

Bother it... Cressida thought, before replying to the now familiar voice. 'Yes, DCI Andrews?'

'You know this dome makes voices travel—'

'Like that of the Whispering Gallery at St Paul's Cathedral, yes I know.' Cressida raised her eyebrows at Ruby and then across to where Andrews was standing the other side of the great hall, by the door to the library.

'So you'll want to explain to me why you just accosted Mr Harper-Ashe, and who you were talking to when you declared Basil to be the man we're looking for.'

Cressida picked up Ruby and hurried over to the library so that she and Andrews could talk more discreetly. The last thing they needed was for another conversation to be overheard.

'I'm so sorry, Andrews. I thought if I quizzed William, and then you did, well, then we could compare notes. And as for the other person I was talking to, well, I'm afraid it was no one more inflammatory than this small pup here. She really is an awfully good listener.'

'I see. Come on in then, let's "compare notes", as you say.'

'But you haven't had a chance to speak to him yet?' Cressida queried, following the chief inspector into the library.

'No, but I'm sure you'll tell me exactly what he's going to say.' He looked somewhat resigned to the matter.

'The only headline was that he knew about Basil and Petronella's affair, and he's not best pleased about it either. As much as I respect Alfred and John, they seem to be much happier about their sister marrying Basil Bartleby than William does. Though I suppose they might not know about the money laundering...' She looked pensive.

'The what? When did you find that out?' Andrews looked flabbergasted.

'Sorry. William mentioned it yesterday, before news of the affair broke – well, as in before I challenged him about it. He said Basil had been interested in investing his small... Oh, hang on.'

'Yes?' Andrews looked to Kirby, who whipped his notebook out, licked his pencil and nodded in readiness.

'The other day Dotty said that Basil was going to be looked after financially by a large endowment from his aunt. He shushed her, and I thought it was only an impropriety thing, but maybe even he felt squeamish talking about inheritance he didn't have. In front of her brothers, who might have started asking questions... Anyway, William said the opposite and that Basil had been in trouble for some "clerical errors" that saw him try to raise funds or clinch deals under the name Boris Berkley. But, despite that, William's father had been willing, due to their cash flow issues, I should imagine, to take Basil's investment of his "small inheritance".'

'Right. So Basil isn't as rich as perhaps the Chattertons think he is.'

'And might want to silence anyone who could let that slip to them...'

'That's quite the accusation...' Andrews looked stern, but Cressida could see he was taking her seriously.

'You'll call him in though, for an interview, won't you? And I'll—'

'Stay out of trouble as much as possible, please, Miss Fawcett.'

'Of course, and now I really must go and see Dotty...'

Before she could finish, the library door was flung open and Dotty ran into the room.

'Oh Cressy! There you are! I... Oh Chief Inspector, sorry, I... I just need...' Dotty was red-rimmed of eye and flushed of cheek. Any suspicion Cressida recently had of Basil calling off his relationship with Petronella was quashed in this instant.

'Dotty, oh Dotty.' Cressida dashed over to where her friend was standing. 'Has he?'

The question was enough to provoke a wail from Dotty, who nodded while sniffing.

'Come on, let's get you up to your room, old thing,' Cressida cajoled her, while quickly turning round and mouthing a goodbye to Andrews. The murder investigation was exceedingly important, but it could wait while something much more critical was attended to: her best friend's broken heart.

It took a full half an hour for Cressida to get out of Dotty what Basil had actually said to her. There'd been angry outbursts and moments of introspection, along with certain words that turned the air bluer than a bad day on a fishing boat, but Dotty was finally calmer and now only hiccupping occasionally as her diaphragm caught up with her breathing.

'He said that he'd met Petronella,' sniff, 'in South Africa, and although he thought he could forget her and make a nice life with me,' sniff, hiccup, 'he realised that when he saw her again, he loved her...' Dotty sniffed and hiccupped and sobbed a bit more.

This wasn't news to Cressida, but she couldn't say a thing, only inwardly curse the hateful man.

'How could she sit here and take tea with me and Mama and you and talk about her "beau" while all the time she meant Basil. I feel such a fool.' Dotty's shoulders slumped once again in a fresh bout of sobbing.

Cressida handed Dotty a handkerchief and pulled her closer to her, her arm around her friend's shoulders as they sat on the edge of her bed. *Men really are the limit*, Cressida thought to herself.

They stayed, Cressida consoling Dotty for a while and occasionally talking about how men were absolutely *the worst*, until the gong for lunch was sounded.

'Gosh, I don't know about you, but this has been such a long morning.' Cressida gave her friend another squeeze around the shoulder and released her. 'Now, Dot, I don't suppose you much fancy the dining room, but can I ask Mildred or Mrs Climpton to bring you up a tray?'

'Oh, yes please. I wish losing a fiancé made me lose my appetite too, then I could be effortlessly sylphlike like you, chum, but, alas, no. My heart might be broken, but sadly my stomach is still rumbling.'

'You're lovely just as you are, Dotty dear, not a pound or two more or less, and, today of all days, should eat exactly what you want. I think roast chicken is on the menu, which is good, as it'll have to be something exceedingly tempting to get me into a room with Basil.'

'I can't even bear to hear his name, Cressy.' Dotty sobbed again.

'I know, dear. I know.'

.   .   .

The dining room was a subdued place, with only Cressida, Lord and Lady Chatterton, their sons and Edmund Priestley. Basil had wisely made himself scarce, and even though he had to be available for the police if needed, Cressida rather suspected that the local inn might have had a new and very sudden guest appear. The talk around the table tumbled between the possibility that there was a murderer on the loose, and who it could possibly be and, of course, poor Dotty and her broken heart. Even her father, who Cressida had barely heard say a thing all the time she'd been at Chatterton Court, mumbled something about a 'very rum affair' and 'badly done by Bartleby' to Alfred, who agreed, while looking utterly thunderous about it.

'I'm so glad you're here with us, Cressy, dear.' Lady Chatterton leaned forward across the table to speak to her. 'Dotty thinks the world of you, as we all do, and I know your presence will be bringing her great comfort.'

Cressida nodded, but couldn't help but blame herself for the part she'd unwittingly played in hastening Basil's admittance of the truth.

'I only wish I could do more for her, Lady Chatterton.' Cressida meant it. She wished she could find Dotty the best of men, the nicest of husbands, someone who would treat her, and the local squirrel population, one hundred times better than Basil had. Luckily, they were young, their debutante year hardly a memory it was so recent, and they had the social season ahead of them.

Lady Chatterton, much like her daughter seemed able to, read Cressida's mind. 'I hope you'll be at all the parties, and balls and things, won't you, Cressida dear?'

'Yes, yes, of course. And Dotty will be swept off her feet, I promise. She'll be engaged again before the leaves fall, I can feel it.'

'Thank you, dear. And you too, you must find a husband.'

Lady Chatterton looked as concerned for Cressida's welfare as her own daughter's.

'Oh, I don't know about that, Lady Chatterton, I'm fine with my—'

'Little motor car and independent means,' Lady Chatterton rather shrewdly observed. 'There's more to life than driving fast and spending money, dear.'

Cressida smiled at her hostess and tucked into her roast chicken.

More to life than driving fast and spending money... she thought to herself and then chuckled as she slipped a beautifully crispy piece of chicken skin under the table. *Why of course, there's pugs too!*

The conversation around the lunch table went from talk of dastardly Basil back to the tragic deaths and from them to the lost diamonds. Cressida listened in and nodded along, all the while thinking about the comings and goings from this great house. Diamonds had been stolen, lovers had met, victims had been killed and no doubt a thief and murderer was currently either as far away as could humanly be possible or was planning that very escape right now. Was it William Harper-Ashe and his need to sell diamonds to save the family mine? Had the major owed Edmund or Basil substantial amounts of money? Was Cardew at this very moment sending off her evidence to Maurice or disposing of it, thinking he was saving his skin in doing so? She couldn't think that any of the Chattertons would do such a thing and her mind turned back to Basil and his philandering ways. How dare he ruin the happiness of her friend. And though she hadn't wanted to see him this lunchtime, she most certainly still wanted to give him a piece of her mind.

'I assume he who shall not be named has biffed off to the Barley Mow?' Cressida asked Alfred, who was about to answer when John chipped in.

'That's right. There hasn't been much study of it, but I think it's statistically unlikely that couples who stay under the same roof once an engagement has ended end up back together. Might be a good thesis subject though,' he mused.

'Thank you, John.' Lady Chatterton shushed her youngest child.

'Yes, the toad decided he'd be more welcome there than here, and he wasn't wrong,' Alfred added. 'Edmund, you just took your car out for a spin, didn't you, did you see him there?'

Edmund frowned at Alfred, obviously trying to remember if he'd seen the blighter. 'Didn't spot him. Sorry. Wouldn't be surprised though.' Edmund concentrated on eating again and Cressida felt a pair of eyes on her. She glanced up and saw Alfred looking at her intently.

'You knew, didn't you? About the affair.' His voice was low so that no one else could hear him.

'Yes. I didn't know you did...' Cressida suddenly panicked that perhaps Alfred had been the one to bash Petronella over the head. It unsettled Cressida how much this upset her.

'William told me this morning as I saw Basil putting his case in his car. Cressy,' Alfred looked at her, 'you will look after Dot, won't you?'

Cressida looked at Alfred, his kind eyes, which were so like Dotty's, imploring her to do what she would do most naturally anyway. She answered him. 'Of course, Alfred. I've left her in the safe paws of Rollo and I'll spend the rest of the afternoon with her. But first, Basil Bartleby is getting a piece of my mind.'

36

Cressida stopped by the boot room and picked up the dependable wax jacket she'd borrowed the last time she'd driven out. Stylish it may not be, but compared to the white driving overalls the nice man in the car garage had advised she wore on each journey, it was haute couture.

'Or *haute car-ture*, eh, Rubes?' she said to her small dog, who was still licking her lips after the extra piece of chicken she'd snaffled from the dining room.

With wax jacket on and small dog in tow, Cressida walked through the stables and waved at the grooms who were brushing down the fine racehorses recently back from the gallops. They were excellent beasts, but not a match for her car, she thought as she hurried through the courtyard and out towards the more modern garaging.

The door was unlocked as before and she opened it up and went in. The Rolls, graceful yet large, was still the first car she came across and then the Crossley Tourer that had been the major's. *I wonder what they'll do with it?* Cressida thought to herself as she let her hand drift over the wheel arches, smarting slightly at the recognition of the scratch marks that Ruby had made when she'd scampered in and found the paper bag with the waistcoat. Next to the Tourer was Lady Chatterton's Standard, still full of Debenham & Freebody catalogues and discarded coats.

'Come on, Rubes,' Cressida hastened her pup along, passing Edmund's car, still there with its gazetteer in the front seat.

She walked around the sporty Crossley to her own car, stopping to delve around in the luggage hold hoping to find a scarf. Finding a rather natty silk number, she tied it around her head, remembering the tangles in her short bob after her drive out yesterday, and while she knotted it under her chin, she noticed the strangest sound. A very gentle *dink dink dink*. It reminded her of Jacob pickaxing the ice blocks, but she was too far from the icehouse for that sort of noise to carry. Shrugging off its oddness, with her mind on something far more all-consuming, she fired up her motor and left the garage, and then the grounds of Chatterton Court in her wake.

The Barley Mow was a larger-than-average English inn, being able to accommodate six or seven bedrooms on the upper two floors and a decent saloon bar and dining room downstairs. It still had a door with a sign that said 'No wimmin' between the saloon bar and the entrance hall, but it was wedged open with a thick chunk of wood and several old coats hung over it.

The landlord, who was standing behind the bar in the saloon wiping clean glasses, beckoned her through. 'Pay no 'tenshon to that sign, miss,' he called over. 'Ever since the war when all we had was wimmins' committees in here keeping us going, we've been meaning to get rid of it. Tends to get hidden by all the coats anyways.'

'Thank you. And good afternoon.' Cressida strode in towards the bar and smiled at the cheerful landlord. It was a smile, however, that only thinly veiled the reason for her visit, which was to tear ten strips off Basil Bartleby and see him hang his head in shame for how he'd treated Dotty.

The landlord could obviously tell something was amiss. 'You look like you fair built up a good head o'steam o'something, young lady.' The landlord looked at her quizzically and Cressida sighed and nodded.

'You're not wrong.' Her eyes scanned the back bar, wondering what tipple she might have to help steel her nerves. A head of steam she might have, but she was worried her bones might turn to jelly once she was face to face with Basil. 'Gin and soda please. Double.'

'Coming right up, miss.' The barman turned to the bottles and poured her a generous measure of a clear liquid that she hoped was gin. It was hard to know since it came out of a plain stoneware bottle with a simple cork closure. She watched as he squirted some bubbly water into the glass from the soda fountain before placing the drink on the bar in front of her.

'Thank you.' Cressida passed over a few coins and hoped he didn't see her hand shaking as she did so. 'I'll take this through to the parlour if that's all right? And do you happen to know if there's a Mr Bartleby staying at the moment? I believe he is.'

'And I believe you are right, miss, though you can check in the visitor book. It's open on the table in the hallway out there. That's where we check in the overnight guests as they happen.'

'Thank you.' Cressida picked up her gin and raised the glass to the landlord, who nodded in appreciation. She then went back out of the saloon bar and towards the parlour. Old pubs like this would have always had parlours or dining rooms, places where in the last century travellers of both sexes could have rested while their horses were changed in the stables behind the pub. Old coaching inns were often made up of higgledy-piggledy rooms and corridors, being such historic buildings.

She walked through to the dark wood-panelled entrance hall, where, sure enough, a visitors' book lay open on a table by the bottom of the stairs to the bedrooms on the floors above. Behind the table there were a few hooks with keys hanging on them. She walked up to it and put her drink down. There it was, Basil's name the most recent in the column marked 'guests' and the time of his arrival only a few hours ago.

Cressida uttered a blue word or two under her breath but stopped when she saw the other names in the book. *Max Andrews... so that's his name, Max.* Cressida smiled. *Oh and Sergeant Kirby... Quentin!* Cressida chuckled to herself. Then, logged a few days earlier, another name caught her eye... *Now that is interesting...*

'What do you want?' Basil barked at her from the turn in the stair by the reception desk.

Cressida looked up and forgot all about the names in the guest book. Caught unawares by Basil's sudden appearance, she felt tongue-tied.

He stood there, one hand on the carved newel post, and eyed the fizzing drink standing next to her. 'On the sauce again, eh? Not sure you were ever a reliable witness.' He spat the words out at her.

Cressida looked down at the drink, then up at Basil. There were so many things she wanted to say to him, so many ways she wanted to explain why what he had done was a horrid and thoughtless thing. To be so careless with her dear friend's heart, not to mention embarrass the family, all of whom she held dear to her. And the questions she had about his 'clerical error' and his meagre, or otherwise, inheritance and how perhaps they might all be motives to steal... and to kill... But none of these words came to her clearly and comprehensively and as Basil nonchalantly took the last few stairs towards her, a sneer on his face, she did the only thing she could think of doing in that moment...

Seeing him now, sodden, with the gin and soda streaming down his face and wetting the front of his shirt, gave her more pleasure than that time her horse came in during the Derby. More satisfaction even than when her colour scheme proved to be just the thing for Lady Staveley's summer house, and Cressida allowed a smile to spread across her own face, while he stood scowling.

'Whaddya do that for...' He tried in vain to brush the liquid off him, wiping the stinging fizz from his eyes and making it worse.

'That's for being beastly to Dotty.' Cressida turned on her heel and headed out across the flagstones of the old coaching inn's hall into the bright sunshine outside. Basil Bartleby hadn't got even half as much as he deserved, but it was a few pence well spent and, boy, had it felt good.

Ruby wagged her tail excitedly at Cressida as she approached her car.

'Job done, little pup,' she said to her as she opened the driver's door and slipped down into her seat. 'Now vengeance has been had for Dotty, we can turn our minds back to justice, and find ourselves the Chatterton Court killer!'

37

The Bugatti purred into action and Cressida, still on a high from her escapade with the gin fizz, gunned it back towards Chatterton Court. Thoughts were buzzing through her mind as she raced towards the house. She hoped the parcels had reached Maurice and she intended to call him as soon as she was back. And there was still something that William had said earlier about his sister that had caught at the edges of her mind. Like a snagged thread on an unbound hem, it was working its way loose and she couldn't quite find the right end of it to pull it clear...

She pulled into the garage at Chatterton Court and cut the engine. She was pleased the large garage doors had been left open, and even more pleased that no one was tinkering around inside. She needed to think.

Cressida sat there for a little bit drumming her fingers on her steering wheel, coming up with her plan of action. Firstly, she needed to speak to Maurice, or see if he'd left a message for her with the staff. Then she needed to speak to Andrews again, see if he'd managed to speak to anyone else in the house. As she thought things through, she heard that *dink dink dink* noise again.

'Huh,' she said out loud and then, when she realised what she was hearing, thought to herself, *An engine cooling down. But which car had just been out when I came into the garage earlier?*

It was a thought that was still occupying her mind, again for a reason she couldn't fully work out, when one of the house-maids found her in the boot room as she hung the wax jacket up.

'Excuse me, ma'am.' The young maid curtsied and Cressida smiled at her.

'Yes.'

'Begging your pardon, but there's a message for you from London, miss.'

'Ah, excellent. Liberty?' Cressida tidied her outfit, having shrugged the coat off, and was pulling down her sleeves prop-erly when the maid replied.

'That's right, miss. A Mr Sausage, I think he said.' The maid blushed as she said this, but Cressida laughed.

'Almost right. Sauvage. He'd appreciate you having a stab at getting it right.'

'Oh dear, miss, I am sorry.'

'Not your fault at all. It's French. They almost always plan their names to trip us Anglo-Saxons up.'

'Yes, miss,' the maid replied, too polite to assume she could joke around with a house guest.

'Did he leave a message?' Cressida said kindly, hoping the young maid wouldn't be scared for life now of ever saying a French name again.

'Just to call him, miss. At the shop, miss.' She curtsied and was about to leave when Cressida asked her another question.

'And Lady Dorothy? How is she?'

The maid looked sadly up at Cressida. 'Not well, miss.

She's still in her bed and not wanting broth nor hot chocolate to cheer her up.'

'Oh dear.' Cressida looked down and saw the shining eyes of Ruby gazing back up at her. 'Good idea, pup.' Cressida looked back at the confused maid, who obviously wasn't used to witnessing house guests talk to their pets. 'Could you take Ruby up to Dotty? And tell her I'll be up shortly? Thank you.'

Mercifully, Ruby let herself be picked up by the cautious maid, who no doubt had heard tell of Ruby's nipping of Jacob when he'd tried to take her away from her mistress. This time, though, the little dog snuffled a lick to the maid's cheek, which made her giggle, and Cressida smiled as the two of them headed upstairs. However much she'd like to be up with Dotty too, Cressida had a phone call to make.

'Operator? Liberty of London please. Upholstery and furnishings department. Yes, I'll hold.'

She waited while the call was put through.

'Mr Sauvage? Cressida Fawcett.'

'Ah, Miss Fawcett.' Maurice's familiar voice was a balm. 'Thank you for returning my call. I didn't want to leave a message with the staff and have done with it, in case one of them was in on it, if you know what I mean.'

'Quite right, most conscientious of you, Maurice. And can I ask, did two very similar parcels recently arrive with you?'

'Why, yes. Hence my call. A young footman called Jacob came bearing them, said he'd been told by both you and the butler to bring me these. Ran in and out at such a lick that it caught me off guard and I didn't have the damask samples ready for you—'

'Samples can wait for now, Maurice. But tell me, both parcels had lead discs in them, yes?'

'Yes, dear girl, what of it?'

'Nothing...' Cressida didn't need to go into details with Maurice but noted that Cardew had followed her request, even if he had delegated the actual journey to Jacob. 'Have you any thoughts on what those strange little bits of lead are?'

'Indeed I have.'

Maurice continued, confirming a suspicion that Cressida had been harbouring since she'd found the discs in the velvet box the diamonds should be in.

'Thank you, Maurice. It's as I suspected, but I still can't fathom who or why...'

'You know there's an old adage we live by here in the fabric world. "Measure twice and cut once".'

'What do you mean?' Cressida held the hearing horn of the telephone closer to her ear, as if hearing him better would help her decipher his riddle.

'I mean, check, check and check again. If you can't think of who did it, retrace all the steps you've taken and see who was there, or who could have been there. Check, check and then cut. Or in your case, get that nice policeman to arrest.'

'I see.' Cressida smiled and nodded. 'Thank you, Maurice. I shall catch up with you back in town. And I'm sorry Jacob couldn't wait around for the fabric samples. Fear not, though, I feel Lady Chatterton might be closer than ever to getting some new curtains! Cheerio.'

Cressida disconnected the call. Her conversation with Maurice had been illuminating and his advice stayed with her. *Measure twice and cut once... check, check and check again.*

38

Cressida now had an inkling where the diamonds might be hidden. Maurice had all but confirmed it to her, but she still wasn't sure who was responsible for stealing them... and worse, killing to cover it up.

But more important than any of that right now was Dotty and her broken heart. Cressida left the telephone room and went through the great hall up the stone staircase towards Dotty's bedroom. As she climbed the stairs, she looked at the crystal chandelier, hanging there sparkling like diamonds in the sunlight that was shining through the glass cupola above it. That the diamonds had originally been hiding up there she was in no doubt; the death of Harry Smith and the piece of waistcoat silk found on the scaffold which had been there proved that in her mind. But who would want to hide diamonds in a chandelier that would then be nigh on impossible to get to once the scaffold was down?

Measure twice and cut once... Maurice's words came back to her. Once she'd seen Dotty, she would retrace everything she'd found out and see if it helped make sense, like a pattern for dressmaking or a particularly complicated set of drapes.

. . .

'Dotty?' Cressida had knocked softly and opened the door. She was greeted at first by Ruby, who inelegantly plopped off Dotty's bed and waggled her little tail as she waddled to the door. 'Oh, hello Rubes.' Cressida bent down and picked up her dog, graciously accepting the face licks and excited snorts that came with her. Rollo, the Chatterton spaniel, greeted her too, with more snuffles and a few soft licks.

'Is that you Cressy?' The voice came from the mound under the bedclothes.

'Yes, dear. Just me. Are you under there?' Cressida let the spaniel out of the room and then walked over to the bed, popped Ruby back where a round indentation in the eiderdown showed she'd been nestled, and poked the talking mound. 'What ho, Dotty.'

'What ho, Cressy,' the mound replied. Then it sniffed.

'Oh Dotty. I'm so sorry you've been so badly treated by that absolute rotter.' Cressida sat down on the bed and placed her hand over the mound. 'If it makes you feel any better, I just threw a mediocre gin fizz all over him at the Barley Mow.'

'What?' Dotty threw the bedclothes off her, revealing a damp and red blotched face with chestnut-haired bob all awry around it. 'You did what, Cressy?'

Despite worrying about her friend's appearance, Cressida was pleased to see some life in her. She knew that any jilted lover, be they calm and reposed or taken to their bed as Dotty was, could always be enticed by news of their ex-lover, especially if it involved a comeuppance.

'I went to go and give him a piece of my mind. And it happened to involve me going to the Barley Mow.'

'Gosh, I haven't been there since you and I did that—'

'Yes, quite. Anyway, thought I better buy a drink rather

than just searching the place and I was checking the guest book when Basil came upon me from the turn of the stairs.'

'And what did he say?' Dotty had reached across to her nightstand and found her round-rimmed glasses, which were now being pressed studiously up the bridge of her nose as she sat herself up against the pillows on her bed.

'Well, frankly, he was rude about my drinking. Now, if he'd had anything else to say, about you for example, or his beastly behaviour, I would have heard him out, if only so that I could report back to you, chum. But he implied I was a terrible drunk, so I had to soak him.'

'Gosh.' Dotty wiped her nose and sat up straighter. 'So he didn't say anything about me?'

'I'm afraid after the sloshing I didn't give him much chance.'

Dotty's face had crumpled into a sad pout and her glasses were slipping back down her nose.

'I think he behaved appallingly, if it's any consolation. And everyone else does too.' Cressida tried to comfort her friend but could see it wasn't doing any good. She tried another tack. 'And you're much, much better off without him, chum. If he does make a go of it with Petronella, and more fool her, I say, if he does, then at least those two are both the early-rising, outdoorsy types. And you've never really liked the outdoors, have you?'

Dotty sniffed. 'My hair frizzes in the rain and horses don't seem to like me.'

'Beastly creatures.' Cressida nodded. To her surprise, Dotty carried on with her grievances against the great outdoors.

'Gnats seem to home in on me, I never seem to have the right clothes and cows often loom at you from sodden fields on walks that are supposed to be healthy but on which you only ever end up with a running nose and a twisted ankle.'

'Cows are the worst, that's true.' Cressida nodded again. 'So, you see, you'll find someone who'll be much more like you and love the indoors. Someone excellent at charades and with a love of the library.'

'Books don't give you allergies, Cressy, that's all I can say.' Dotty sniffed again and Cressida got up and fetched a handkerchief from the dressing table while Dotty continued. 'And you say it was a very mediocre gin fizz?'

'Yes. Warm and the gin was of unknown origin. Quite stung the eyes, I should hope. And, Dot, there are heaps of lovely young men out there who can think of nothing better than sitting reading a book all day and doing some light comic acting in the evenings.'

'Will you come with me?' Dotty asked, having blown her nose again and pushed her glasses back up to the bridge of her nose.

'Where to, Dot?'

'To the parties and balls. Where I'll meet these chaps?' Dotty looked at her expectantly. 'That's if any of them will have me.' She looked downcast once more.

'Of course they'll "have you", Dotty. You're a catch. Not only are you one of the most kind-hearted and generous people I know, you're a whizz on the pianoforte and a jolly good laugh. And when you're not so blotchy, you're pretty as a peach, chum.' Cressida could see Dotty flushing, but at last it was the good type of redness, the sort that bloomed on happy cheeks, not sad ones. Cressida continued, a twinkle in her eye, 'Oh, and there's that small factor of the Chatterton fortune... You and your inheritance will be batting suitors off, Dotty.' Cressida raised an eyebrow at her friend, the corners of her mouth twitching as she held in a giggle.

'Oh, Cressida.' Dotty found a pretty little silk cushion and threw it at Cressida's head.

'See, that's the spirit.' Cressida laughed. Then she paused, frowning as she thought about something.

'What is it, Cressy? Mentally running through your little

black book for me? Must have own teeth, lacks penchant for shooting squirrels...' Dotty started to reel off her 'must haves'. Ruby stirred at the mention of squirrels but otherwise stayed curled up, a small, solid snoring ball of pugginess.

'Inheritance... it does make sense you see...'

'Cressy?' Dotty interrupted her thoughts.

'Oh Dotty, sorry. Away with the fairies there. But speaking of your inheritance, I think I might know exactly where your mother's diamonds are hiding.'

39

'Cressy? Do you really?' Dotty looked at her in awe.

'I think so... Fancy coming to see?'

'Oh, rather. Yes please!' This news was enough to get Dotty out of bed and running a brush through her hair. 'Where do you think they are?'

'All shall be revealed. I need to speak to DCI Andrews first, he's been good enough to let me in on his investigation now, so I think he'd like to be kept in the loop. Ready?'

'Ready.' Dotty pushed her glasses up her nose and scooped up Ruby from her bed. 'Let's go.'

The two friends headed down the stone staircase and all but bundled their way into the library, where Andrews and Sergeant Kirby were heads together going through notes on the desk.

'Chief Inspector, Sergeant Kirby!' Cressida called out, not giving in to the urge to call them Max and Quentin...

'Miss Fawcett, any news?' Andrews turned to face her, and she noticed again how tired he looked.

'Yes, tons. Firstly, before he dobs me in, I confess to chucking a glass of gin fizz over Basil's head. It's up to you to ponder if that constitutes a crime against the Crown, but I take full responsibility.'

Andrews sighed, though Cressida could see the creases around his eyes twitching with mirth. 'And?'

'And, I think I know where the diamonds are,' she said rather triumphantly. 'Follow me!'

The four of them, and Ruby of course, excitedly left the library and headed to the ballroom, where the ghastly curtains still dominated the decor. Even tied back with their elegant gold ropes they were far too colourful for the room, its softly aged wooden sprung floor crying out for something more gentle.

Cressida put these thoughts aside and headed for where she could see, despite the voluminous folds of the curtains, the hem that didn't sit right.

'Can you fill us in at all on your thoughts, Miss Fawcett?' Andrews asked, a little exasperated.

Sergeant Kirby was trying his best to poise his pencil ready to make notes in mid-air.

'My friend Maurice Sauvage at Liberty confirmed what I suspected. The lead discs we found in the velvet jewellery box were in fact hem weights. They're used in curtain making to ensure the curtains hang correctly and don't spring up or give way to annoying creases and all that. The odd thing about these curtains is that, although they are exquisitely made, I noticed something off about the hem. I'm kicking myself now for not putting two and two together then, but, of course, we didn't know that the diamonds were still in the house, despite my theories on the chandelier.'

'I see. And you think the thief, who still had the original box about his—'

'Or her,' Cressida interrupted the inspector.

'Or her,' he accepted the possibility, 'person, then used it to dispose of the lead weights that had to be removed from these curtains? Kirby, could you do the honours and check that hemline.' Andrews gestured over towards the curtain that wasn't hanging right and Kirby quickly put his notebook away and hurried over.

'I think that's exactly what happened,' Cressida agreed, while not being able to take her eyes off where Kirby was feeling along the hemline. 'I still don't know who yet though.'

Cressida, Dotty and Andrews fell silent as they watched Kirby search the hemline some more. He looked back at them and shook his head.

'Keep looking, man,' Andrews said. 'Check all the hems.'

'I don't understand,' Cressida huffed as the final hem was searched and nothing revealed. 'I'm sorry, I was sure—'

'It was a good theory, Miss Fawcett.' Andrews sighed and gave Kirby the nod of permission to stop searching. 'As good a theory as we've had anyway.'

'Measure twice and cut once...' Cressida whispered to herself, but Andrews and Dotty looked at her quizzically. 'Sorry, it's just something Maurice reminded me of. In upholstery and curtain making, the first rule is to measure twice and cut once, because, well, you only get one chance at the cutting, don't you?'

'Yes?' Andrews cocked his head as he answered her somewhat rhetorical question.

'I'm going to have to go over the whole thing again. With all the clues. We can do this, Andrews, I can feel it. The thief, and the murderer, are within our grasp... I just need to measure it all again, as it were.'

Andrews blew out his cheeks and gently nodded his head. Cressida thought he might be about to dismiss her and Dotty as pointless wastes of time in this whole business, but instead he looked at her and simply said, 'To be honest, Miss Fawcett, I've not been having much luck with cases these last few years, so if you can help me solve this one, I'll be grateful. What would you like me to do?'

Moments later, the four of them were huddled around the desk in the library again.

'Chief Inspector,' Cressida started the meeting. 'I think we need all the physical clues around us. That way we can see them and keep them in mind while we retrace the steps of what happened, right back to the night the diamonds were stolen.'

'Kirby,' Andrews delegated the task by calling on the sergeant. 'Can you find the evidence bags and bring them here please?'

'Yessir.' The sergeant jumped to it and made to leave the room.

Cressida looked at Andrews and he answered her before she could ask the question.

'We thought it safer to lock the evidence in our car, rather than leave it lying about.'

'Quite right,' Cressida replied. 'Especially as someone in this house is a murderer.'

Dotty blanched and Cressida reminded herself that her friend had had an utterly awful day so far and reached out to touch her arm.

'I'm sure it's not a Chatterton.'

Dotty nodded. 'I know it's not. I know it's not.'

Cressida wanted to say *Basil, on the other hand, is very high up on my list of suspects, as is his 'athletic' girlfriend*, but she kept it in, thinking it better to wait for the evidence bags before she expanded on any more of her theories.

Luckily, Kirby soon reappeared carrying a wooden box that had once housed twelve bottles of vintage port and now had the brown paper bags used for collecting the items of evidence in them.

'Right, thank you, Kirby.' Andrews cleared his throat and started to lay out the bags on the desk. He read from the labels on the bags. 'Number one, we have the small scrap of fabric found by you, the Honourable Cressida Fawcett on Saturday the eighteenth of April 1925.'

'Oh yes, there it is.' Cressida arranged it on top of its bag when the inspector had taken it out.

He carried on. 'Number two is a waistcoat found in the footwell of Major Elliot's car by the Honourable Cressida Fawcett on Sunday the nineteenth of April 1925.' He raised his eyebrows at her. 'Number three is a burnt piece of paper found by the Honourable—'

'Yes, yes, Andrews, I get the point. I've been a busybody.' Cressida unfolded the waistcoat and smoothed out the back where the tear was as she spoke. She nurtured a strange combination of embarrassment and pride at how many of these clues she was responsible for.

Andrews drew breath and continued the roll call. 'Potential clue number four, the velvet jewellery box and the remainder of what was in it. I'm referencing, of course, the lead discs that have now been identified as curtain weights by Mr Sauvage of Liberty of London.' He looked up from his notebook at Kirby, who was getting the black velvet case out of a brown paper bag.

'I knew I'd seen something like them before,' Cressida insisted. 'I think my cousin used them to skim across the lake at Mydenhyrst when he came to stay for the holidays and Mama would go spare when she realised he'd cannibalised her drawing-room curtains to do so.' Cressida shook her head, the memory of curtain desecration lingering.

Kirby continued pulling out clues and pieces of evidence, such as the moustache net and the medicine bottle from beside the major's bed, until the desk in the library was heaving with items.

'Gosh,' Dotty whispered, looking at the desk. 'What a lot of clues, yet I don't know about you, but I'm still none the wiser.'

Cressida looked at Andrews, who shook his head. 'Nor are we, Dotty,' she said to her friend, who was still holding a now gently snoring Ruby in her arms. 'But now we have our fabric out, so to speak, we start our measuring...'

DCI Andrews looked at Cressida. 'You're speaking in riddles again.'

'Not riddles, but reasoning. We need to go over the whole thing from the beginning. John's right: things don't just happen in threes, or fours. All of this' – she swept her arm over the desk – 'has to be linked somehow. And going back to the beginning should help us with that.'

Andrews nodded and Kirby flipped over a new page of his notebook.

'Come on then,' Cressida ushered them all out of the room and with Ruby comfortably nestled in Dotty's arms they traipsed up the wide stone staircase and onto the upper landing.

'I do see the logic, Miss Fawcett,' Andrews told her as they stood outside the closed door to Lady Chatterton's bedroom. 'But the local police investigated here and Kirby and I later found nothing that wasn't in their original report.'

'And do you have that report, Kirby?' Cressida turned to the young policeman.

'Yes, miss, hang about.' He flicked back several pages of his notebook. 'Right, it says the lady of the house came up to discover her room in disarray—'

'I'll stop you there, Kirby. Apologies all, but back downstairs we go. We've started this far too late on in the series of events. Dotty, where were you when the lights went out?'

'Well, we were all in the drawing room, I think. Yes, definitely. John was looking at his atlas and Mama and I were planning menus for the weekend.'

'Right, come on...' Cressida led the small party back down the stairs.

'What ho!' John called to them from the hallway as they were halfway down the stairs.

Edmund was with him and looked on with mirth at the bizarre image of two policemen and two gentlewomen and one snoring pug en masse.

'What are you all up to? Can we join in?' Edmund asked, and almost as soon as he'd said that, Alfred appeared from the library.

'Hello, you lot. Any thoughts as to why a burnt bit of paper and some fabric are floating around the library floor? Afraid the spaniel almost made off with that hideous moustache net of the major's too.'

'Kirby!' Andrews turned to his junior officer. 'Secure the evidence!'

The two policemen ran down the remainder of the stairs and barrelled past Alfred and the other chaps in their haste to get to the library.

Alfred looked on in bewilderment. 'Good job none of us are murderers, isn't it?' he asked rhetorically and looked up at Cressida and his sister. 'How are you doing, Dot?'

A kind word from her brother was enough to cause Dotty's tears to flow and Alfred looked at Cressida apologetically. Cressida, in turn, was looking at Ruby somewhat apologetically as the small dog was bearing the brunt of Dotty's running nose and teary sniffles and so Cressida lifted the pup from her arms and whispered to Dot that it might be worth her heading up to her room and that she'd follow her up.

'Sorry,' Alfred apologised again when Cressida came down to join the three of them.

'It's not your fault, Alfred. That Basil did a number on poor Dot and now I think she's worried she'll never find a nice chap.'

Alfred looked at Cressida and she would have given five

bob to have known what was going on inside that handsome –
yes, she had to admit to herself, handsome – head of his. They
were interrupted by Edmund asking Alfred if he thought it
would be all right if they went out for a ride. Cressida nodded
an adieu to Alfred as he played host, but thanks to the peculiar
acoustics of the hallway, heard the young men's conversation as
she climbed the stairs and they walked away.

'How long do you think that chappie wants to keep us
here?' Edmund asked. 'Not that I'm not enjoying the Chatterton hospitality, but I've got half an eye on Saucy Sue running
the 1000 Guineas in Newmarket at the end of the month and
rather thought I might motor up there and stay a few nights
with some of the other Mutton Pie-ers, enjoy the racing, you
know.'

'Top up the allowance with a win?' Alfred asked, unable to
answer Edmund's question.

'Got to make hay while the sun shines,' Edmund replied.

'Yes, heard you were having the taps cut off on your next
birthday, rum shame.' It was John's voice. 'But the odds on
Double Chance are pretty decent after the Grand National win
and I know a good bookie who'll add in an each-way bet...' The
voices trailed off, but that loose thread Cressida had started to
pull while in her car earlier, the one snagging in her mind,
started to unravel a little bit more.

40

'Ah, Cressida dear,' Lady Chatterton called to Cressida from the top of the stairs. 'Did I hear you all outside my bedroom a moment ago?'

Cressida blushed and hoped Lady Chatterton would mistake the pink in her cheeks for the sunbeam that was cascading through the crystals of the chandelier from the cupola above. 'Yes, sorry, Lady Chatterton, we were... well, I was—'

'Is Dorothy with you?' Lady Chatterton asked, and Cressida could see that deaths and diamonds aside, her daughter's welfare was actually what was uppermost in Her Ladyship's eyes. 'You are good spending time with her in her darkest hour. Her father and I are livid at Basil for letting her down, but we're so grateful that you're here. She really does look up to you, you know.'

'Oh, I don't know, Lady Chatterton, I don't think I'm being much use.' Cressida had climbed the stairs and was now looking towards the very shut door of Dotty's bedroom.

'Well, I'll tell you how you can be if you'd like?'

Cressida looked at her hostess, a million loose threads vying for attention in her mind. But she was unable to say no to any request of dear Lady Chatterton and so nodded.

'Be a dear and leave Ruby here for a moment and pop back to your room and fetch Lady Adelaine down. I know she'll be looking lovely on your chest of drawers, but now the scaffolding has gone, she can come back down to sit next to Sir Roger. Hated each other in real life, dare I say, but their effigies do look so handsome together here in the hall.'

Grateful it was an easy enough errand, Cressida replied, 'Of course, I'll be back in a jiffy.' She let Ruby down, who happily snuffled around the landing while she headed back to her bedroom to find the pretty alabaster bust of the long-dead Lady Adelaine. The sculpture was just as she'd left her, and Cressida picked her up and carefully brought her down to the main hall, where Lady Chatterton was now waiting. 'Here you are,' Cressida said, a somewhat disembodied voice from behind the ghostly white visage of Lady A. 'Where would you like her?'

'Wonderful. Over here by Sir Roger. Careful of the ledge though, it's not as deep as the trompe l'oeil makes out. The Chatterton who came up with the decor for this room ran out of cash after the cupola was built so had to make to do with painted niches and all sorts of mottled arty effects to make some of this plain old plaster look like marble.'

'How marvellous.' Cressida looked more closely at the painted 'niche' that she put Lady Adelaine into. Lady Chatterton was right, the ledge for the bust was just deep enough, but the paintwork behind the ledge made it look like there was a generous niche, carved out of stone, in which the sculpture could sit like something in the British Museum. 'It really is a work of art in its own right.' Cressida stepped back and wondered at the skill of the artist who had created it.

'All the rage in the eighteenth century when folks ran low of marble-buying funds. Anyway, thank you, dear. Ruby is around here somewhere. I'll let you get on. This whole weekend has

been a nightmare, but I'm so glad that you're here with us.'
Lady Chatterton squeezed Cressida's arm and then left her
alone in the great hall with Ruby, contemplating her navel
under Sir Roger's bust.

Cressida looked at the trompe l'oeil niches again in the great
hall. *Something that on closer inspection appears to be
nothing...* She held onto that thought as she pushed open the
green baize door that led to the kitchens. Andrews and Kirby
were still more than likely playing chase the evidence around
the library floor, so with Ruby at her heel, Cressida started her
walk-through of the robbery again.

Standing out on the terrace, Cressida looked up at Lady
Chatterton's bedroom window. The local police had been right
about the drainpipe being so close to the window and easily
slide-downable by someone athletic... She cocked her head on
one side, remembering that thread she'd been trying to pull out
of her mind since she'd spoken to William this morning.
Petronella had excellent upper body strength... she thought to
herself. *That's what I was trying to make sense of...* Could the
South African diamond heiress have been the one to break into
Chatterton Court before arriving for the weekend house party,
where she had not only intended on snaring Basil back for
herself but also flogging the now-vulnerable Lady Chatterton
some new gems?

Cressida bit the inside of her lips in thought. She'd heard
the Harper-Ashes talking and Petronella had been quite firm
with her brother. It had sounded like she only had one thing on
her mind, and that was Basil. Still, there was something else
about Petronella that nudged the periphery of Cressida's mind
and refused to come to the forefront.

'Oh, darn it, Rubes.' Cressida stamped her foot on the York
stone of the terrace in frustration. An unexpected crunch under

her shoe distracted her from her vexation. She lifted her foot up gently and looked to see which poor snail or bird egg had been squished and was surprised that neither of those things had been the crunch. 'Now that is odd.' Cressida looked at the dark orange crumble on the stone. She squatted down as best her pencil skirt would allow and peered at it. The fragments of terracotta must have been left over from a smashed tile. Cressida stood up so quickly she felt a little dizzy, but that didn't stop her from darting across the terrace and taking the few steps down onto the lawn from where she could see the roof and, among the uniform tiles, she spotted a hole where one was missing. 'Aha...' she said to the patient pup beside her, who was wagging her tail. 'Of course. It's like the trompe l'oeil and the fact the drainpipe is still green. And, Rubes... oh by Jove, I think I've got it! Of course the diamonds weren't in the curtains because of the ticking of that engine. And those footsteps with no flushing... I knew I recognised that writing too... Oh Rubes. It's so obvious who it is... Come on, let's find Andrews and Kirby... I think we're about to solve a murder!'

Cressida ran back into the house, hoping to come across Andrews, Dotty or even Sergeant Kirby. She stood for a moment in the great hall and listened in case she could hear anyone's voices. For once, the whole house was still, and despite there still being a great number of them lingering after the weekend, not to mention the household servants, there was no one around.

'Where is everyone, Ruby?' Cressida asked and Ruby panted some sort of answer to her, that Cressida had to admit she didn't understand.

A movement from the top of the stairs caught both their attention and she looked up.

'False alarm, no one there, Rubes,' Cressida said, walking into the centre of the great hall. She looked up at the sparkling chandelier and thought about her theory regarding the diamonds. The crystals sparkled like the finest cut gems and they glinted and shone in the wonderful light that was streaming in through the glass cupola. She raised her hand up to shield her eyes from the glare and moved back away from the centre of the room so that she could see the crystals without squinting.

Another noise from above startled her. This time, it wasn't a tread of a footstep on the landing carpet, but the sound of a scraping, scratching, grinding sort of action. Still blinded by the brightness of the sunlight, Cressida spun around, trying to work out what she could hear. It was like grindstones clashing, or... She noticed that the bust of Lady Adelaine was no longer in her shallow niche. Cressida had only just put her there herself before she went out to the terrace. And now she was gone... And there it was again, the sound of stone being pushed along stone... or alabaster being pushed across stone.

Cressida looked up, her eyes straining against the light coming into the great hall from the cupola. But she did see something, something white and Lady Adelaine-shaped teetered on the edge of the stone balustrade above her.

Cressida screamed, but her voice caught in her throat and she was frozen with terror at the sight of Lady Adelaine wavering one last time before starting her deathly plummet to the ground below, precisely where Cressida was standing.

41

The crash of the alabaster bust reverberated around the great hall of Chatterton Court, causing the other busts to wobble in their niches and the huge chandelier to sway and tinkle. White shards of the antique sculpture scattered all over the marble floor of the hall, each one jagged and pointed and sharp as scalpels. The largest of these vicious pieces lay inches from Cressida's head, which in turn was huddled to the ground, her hands over it as she crouched protectively over Ruby.

The silence that the smash had shattered, as easily as the alabaster bust had, was replaced by calls and shouts from throughout the house. Cressida could hear voices coming closer and knew she should get up and flee, assuming one of those voices was the person who had just pushed the bust of Lady Adelaine over the balustrade. But she couldn't move, her joints seemed fused into position and her heart was beating so loudly it felt like it was about to burst from her chest. Ruby, who had been as startled by the crash as Cressida had, recovered herself more quickly and Cressida used the rhythmic panting of the small dog to calm her own breathing.

'Miss Fawcett!' DCI Andrews was the first to the scene,

Sergeant Kirby close behind him. He knelt down next to Cressida's hunched body, his arm instantly over her back, his voice hushed so as not to alarm her, but full of tension too. 'Miss Fawcett, are you all right? Can you hear me? Miss Fawcett?'

Cressida concentrated on her breathing, aware of the kindly voice next to her but unable to focus on it. Instead she kept replaying in her mind the sight of the bust falling towards her and Ruby, Lady Adelaine's face rushing down to meet hers. She was dead, she knew it. She must be? But the voices around her didn't sound like the heavenly host, or if her luck was out, the demons of hell. They sounded like the hysterical maids and concerned gentlemen of the family, voices she'd heard three mornings running when it had been someone else, someone else's body, in the same predicament as her.

Lady Adelaine was smashed all around her... it was coming back in flashes. Her white porcelain face, like a ghost that screamed towards her. Yet there was another face, smaller and further away, obscured by the balustrade and hazy in her terrified vision. Chestnut hair...

'Miss Fawcett?' Andrews' arm was cajoling her into a sitting position and she let him help her upright.

'R-Ruby?' Cressida picked the small pup up as she stood, shakily staggering a few steps and letting Andrews and Kirby support her.

'She's fine, not a scratch,' Andrews' reassuring voice comforted her. 'You're both unharmed. Come and sit down, you've had a horrible shock.'

DCI Andrews led Cressida into the library. She noted the evidence bags all neatly labelled and was surprised that her memory recalled the run-in the clues had with Rollo in amongst all the other horrors she was processing.

'Cressy!' A dishevelled but otherwise determined Dotty was suddenly through the library door and at Cressida's side. 'Cressy, what happened? Are you all right?'

In moments, Lady Chatterton and Alfred were by her side.

'Cressida dear.' Lady Chatterton sat herself down on the chintz sofa next to Cressida and held her hand. 'Please say you're all right. I couldn't bear it if another... oh.'

'Mother,' Alfred crouched down in front of Lady Chatterton as she recovered from her faint and took her hands in his. 'Sorry, Cressy. We're meant to be comforting you... Mother, are you well?'

'Yes... yes...' Lady Chatterton sounded most feeble and Alfred asked Kirby to ring for tea. 'Hotter and sweeter the better please!'

Andrews mimicked Alfred's position and crouched down in front of Cressida. 'Miss Fawcett, tea's on its way. Are you quite well?'

'Yes, I think so.' Though Cressida was still holding fast to Ruby and her pulse still beat extraordinarily quickly. 'I just didn't think... but I suppose this proves it.'

'What is it, Miss Fawcett? Is everything all right?' The inspector looked concerned.

'Yes.' She lowered her voice to a whisper. 'I think so and I think I've worked out who it is. Who's been stealing and killing in order to... well, I can go into all of that later.'

Cressida released her grip around Ruby in order to place a finger to her lips and the small dog took the opportunity to plop off her lap and go in search of crumbs. Cressida, still slightly wobbly from the shock, got up off the sofa and indicated to Dotty that she should take her seat and comfort her mother while she and Andrews moved towards the desk.

When out of earshot, she asked him a question. 'Andrews, about Petronella. Do we have a report yet from the hospital?'

He consulted his notebook. 'Yes. Came through this afternoon after William visited. The nurse said it was a blow to the very crown of the head; a sharp instrument but not a knife.'

'Like a tile. Falling from the roof perhaps?' The similarity to her own position wasn't lost on her.

'That's exactly what the nurse at the hospital said actually.' Andrews flicked his notebook shut on the desk. 'So?'

'So, trompe l'oeil. I'll explain what I mean in a bit. But first, could I beg a favour of you? Could perhaps Kirby fetch Basil back from the Barley Mow? And ask very nicely of the house-maid he likes...' She saw Kirby blush. '... And see if she could find all the Mutton Pie Club waistcoats? And, Andrews, could you gather everyone together for me? I have a suspect in mind.'

Cressida picked up Andrews' notebook. She wrote a name on the pad and passed it back to him, watching as his eyebrows raised in curiosity.

'Why—'

'Walls have ears, Inspector.' She glanced over to where Dotty, Alfred and their mother were gathered on the sofa. 'I'd rather not say out loud, just in case. But let's meet back here, with everyone, in about half an hour? I've got another inkling of where the diamonds really are.'

'Right you are, Miss Fawcett.' Andrews turned to Kirby. 'Sergeant, you heard the young lady. Off to the pub please to pick up Basil Bartleby. I'll corral the other house guests back here. But, Miss Fawcett...'

'Yes, Andrews?'

'I can't have you going about on your own. Not after what happened. You're still shaking, for goodness' sake.' He looked concerned.

'I need to do this as subtly as possible. If I tramped around with an escort, I fear our suspect would realise and make a run for it.'

Andrews frowned. 'You remind me of your father, Miss Fawcett. He'd never take his own safety seriously when others needed help.' He sighed. 'So be careful. And good luck.'

'Thank you... I hope I won't need it, but right now I'll

take it...'

Cressida, her shawl wrapped around her to keep off the afternoon chill, left the library through the French doors that led onto the terrace. Her steps were faltering and flashbacks to her near miss in the great hall almost felled her. As she walked down the steps from the terrace to the lawn, she glanced back up at the house. The drainpipe was just as she thought.

'Impossible...' she murmured to herself. 'Not in that state anyway.' She shook her head, annoyed at how long it had taken her to notice what was glaringly obvious to her now. Casting her eye even further up, she saw again the missing tile from the roof. 'So obvious too, when you think about it...' She sighed, then turned and stalked across the lawn to the thicket of trees and the icehouse.

Ruby, who had padded along with her amiably from the library put on a sudden turn of speed that looked rather comical, but Cressida trotted along to keep up with her.

'I reckon you know exactly what we're going to find, don't you, Rubes?' Cressida asked her as they entered the shade of the woods.

The sun was low in the sky now anyway and the forest floor felt soft and damp under her feet. A shiver came over her as the warmth of the sun disappeared from her back and her eyes adjusted to the gloom of the woodland. She pulled her shawl closer around her. If the murderer had followed her from the house... She looked around and checked time and again, but she was on her own.

'It's not far luckily, Rubes,' Cressida said to herself more than her to her dog. Her steps became more purposeful the closer she got and she reached the dome and igloo-like entrance tunnel of the icehouse in no time at all. 'Well, here we are. Fancy having a sniff around, Rubes?' Cressida bent down and ruffled the short fur between Ruby's ears. Taking that as a starting pistol for a race, the little dog bounded off around the dome, sniffing and pawing at various mounds of soil and old leaves. Cressida looked too, peering up and over the top of the dome to see if she could spot anything glinting in the last few rays of light that were coming through the tree canopy.

A few more moments passed, then to Cressida's delight Ruby yapped and her besotted owner rushed round to where she was standing, panting and looking about as exceptionally happy as a dog could look. And as exceptionally glamorous, as dripping from her mouth was the most beautifully set diamond necklace Cressida had ever seen.

'Oh Ruby, you clever, clever pup.' Cressida knelt down beside her and gently eased the necklace out of her mouth. She held it up and saw how it sparkled, even in the dwindling light of the late afternoon. Looking down, she noticed more gems in the rough patch of twigs and leaves that Ruby had been snootling around in. The matching bracelet and earrings were all there, lying on the ground, yet perfect and completely undamaged. 'You might be a Ruby by birth, young pup,' Cressida picked up her dog in one hand, the other cradling the precious jewels, 'but today, you are a total diamond.'

Cressida slipped the diamonds into her pocket and carried Ruby triumphantly across the lawn. She was now surer than ever that she'd identified the thief, and killer, and could explain all the clues they'd found over this most troublesome of country house weekends.

'I shall look forward to the peace and quiet of London. Never has someone at The Ritz tried to kill me,' she whispered to Ruby as she approached the open French doors of the library, and then put the dog down as she walked in.

The bulbs in the new electric lights were burning bright and Cressida realised that her eyes had become adjusted to the gloaming outside. She blinked now at the well-lit faces that all turned to her as she entered. Lord and Lady Chatterton were seated on one of the chintz sofas. Dotty was perched next to her mother, all three of them looking thoroughly washed out and exhausted by the whole affair. Basil, recently accompanied back from the Barley Mow, had the decency at least to stand on the other side of the room, while Alfred and John stood with arms crossed by the fireplace, acting as guards between their sister and her ex-fiancé. Edmund sat down on another of the chintz chairs, his arms crossed too, but looking less protective and more crotchety, as if he were being kept from being somewhere more important. William looked tired too and somewhat twitchy, his sister obviously still too unwell to leave the hospital and he perhaps right now would prefer to be by her side. Andrews and Kirby were standing by the desk and Andrews welcomed Cressida in just as Cardew entered the room, and closed the door behind him.

Andrews quietened the murmurings of the guests. 'My lords and ladies, gentlemen. Thank you for all staying here at Chatterton Court while we've investigated the deaths of both Mr Harry Smith, the chandelier cleaner, your friend Major Elliot and the attack on Miss Harper-Ashe. Not to mention the theft of Lady Chatterton's diamonds.'

'And Cressy almost being finished off too,' Dotty stuttered, and Cressida smiled at her comfortingly.

Andrews continued. 'Yes, Lady Dorothy, that as well. As you know, this case has been a conundrum from start to finish and despite my best efforts to solve it myself, I have to admit that the Honourable Cressida Fawcett here has cracked it.' He turned to her, gesturing for her to stand more centrally in the room. 'The floor, as they say, is yours, Miss Fawcett.'

'I say,' Basil piped up. 'What rot is this, what? Some sort of parlour game? You know how I hate those.'

His outburst made Dotty sigh and Cressida, while desperately trying to keep all of her ideas straight in her head, could also see how hard this was for her friend.

'Miss Fawcett,' Andrews urged her. 'We're all waiting...'

42

'Yes, indeed, sorry, Chief Inspector.'

Cressida cleared her throat and smoothed down the front of her skirt. In so doing she felt the bulge in her pocket. At least she knew where she could start.

'Lady Chatterton,' she reached into her pocket and pulled out the diamonds, 'I believe these are yours. Sorry about the twigs and the odd woodlouse. But nothing a bit of spit and polish won't get rid of.'

The atmosphere in the room changed almost immediately.

'Oh Cressida!' Lady Chatterton blurted out. 'My diamonds!'

'Cressy!' Dotty exclaimed. She looked around at the other faces. All but one was looking in awe at the sparkling, if somewhat muddy, gems that were now being passed between Lady Chatterton, her husband, daughter and sons.

'Where were they, dear?' Lady Chatterton looked up, holding her dangling earrings against her ears as if trying them on in the mirror at Asprey.

'They were loosely concealed in the dirt by the icehouse. Hence the bugs. Sorry.' She did a quick check to see if any creepy-crawlies had made a home in her pocket and then continued. 'I had a hunch they'd be there because the chandelier had been rumbled, and the curtain hem deemed unsatisfactory, so the thief had no option but to get them as far away from the house, while not causing suspicion by running away. The icehouse fits the bill as it can be approached by the back lanes out of sight of the house, easy enough for the thief to drive up in his car and sling them out, return back to the house pronto and then pick them up again once all this is over.'

'His...' John looked around the room.

'Yes. Dotty and Lady Chatterton were never in the frame.'

'Can you explain why, Miss Fawcett, for our records, of course.' Andrews looked apologetically at Dotty and Lady Chatterton, who still seemed so enamoured with the diamonds that they hadn't clocked what he'd said.

'Of course, Chief Inspector. Not only is Dotty my friend, but she of all people, excepting Lady Chatterton, had no motive to steal them. She would inherit them herself in time. Plus, she was with her mother throughout the whole evening of the theft, so there was no time when she could have run upstairs and ransacked her mother's room.'

'And Petronella?' Andrews asked.

'I toyed with the thought that she's perfectly capable, physically, of getting down that drainpipe, what with all the exercise she does. Not to mention I overheard her and William talking about pushing diamonds onto Lady Chatterton, to replace her old ones... Oh and she was wearing a light-coloured silk dress the night of the first murder—'

'What would that have to do with it?' William asked, and Cressida looked at him.

'I'm sorry, William, I'll get to that. As for Petronella, though, she's been hospitalised since this morning so couldn't have been responsible for the diamonds' final move today. And there's no suggestion that she or her brother were in the area on Wednesday night.'

'Who attacked her?' William asked, taking a step towards Cressida.

'No one, William. I'm afraid Petronella was the victim of nothing but an accident. Or divine intervention perhaps, if you're disposed to think about it that way.'

Basil huffed but Cressida could see Dotty trying her best not to smile.

'But she was hit by a blunt object,' William countered.

'Yes, she was. And it was odd because her "attack", as we all thought it to be, was the most obvious of the lot. The cleaner, Harry Smith, might have fallen by accident. Dear Major Elliot might have had a heart attack in his sleep, but Petronella was definitely hit over the head by a blunt object. Except, like the trompe l'oeil in the great hall, it's not what it seems.'

'The trumped-up what?' Basil interjected.

'Tromp l'oeil, you imbecile,' Cressida took great pleasure in correcting him. 'If you spent more time with books rather than guns, you'd be able to at least translate from the French. It's a form of decorative art, very popular in large houses like this, where artisans painted the effect of stone or marble, and even sometimes the perspective of a niche or archway, in order to create dramatic room schemes in a more economical way. And in so doing they create a mirage. They flip reality on its head. Like the two deaths that could have been accidents that were in fact murders, and the one we definitely thought was an attack, which was actually an accident. Petronella was simply in the wrong place at the wrong time and the unseasonably warm weather had obviously dried out the terracotta on one of the roof tiles to the extent that it cracked and fell during the high winds. And knowing what I know about their clandestine relationship, I think she might have been out there to meet Basil—'

'Definitely in the wrong place then.' Alfred narrowed his eyes at Basil, who nodded his head resignedly.

'Yes,' agreed Cressida. 'And the tile hit her here, on the crown of her head. Isn't that right, DCI Andrews?'

'Yes, the hospital confirmed by telephone earlier that the injury is consistent with a blow from very high up, what I mean is not a sideswipe from arm height, even from a very tall person.'

'Thank you, Inspector. I thought as much when I trod the crunchy, deteriorated terracotta under my foot. It was a different colour to the broken pot shards too. The tile must have hit her and then smashed to smithereens on the terrace as she fell. No sign of a weapon, you see, as it was smashed and then destroyed by the rain. So, Petronella was the reddest of herrings in all of this. Even down to me wondering if her excellent upper body strength could have meant she could cope with that drain-pipe... Which brings me back to the original robbery.

'The night that the diamonds were stolen, we know that the house had had its main electric switch turned off, Lady Chatterton's bedroom was ransacked, the diamonds taken from their box and the window was left open. Footprints, an army-style boot no less, were found in the flower bed below. So, under-standably, the local police deduced that the felon had entered through the house, cut the power, slipped upstairs and then out down the sturdy drainpipe next to Lady Chatterton's window.'

'That's about the gist of it,' Andrews conceded. 'And no blame can be put upon them for thinking so.'

'Quite. It was easy enough for all of us to leap to the same conclusion, but for a few things. Firstly, my friend Maurice Sauvage from Liberty told me that there had been no chatter on his network of contacts regarding the fencing of the jewels. Not two days later when we read about it in the papers, or over this weekend when I telephoned him. That's important when we think about the motive for the theft.'

'It's not hard to come up with a motive for stealing two

thousand pounds' worth of jewels, surely?' Lady Chatterton said, still clasping her precious stones to her chest.

'No, and their value was certainly the reason why they were taken, but then the fact that they weren't turned into ready cash on the black market as soon as they were stolen really tells us more about the identity of the thief.'

'I don't follow,' Basil stated. 'Is this some sort of psycho-analysis mumbo-jumbo?'

'No, Basil. It's just plain logic. Something you boasted to me that you had in buckets on Saturday morning when you were worming your way out of my suspect list and putting all the heat on the dear major.'

'Oh Basil.' Dotty looked at him. 'How dare you!' She crossed her arms, having pushed her glasses up her nose.

'The thief needed money, you see,' Cressida continued. 'But not yet. Hence concealing the diamonds in the chandelier, a perfect hiding place for them if you knew you could leave them, hiding in plain sight, until you came back to collect them the next time the chandelier was cleaned.'

'How did you know they were up the chandelier?' John asked.

'It all started to make sense the more you looked at the situation. Why had the electricity to the house been cut? So that the thief could safely hide the diamonds in the chandelier by moonlight. Why did one of the maids say she heard the scaffolding tower wobble while the power was cut? Because someone was scaling it in the dark.'

'Cressy dear, you're losing me. Go back to the motive,' Lady Chatterton prompted.

'It's all about inheritance. Or lack of it. There was talk this weekend of the vagaries of inheritance, the rum hand that some of these younger sons feel they've been dealt. Some, like Basil only have a small one—'

'I say—' Basil interjected, but Cressida and Dotty simultaneously shushed him.

'It is small, Basil, and all invested now in the Harper-Ashe diamond mines, which means that, like William, I'm sure you'll do all right in the end. You might be feeling the pinch now, hence gambling so much at the Mutton Pie Club tables, but in a few years, you'll be rich enough. And John, of course, will be looked after in the same manner Dotty is, and Alfred will inherit this whole estate one day. You, Edmund, well, you're getting the "taps cut off" at your next birthday, so—'

'But what of it? You didn't find those gems about any of our persons, did you?' Edmund retorted. 'I'm not sure I believe this chandelier nonsense. As the police said, the chappie obviously pegged it down the drainpipe and off past the icehouse, where the stupid idiot must have dropped them.' He looked around for agreement from the others.

There was a pause before Cressida answered him. 'You didn't though, did you, Edmund?'

43

The guests in the room either gasped or shouted out in surprise at Cressida's accusation.

'How dare you accuse me like that!' Edmund jumped up out of the armchair, but before he could take any steps towards her, Andrews and Kirby had him by the wrists and secured into a solid pair of cuffs.

'I'll explain! I'm sorry, everyone, please calm down.' Cressida could feel her own heartbeat hammering against her chest as she mentally recounted the things she'd seen and noticed that had brought her to the conclusion that Edmund was the murderer.

'Cressy, are you sure?' Dotty looked at her, anguish in her face, and Cressida felt terrible that this horror had been brought down on such a lovely family as the Chattertons. She only hoped that her explanation would help soothe them and reassure them that they were in no way responsible for what had happened under their roof.

'Firstly, the drainpipe was never used as a getaway. And I know this for two reasons.'

'Which are?' Edmund all but snarled at her from his cuffed

position back on the chair with the firm hand of Sergeant Kirby on his shoulder.

'Well, that drainpipe was never used as a means for climbing, or rather sliding down. I remember looking at it when I first tried to retrace the investigation of the local bobbies and thinking how I'd hate to get that green algae on my evening wear. And then, of course, it came to me... why would there still be so much algae on it if someone had recently slid down it? The boot prints could easily have been made once the thief had come back down the stairs with the diamonds and was making their escape through the house.'

'But why risk coming back through the house, Cressy?' Dotty asked, this time properly engaged in the conversation.

'Well, one very good reason. Or maybe two, depending on how much Edmund fancied his chances on the drainpipe. They're not everyone's favourite means of getting about. But, more importantly, it was so that he could use the cover of the dark house to hide the diamonds in the chandelier. With the lights off and the chandelier in utter darkness, he could use the light of the moon through the cupola to navigate up the scaffold, hide the diamonds in the crystals and then leave through the house. He couldn't risk going back the way he came through the kitchen as no doubt the staff would be more inconvenienced by the blackout than the family, who were rather used to them and comfortably going about their evening. So, he probably exited through these French doors, hoping the darkness in the house meant no one would see him on the terrace planting the footprints and then scarpering off to his waiting car, that I think must have been idling by the lake. You can get to that spot very easily from the back lanes and no one would spot a car pull up there from the house.'

'But why would anyone hide the diamonds in the chandelier? Especially if they were stealing them to bolster their inheritance?' It was William who was inquisitive this time.

'Well, this is where it all comes down to the type of inheritance you have. You, William, and Basil, for example, are strapped for cash *now*, but will make good on your inheritances or investments eventually. If you stole diamonds, you'd have had them fenced and cashed and be on the Riviera as soon as you could, living it up with your ill-gotten gains. But Edmund here, well, he has a healthy allowance *for now*. So he can afford to wait and not risk having the diamond theft being traced back to him.'

'I still don't understand the timing of it all though, Cressida dear?' Lady Chatterton asked.

'Edmund knew he was coming to this house party this weekend. Now, most of us who were invited received a telephone call from Dotty on Friday morning checking we could still come. I was in London when I received the call, but Edmund...'

'Oh, yes, I couldn't get hold of Edmund!' Dotty piped up.

'Told you I was already on my way. Nothing illegal about that,' Edmund gruffly added to the conversation.

'No, but in the front seat of your car, I found your road atlas, a sort of gazetteer with a natty bookmark that you can pencil in your journey. Odd that yours brought you so close to Chatterton Court, yet not all the way here, wasn't it? And when I visited Basil at the Barley Mow,' she paused and glanced at Basil, who looked as peeved as she hoped he'd be at the memory of the gin fizz he'd had chucked at him. 'Well, when I was there, I spotted your name in the guest book for Wednesday night. Why book yourself in for the night at the local inn, when you were a friend of the family and no doubt welcome any time you like?'

'Exactly. I could have done this whole thing while I was here if I'd wanted to. Why make a fuss about staying nearby and flicking the electric?' Edmund looked a bit too smug for Cressida's liking.

'Well, that's simple, Edmund. It all went wrong for you when the scaffold never came down. You had anticipated the cleaners to be done on Wednesday and to be removing the scaffold on Thursday ready to hang those ghastly curtains. More on them later. Hence why you had to break in on Wednesday evening to steal and then hang the diamonds, safe in the knowledge that they would stay hidden in plain sight among the crystals for another year until the cleaners came back for the next spring clean. It was your family who recommended the cleaning firm to Lady Chatterton, and although I don't for one moment suspect your parents of playing a part in this, it would be easy enough for you to get hold of the cleaning firm's details and ask after their availability, posing as a client perhaps.'

'This is all circumstantial supposition,' Edmund all but growled.

'But it's true though, isn't it? And in a year's time, as you know Lady Chatterton would be having the *annual* clean again, you could wangle yourself an invitation back to the house, or dare I say it, break in again, and retrieve the diamonds before the cleaners had a chance to notice they were up there. Then you could fence them long after the heat was off from their initial disappearance.'

There was another round of gasps, mostly from the Chattertons. 'That's a dastardly plan indeed.' Alfred looked shocked at the thought, but Cressida could see that it was all making sense to them. 'So Edmund hid the diamonds, but made it look like an unknown thief had crept down the drainpipe and made off with them, while all the time hiding them right in front of us?'

'And there they would have stayed, except that Harry Smith, the cleaner, *did* find them.'

'How did Edmund know he'd found them? Wouldn't he just take them and go?' John asked, looking around the room to see if anyone else would be nodding in agreement with his logical point of view.

'How could he, when the police were still searching? And I hate to say it, but someone from his walk of life wouldn't have stood a chance if he'd been caught in possession of them. No, he saw them hanging there and started formulating his own plan, asking the other servants how they'd go about spending a windfall, making it sound like he was inheriting some money. Young Jacob, the excellent footman you have here, told me that he'd gone as far as asking some of the "gents" about how to live the high life. It was unfortunate that one of them was you, Edmund.'

'I was there too,' William admitted, his voice quiet and contemplative. 'And you, or Jacob, are right. He was quite the peacock about it, barrelling up to us as if he were our equal and bragging about having recently come into some wealth.'

'His garrulous ways cost him his life. Boasting about his lucrative find, however cryptically, was enough to tip Edmund off,' Cressida explained.

Ignoring Edmund, who harrumphed and murmured the words 'circumstantial' and 'poppycock' a few times, Cressida continued:

'When the major was killed, I took it upon myself to search his room, and within it I found this note. DCI Andrews, do you have it?'

'Yes, Miss Fawcett, Kirby?' He reached round and found the note which was carefully placed in one of the brown paper evidence bags.

'Thank you, Kirby.' Cressida took it from him. 'As you can see, there are words still unburnt and you can clearly make out the words "diamond" and "chand", which I took to mean chandelier. And the number six, which I think was the agreed rendezvous time. You sent this note to young Harry Smith, having spoken to him on Friday evening, soon after you arrived, Jacob told me that. I assume you climbed the tower and waited for him up there. He was expecting some sort of parlay, but instead you retrieved the diamonds from their hiding place, got the note back off him and pushed him to his death.'

'You found that in the major's fireplace though,' Edmund harrumphed. 'How do you know it's not his and he wasn't the one to steal the diamonds in the first place?'

'Because this handwriting matches the scribbles on your gazetteer, Edmund.'

There were gasps as Kirby fetched out of a bag the gazetteer that had been sitting plain as day in Edmund's car. He opened it up in order to show the assembled family and guests the bookmark, and, sure enough, the writing was a match.

'I think you planted it in the major's bedroom. There were other things too, Edmund, that slot into place now I know. The velvet case for the diamonds was stolen from Lady Chatterton's room on Friday night too, no doubt in the early hours of the morning before your deadly rendezvous with Harry. And you accused me of having "magpie eyes" myself when I pretended to be interested in William as a suitor.'

'William, really?' Alfred interrupted.

'I was pretending, Alfred. Anyway, Cardew said you were seen near the scaffolding tower when I was up it retrieving this.' She took the piece of silk out of one of the evidence bags and held it up.

'You mentioned Petronella's dress being silk, Cressida, is that what you meant?' John asked.

'Yes. This scrap of fabric caught my eye fluttering high up on the scaffolding tower on Saturday morning, not long after Harry had been killed. I think Edmund noticed and tried to stop me as this small piece of cream silk, far from being from Petronella's dress, or part of the Chatterton livery, is an exact colour match for the Mutton Pie Club waistcoats.'

'You haven't been through and checked all of our waistcoats though?' William asked.

'I didn't need to. I found one, one with a rip that exactly

matches this small piece of fabric, and I'm pretty sure we can prove that it's yours, Edmund.'

'How, Cressy?' Dotty asked, intrigued.

'Well, everyone else who might have had motive or opportunity to be up that scaffolding tower had some sort of stain on theirs. William's was smeared in gravy from a pie, the major had jam down his from the roly-poly pudding. Alfred, your grease stain is from—'

'Madame FiFi's House of—'

'Quite. And even Basil sloshed a cocktail on his. John's is clean, miraculously, seeing how clumsy you all are, but he has an alibi for the diamond theft as he was in the drawing room with his parents and Dotty while it was happening. And you swapped to your Mutton Pie Club cummerbund, Edmund. You told me you'd spilt something on your waistcoat, but I think you disposed of it, didn't you, after you'd ruined it—'

'You can't blame me for it ending up in the major's car.' Edmund looked infuriated at Cressida.

'I never mentioned the major's car. DCI Andrews, did you?'

'No, Miss Fawcett. And neither did Kirby. Edmund Priestley, I'd suggest you've been hoisted by your own petard.'

Edmund grimaced at them both. 'Bet you're pinning his death on me too, are you?'

'You bet your life I am.' Cressida looked at him, her choice of words sending a chill through the other guests as the colour drained out of Edmund's cheeks.

44

'Cressy, this is serious. Edmund could hang...' Dotty whispered it, but everyone in the library could hear.

'I won't hang, dammit.' Edmund shook his cuffed wrists. 'This is all nonsense. You, policeman chap, you should let me go or arrest me, but this is undignified.'

'I'm sure Miss Fawcett has more up her sleeves,' was all Andrews said, and Cressida saw Sergeant Kirby's hand press down further on Edmund's shoulder.

'Quiet right. Poor Major Elliot. He saw you, didn't he, Edmund? When you were hiding the diamonds again.'

'How could you possibly prove that?'

'Well, I wasn't the only one who heard what he was saying to you over the card game that night. At the time, I thought he was drunk. In fact, I think you insinuated he was, so the other chaps wouldn't pick up on what he was saying, but he outright accused you of hiding the diamonds in the hem of the curtains. "Hemmed in by a pie of clubs" was what he said when you asked him where his three of diamonds came from – three, I assume to indicate the full set of necklace, bracelet and earrings.' Cressida paused, letting it all sink in. A few nods of recognition from the fellow gamblers that night gave her the courage she needed to carry on.

'I heard someone out on the landing the night the major was killed. Footsteps that I assumed was a late-night bladder call like me, but there was no gurgling from the cistern when I got to the bathroom.'

'Could have been any of us!' Edmund answered back.

'So the major was definitely murdered, then?' Dotty asked, her voice wavering.

'Undoubtably, I'm afraid, Dot.' Cressida sighed. 'He always slept with that moustache net over his whiskers, didn't he? And there was no sign of him waking in the night and taking his medicine; the bottle top was screwed on tight and his glass of water untouched. The police, and I, found the moustache net on the floor of the bedroom with the discarded pillow. It shows that there was a struggle as he was suffocated, the net coming off his face as the pillow was finally pulled off him once he'd... well, once he'd stopped struggling.'

Lady Chatterton wiped a tear from her eye. 'Oh, the poor major. He was such a dear, sweet man. Always looking out for other people.'

'That's what Alfred told me. That the major was the sort of chap who'd let you sort out your own mistakes. I think the cryptic clue he gave Edmund during the card game was meant to be one of these warnings, a sort of shot across the bow giving him time to repent and return the diamonds.'

'And own up to killing Harry Smith?' Dotty asked.

'I'm not sure the major knew about that, but he must have seen Edmund moving the diamonds about. But instead of repenting, Edmund doubled down and decided the major needed to be silenced. For good.'

'The major did look as if he had the weight of the world on

his shoulders on Saturday evening,' Lady Chatterton said sadly. 'I thought, after what happened to him, that it might have been some prescience of his heart trouble, but he must have been carefully weighing up how to deal with Edmund. Him giving you a chance, young man, cost him his life and for that I will never forgive you.' She shook her head and Lord Chatterton rested his hand over hers on her lap. This obviously reminded her of the diamonds in her hands and she asked Cressida a question. 'So where did they go then? After the chandelier?'

'Ah, well, I thought I was awfully clever and had worked out that they were hidden in the horrible curtains. You see, I found the velvet box that they came in by the icehouse, no doubt thrown there by Edmund when I saw him crossing the lawn shortly before I bumped into Basil and Petronella.' Cressida risked a glance at Dotty, who was looking stoically at the fireplace. 'Well, in the box, there were these lead discs and my friend Maurice helped me identify them as curtain weights. Why hide curtain weights in a box unless you had put the diamonds where the curtain weights should be? And you yourself, Lady Chatterton, noticed how badly the curtains were hanging.'

'Yes, yes. But why not keep them in his bedroom from then on?' Lady Chatterton asked.

'He couldn't risk having them found about his person or in his bedroom and still needed somewhere safe where there was no risk of them being found by cleaners. Hence the curtain hems. Edmund had slipped in the day after we found Smith dead and replaced the weights with the diamonds.'

'How do you know that?' John asked.

'When I was feeling rather sorry for myself after Andrews here had rightfully told me off for snooping, I went and found Dotty in the ballroom. She said she'd just seen Edmund exit stage left, chased by a spaniel as it were. I think he saw the hems as the next best place after the chandelier for keeping them safe until he could come back in a year's time to collect them. He said they were "bloody ugly things", and men don't usually notice curtains.'

'So now I'm the murderer because I can see what's blatantly obvious. It doesn't take a psychopath to tell you they're horrendous.'

'Steady on, Edmund,' Lady Chatterton cautioned him. 'I did choose those, you know.'

'Also,' Edmund tried to jab a finger at Cressida but found it hard with the cuffs on and Kirby's hand still pressing down on his shoulder, 'if I had slipped the box out to the icehouse, why didn't Basil and Petronella notice me?'

'They were a little, ah... let's say their focus was elsewhere,' Cressida stammered, not wanting to hurt Dotty's feelings any more than she had to. 'They certainly didn't hear me approaching along the soft woodland path. And I had a dog with me!'

'But they weren't in the hem when you looked, Cressy?' Dotty was doing a marvellous job of maintaining her composure.

'No. And that surprised me. But then I remembered last night we spoke about the curtains, all of us again over dinner and, Edmund, you were next to me when I promised Lady Chatterton that I'd have them replaced by midsummer. In fact you spluttered into your wine at the mention of them being used as a coconut shy; I thought you were simply laughing along with the rest of us, but actually you were suddenly very worried that your hiding place was no longer secure. And,' Cressida looked at Andrews. 'Edmund couldn't rely on an invitation back here before then, however charming he comes across.' Cressida raised her eyebrows.

'When did he move them?' Dotty asked.

'When I went to go and find Basil to give him a piece of my mind.' Cressida glared at Basil. 'Before I got in my car, I heard one of the other engines in the garage making the sort of *dink dink dink* noise they make when they cool down and it was only when I returned my car to the garage that I realised what the sound was. And over lunch, you see, John said Edmund had just been out for a drive.'

'So he moved them from the curtains to the icehouse?' Alfred asked, with all of them seemingly finally catching on.

'Yes. I propose that he used his car to drive around to the other side of the lake again, and fling them by the icehouse. It had already been searched enough times, I assume he thought he'd let them lie there for a little while before collecting them on his way home,' Cressida finished.

In a very quiet voice, and with a face quite pale, Dotty addressed the room. 'And Lady Adelaine... that was you too Edmund?'

Edmund stared at his knees, his face giving nothing away. It was Cressida who answered her friend instead. 'Yes, I believe so. I saw someone with dark hair up by the balustrade... We'd all been dashing around trying to find the diamonds and retrace the burglar's steps. Not too subtle of us, and Edmund, who'd come across us in the great hall, could probably see exactly what we were doing. I think dropping Lady Adelaine on me was his final attempt at getting away with all of this.'

'You could have been killed, Cressy!' Dotty looked, wide-eyed, at her friend.

Cressida nodded. 'Or worse, Ruby could have been hurt.' The small dog, who had been exceptionally patient while her mistress had revealed all, snorted in both agreement and disgust and strutted out onto the terrace, her curly tail bobbing along behind her.

DCI Andrews moved forward and looked down at Edmund

Priestley, who was sitting, ashen-faced, in the chintz armchair. 'Mr Edmund Priestley, I'm arresting you in the name of the law.' He read him his rights, and amid gasps and muttering from the assembled guests at Chatterton Court, Sergeant Kirby led him away.

45

The next morning, a brown paper parcel arrived at Chatterton Court, addressed to Cressida care of the family. It was brought to her at the breakfast table, and she left it sitting next to her as she finished off her plate of bacon and eggs. Edmund Priestley had as good as confessed last night after she had presented her case against him, and although it had given her no pleasure to be the bearer of bad news and declare one of the house guests a thief and murderer, she knew she'd got it right. The conversation around the breakfast table had been of nothing else.

'His mother was a funny one too, you know,' Lady Chatterton said. 'I don't want to crow about it, but she always had a scheme about her, if you know what I mean. Make you do something she wanted you to do, and you'd get the blame all right when it all went awry.'

'Mama,' Dotty reprimanded her gently. 'Like you said, best not to crow. Let's hope none of this hits the papers. His family will be heartbroken and Chatterton Court might become synonymous with bad behaviour.'

'You're just worried that'll scare off any more suitors, sis,' John said, not realising perhaps how sore a subject that was.

'Oh John.' His mother certainly realised. 'Eat up. I won't have those eggs wasted, and it might shut you up.'

The family bickered on, but Cressida really was worried about Dotty's feelings, so after breakfast, and with Ruby still enjoying the taste of a rogue sausage that had 'accidentally' fallen to the floor, Cressida caught up with her in the great hall.

'What was that parcel, Cressy?' Dotty asked but without her usual enthusiasm.

'Shall we find out? I should imagine it's the samples from Maurice in London, but you never know.'

The pair decided on the ballroom being the best place to open the parcel and, sure enough, there were beautiful fat quarters of the finest damask in the most beautiful subtle shades. The two friends sorted through them and ordered them in preference.

'I do like that rose pink,' Dotty said. Cressida preferred the pale gold, but nodded an agreement to Dotty and placed the rose pink at the top of the pile.

'Dotty dear, are you all right? I mean, are we all right? I'm so sorry that I—'

'Shush, Cressy.' Dotty turned to face her. 'It's me that should be apologising really. You've done nothing but help and I've been a useless wet moppet. Weeping over blooming Basil and hiding under my bedclothes hoping the world would stand still and everything would go back to... oh I don't know, Sunday last. It was foolish of me, and I didn't help you enough.'

'Oh Dotty, you did. You did. And you weren't a wet moppet or whatever. You've been through the wars, not to mention having had a rather stressful series of murders under your roof.'

Dotty shivered.

Cressida continued. 'I think you've been frightfully brave and although I hope not to come face to face with another murderer, I hope if I do, I have you by my side.'

Dotty smiled at her friend. 'And Ruby?' she asked.

'Yes, of course Ruby. Clever pup found the diamonds at the end of the day.'

'And Chief Inspector Andrews?' Dotty asked, her eyebrow arching. 'He's rather dishy after the gruffness has gone. Not a penny to his name, I'm sure, but—'

'But nothing, missy.' Cressida glared at her friend, but her eyes were twinkling. 'You know my stance on marriage and the grizzled appearance of a middle-aged policeman shan't do anything to tempt me out of it. You, on the other hand...'

'Oh no. He's not my type either. I should imagine he'd be terrible at charades.' Dotty giggled.

'Well, maybe not a policeman for you either, but, Dotty, we will find you a husband, I promise. In fact, I have an invitation down to the West Country next month – a house party like this one, but by the sea and hopefully with fewer murders. Fancy coming?'

'Oh rather.' Dotty beamed at her.

With the goodbyes said and Cressida loaded up into her sporty Bugatti, the family all stood on the front steps to wave her off.

'It was lovely to see you, dear,' Lady Chatterton called. 'And thank you again for finding my diamonds. I'm most terribly in your debt.'

'A pleasure, Lady Chatterton. Least I could do for all the cake and tea and possibly numerous stolen slices of bacon by my little chum here.' Ruby was sitting next to her in the car, panting excitedly for the off.

'It was good of you to let that policeman take all the credit for your work, Cressy,' Alfred said, coming down the last few steps of the ornate front of the house and leaning over her car.

'I think he needed it more than I did,' Cressida replied, thinking of when Andrews had mentioned how he hadn't had much success recently. 'And, you know what, I think my family owes him quite the favour.'

Alfred tapped the side of the car in recognition of what she said. 'See you in London again soon then, old thing?'

'Absolutely.' Cressida smiled at him.

'There's a shindig at the Lanesborough Hotel this weekend, you could entertain us all with that thing you do with the fan and three cocktail glasses—'

'Yes, that's quite enough of that, Alfred.' She warned him from saying much more with a flare of her nostril and a raised eyebrow. 'Bye then all, thank you for having me. And do let me know which fabric you like best, and I'll get those curtains sorted.'

She gave a thumbs up and was halfway down the driveway with a dust cloud churning up behind her before Lord Chatterton, who had barely said a thing all weekend, announced to his family in a forthright way, 'She's right, you know. Those curtains are ghastly.'

A LETTER FROM FLISS

Dear reader,

I want to say a huge thank you for choosing to read *Death Among the Diamonds*. If you did enjoy it, and want to keep up to date with all my latest releases, just sign up at the following link. Your email address will never be shared and you can unsubscribe at any time.

www.bookouture.com/fliss-chester

I hope you loved *Death Among the Diamonds*, the first in the new Hon. Cressida Fawcett series. If you did, I would be very grateful if you could write a review. I'd love to hear what you think – did you like the way she used her 'eye for design' to give her 'an eye for a crime'? Reviews from readers like you can make such a difference helping new readers, who will hopefully love the cosy crime setting of 1920s English country houses, discover my books for the first time.

I love hearing from my readers – you can get in touch on my Facebook page, through Twitter, Instagram or my website.

Thanks,

Fliss Chester

KEEP IN TOUCH WITH FLISS

www.flisschester.co.uk

 facebook.com/flisschester

twitter.com/socialwhirlgirl

ACKNOWLEDGEMENTS

My thanks as always to the brilliant team at Bookouture for breathing life into this manuscript. It's been wonderful working with both Laura Deacon and Rhianna Louise, who have been a great support and amazing to work with on this new series. Also to the copyeditor Jade Craddock and proofreader Anne O'Brien; I hate to think of the typos and mistakes that would have littered this book without you! And, of course, the publicity and social media departments (Kim Nash, Noelle Holten, Sarah Hardy and Jess Readett) who do a fantastic job of getting reviewers and bloggers interested in our books, while Alex Crow and Melanie Price in marketing are possibly the best in the business. So many more within the Bookouture team have worked on this book too, so thank you all.

Thanks also to my literary agent, Emily Sweet, for her enduring advice and friendship, not just on this book but throughout the career I've only had because of her. There's a group of authors I don't think I could do this without, so huge thanks to my Criminal Minds chums (you know who you are), for always being super supportive and downright hilarious most of the time. Victoria, Heather and Rachael – without your pep talks, this series might never have happened.

Special mention to my friend Tet Staveley who helped me come up with some of the ideas for the hiding places for the diamonds in this book – I'm only sorry that the earrings in the ice cubes didn't make it past the first draft!

My family have been a huge support as I wrote this book

and I'd like to especially thank the 'Cherry Hill Lawsons' who have kept a (very special) roof over our heads this year as we navigate the vagaries of the current UK property market. Also, as ever, my husband Rupert, who supports me in so many ways, giving me the time I need to write and frequently suggesting inventive ways to kill people...